DIRE DAYS

DIRE DAYS

The Uncharted Horizons Serial

C. R. Buchanan | Jason Diamond

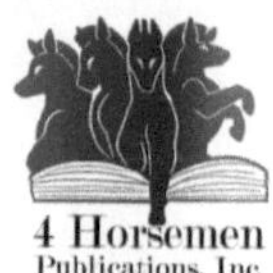

Published By: 4 Horsemen Publications, Inc.

4 Horsemen Publications, Inc.
PO Box 417
Sylva, NC 28779
4horsemenpublications.com
info@4horsemenpublications.com

Cover Illustration by CD Corrigan
Typesetting by Autumn Skye
Edited by Jen Paquette

Library of Congress Control Number: 2024950617

Paperback ISBN-13: 979-8-8232-0741-6
Hardcover ISBN-13: 979-8-8232-0742-3
Audiobook ISBN-13: 979-8-8232-0744-7
Ebook ISBN-13: 979-8-8232-0743-0

Acknowledgements

"I would like to say thank you to everyone that has believed in me over the years and stood by my side along the journey to get me where I am today. You know who you are, and you are loved."

C R BUCHANAN

"Thank you to my friends and family over the years. It is because of you that I became the person I am today."

JASON DIAMOND

TABLE OF CONTENTS

Kepler 442-b is dying at the hands of delusional people. Most live under foolhardy dreams, pretending everything will be alright while ignoring deceptions from lying windows. It is easier than facing the truth.

Armada scientists manipulate animal genomes in desperate attempts to cure Kep Four syndrome, sacrificing their subjects' lives. Vegetation is scant under rusty skies. Dead oceans beneath them, tainted red with sickened, settling air, beat against coastlines no longer welcoming life.

Attempts to correct the climate have failed, and we must endure the mistakes made by our ancestors thousands of cycles ago. Like those of Ancient Earth, humanity pushed too hard. Hope is dead, and soon, there will be no one left to remember us.

My best friend in childhood was a little girl four cycles of age whose name I never knew. I asked her for it once. She said it was a secret, and it was not until reaching my sixth cycle of life I realized she was joking.

We played in a fantasy world with blue skies, cheerful people, and all the fresh food and water needed. It took but a few rotations before my older brother, Comilo, joined us. He was king; we were noblewomen.

Dirty torn dresses, a lack of nutrition, and an absence of toys to play with did not bother us. We carried on in dated respirators pretending to be royalty atop a high castle in a mighty kingdom. The world was ours, and it was beautiful.

Comilo had a large spotted womosa bat that followed him on sight. He was always good with animals. The little girl we played with admired him for it as much as I did, but she never laughed harder than the time we asked my brother's bat to guide us to riches.

We gave it a quick pet for good luck, and Comilo moved his arm up and down—his flight command—only to have it dart off his arm to chase after goneth jumpers for several teks. The little girl chuckled until she coughed. I do not know why she thought it was funny, but her laughter was contagious enough to have all three of us in tears. I will never forget that rotation.

Comilo and I played with her for two cycles before she died. Born under the brown's scythe of starvation and sorrow ... I remained oblivious to how bad it was in Najasa until my brother's death. I think of them, and others, more than I would like to admit.

They are heavy on my mind as I sit on this aged white sofa, awaiting Mother to return. She boils a pot of Kep Four's famous swizzel branch tea in her kitchen while I run through the world in my head.

Mother takes a few spoon-dipped swigs and licks her lips between stirring the pot. "Almost done, McKayla."

I watch her in wonder about how many others from the poverty-stricken ghetto of Najasa she raised me in are still alive. There is nothing else to do in Mother's place but think. Nor is there much to admire. The couch I am sitting on, a matching love seat, an A.I. painting of her and Father on the wall behind me, and a holo news feed are all she possesses besides clothes, food, and drinks. Mother is a minimalist.

She limps into the living room with two gray-swirled cups of olive-tinted tea on a copper tray and places them to rest on an iron coffee table with a plate of reskberries. My family's tradition is to drink tea. We do it in silence every 10th rotation in remembrance of those we have lost.

"Well," she says, "are you going to drink that, or aren't you?"

The tea warms my lips with a flavorful hint of old melon and heifer milk. It thaws the pallet to release cinnamon-scented fumes. Swizzel branch tartness dries my mouth, dissolving to unleash spiced flavors as I remain lost in Najasa. Life was hard there, yet I miss the ignorance that came with youth.

Mother sighs and releases a half-hearted smile upon her first sip. "I miss him more every rotation."

I know who she is talking about. Mother always thinks of Father while she sips. I held him in my heart, but we were not as close as they were. His criticisms over my A.R.S. (Animal Rights Sympathizer) lifestyle were harsh and drove a lasting wedge between us.

The air took him twelve cycles ago. My brother, cousins, nephews, and grandparents died on this planet—astrologically dubbed Kepler 442-b. Only Mother remains for me to chat with since my brother Comilo's suicide, and we only made it because I joined the training program at the Armada.

Being a member gave me free housing and one lung purging to use at any point chosen in life. Living quarters are reasonable, and we may share it with one family member. The choice was simple for me. I had only Mother to choose, but I have seen that decision tear families apart.

Mother finishes her tea and places the empty cup back on the tray. "Ready for the fun part of the tradition?"

"You mean your part of the tradition?" I ask.

"Whatever," says Mother. "What's your poison these rotations?"

I roll my lips together in thought. "Jerleanian."

"Jerleanian?" she asks, picking up the tray and limping to the kitchen on old hips. "Off the old wagon, huh?"

I nod in silence to hide my sadness. I do not enjoy seeing her in pain, but Mother refused to get artificial joints after Father passed. A malfunctioning Class 'A' Excavation Unit crushed his left leg. Doctors had to amputate.

We lived in the wrong district to get Father approved for M.E.R.P. (the mech-engineered replacement program), and we could not afford to replace his limb without it. He spent his ending cycles on one leg until Kep Four Syndrome's cellular lung decay took his life.

Mother and I became eligible for the program when I joined the Armada, but she refused surgical offerings from M.E.R.P.—if they would not help Father, she would not let them help her. She further disdained anything relating to Armada research after my brother's passing. It was their scientists studying Kep Four Syndrome's fault my brother took his own life. My hate for them runs deeper than the Jade Sea.

She returns from the kitchen with two small boxes. The first reads:

Jerleanian reserve - 8212

The other:

Red 49

"You'll love this," says Mother. "It's from your father's collection before he passed. Aged five hundred cycles now."

Mother cannot form fresh memories and thinks I am unaware of its flavor. I will say nothing about it. Instead, I watch as she pulls a few hardened brown drink cubes from the first box and drops them into my glass, rattling them until they break into liquid Jerleanian.

"Here you are." She hands me the glass with unsteady hands.

A mischievous look escapes me. "Thanks, Maddie."

"Hey," she says. "What'd I tell you about calling me Maddie, McKayla Mason?"

Her wide-eyed reaction to hearing the name *Maddie* leaves me thinking about the times I called her by her first name instead of Mother in my youth. We had a teasing relationship. A loving one.

The Jerleanian pulls me further into a nostalgic state. A furious rush warms my throat and slithers into my chest. Father left magic bottled with Mother.

The drink cubes, prefabricated and unstable compressions of liquid, fall apart into their natural fluidic state once jostled. Father preferred them over natural liquid, but not as much as Mother. I raise my glass to her as she rattles burgundy Red 49 cubes into her glass, breaking them apart into liquid wine.

"Thank you," I say.

"I'll make some bezzle berry sopo when we're done sipping," she says.

I cannot help but smile. She knows how much I love the morning dish with its oatmeal-like texture and almond flavor.

"It's good, isn't it?" she asks. "The Jerleanian. Very smooth."

She takes a slow sip of Red 49.

BEEP—BEEP—BEEP

I sigh upon hearing it. A powerful urge hits me to ignore the call and finish my conversation with mother, but I understand I must answer. This rotation is vital to the A.R.S. movement and one on which I will deal my biggest blow to date against the Armada's research practices.

"Pause memory," I say.

Mother freezes mid-sip of her wine. Crows feet signal she grieved a lot in life, which is something I respected because she hid it behind smiles to protect me as a child. She was the most thoughtful person I knew and where I gained inner will. She passed five cycles ago. And I miss her to this rotation.

I lean in to deliver a kiss to her forehead, one she will neither feel nor remember. "I'll see you later, Mother."

My temples tingle as the memory file closes. The furious rush of tea that warmed my throat and slithered into my chest fades to nothing. Cinnamon-scented Jerleanian no longer fills my nostrils; its scented fumes have dissipated. If I want those sensations again, I have to find them in the real world.

I make my way to a still image of myself on an empty wall. It is where Mother's door used to be and a snapshot of myself motionless in the center of my living room. We call them V.P.U., or visual return points. They come equipped with memory files to remind us we are not in reality when visiting the past. Those who visit without a V.P.U. never psychologically return.

I turn back for one last look at Mother. "Exit memory file."

The V.P.U. on her wall expands as I near it, letting me pass through and into my quarters.

1-2
The Window

I take a deep breath as the opening behind me shrinks. The image holds Mother as she was when I left her—frozen mid-sip of her wine for me to return and continue the memento another time. Heavy eyes are hard to keep open. I close them and relax until I am free of the past.

Depression hits me like a wave of fog misting my face. My home feels shadowy compared to Mother's. Although it is a contrasting train wreck of eclectic souvenirs, oddities, and a statement of who I am for others to see upon entry, it does not embrace the heart as Mother's place did.

The living room window catches my attention. I enjoy looking through it and sometimes spend taks gazing into the lush, beautiful world outside my home; but tall green trees with thick, palm-width leaves swaying over romping wildlife do not comfort.

BEEP—BEEP—BEEP

I study the security feed near the door's manual control panel:

CONFIRMED SAFE CALL—QUARTERS ACCESS.

I have given only one person such permission. It must be him. A time of action is upon me.

"Answer," I say.

A physical imaging projection of Dr. Sellers appears at my side. He is attractive, in his mid-40s, and holds the same protective nature for life as I do. He is also 70% European and one of the least-mixed people on Kep Four if you omit the Uprisers from the equation. This unifying look is why I keep my hair partly shaved and dyed a combination of dull Armada green and white highlights at the bangs. Anything to feel less like an Armada drone.

The cycle is 8719 AD, measured by the ancient, and no pure breeds remain on Kep Four. It is better this way. I never understood racism when studying records of Ancient Earth. The definition is clear on what it means, but I cannot grasp the concept of judging in such a way. I only see one race on Kep Four; that race is humanity.

The physical imaging projection of Dr. Sellers steps to square himself in front of me. If anyone considers me their friend, it would be this man. He was paramount in my development and guided me one rotation at a time until I reached my current standing in the A.R.S.

"We're a go, Mason," says Dr. Sellers. "How are you feeling?"

"Ready," I answer.

"Good," he says, placing his hands on my shoulders to give them a hard squeeze. "I'll guide you once you reach the cadet flight building. Be careful, Mason. I mean it."

I nod with stern confidence.

"End transmission," he says.

The physical imaging projection of Dr. Sellers disappears.

An unopened bottle of Jerleanian Reserve catches my attention. The metallic cork pops out to sting my palm when I twist it. Bottles are under pressure in the real world, and their contents hold the proverbial teeth needed to deliver a bite to my liver and motor functions.

I pour three fingers and toss it into my mouth. Although uncommon for me, this rotation will be lengthy. Pent-up energy at the internal edge of rising stress is distracting. I need to shake it before I leave.

The shot hits hard and burns the roof of my mouth with its flavors. I swallow, exhale Jerleanian fumes, set the glass on the table, and walk to the window. I take a moment to reflect on Dr. Seller's words. He is right. I need to be extra careful this rotation. What we have planned is riskier than usual, but time is of the essence. We must be swift.

"Remove screen," I say.

It takes a moment for the window's image to dissipate and show the truth. The visual outside my housing unit shifts to show anyone brave enough to take it in the same grim story: brown skies swirling with pollution-laced air, no visible sun, and not a hint of plant life growing from Kep Four's contaminated soil. The planet was in a weakened state when humanity arrived, but we did this world no justice by being here. We made it worse—nobody can take it back.

I turn and leave the filter down while grabbing a small, black bag, bio mask, and a pair of gray ocular goggles from the table. Everything is going in the same bag, along with my Song Hen. I rarely leave without it. There is something about listening to a Gömböc-shaped song-box I find attractive during downtime. I am a fan of things that refuse to stay toppled.

My head feels lighter. Nerves are fading. Jerleanian is taking hold.

I grab a Farca from the shelf next to the door and stuff it into my bag. They are the only manufactured respirators capable of protecting us on Kep Four. Leaving without one in some areas is a death sentence.

"Exit and lock," I say.

My door opens, and I double-check to ensure I am not forgetting anything, taking one glance into the living room before letting the door shut and lock behind me. Jerleanian is not stopping me from shaking inside. It does not matter. My life holds no importance when weighed against the masses, and this is something I must do.

I stop before moving outside and put on the Farca. The rotten scent of relon (synthetic rubberized titanium) fills my nostrils like decomposing reskberries, but it beats dying from atmospheric intoxication. I hold an ocular goggle over each eye. They suck into place, and I exit housing structure 25.

Nobody is in sight. Light and dark swirls of different browns move with heavy currents of air in a dying world. With every footstep, I feel further lost in a lifeless biosphere that the living loath to inhabit.

Population is sparse by global standards—1,600,000 with sixty-three percent imprisoned—but we live a crowded coexistence. A single continent among five is home to all. Within that, we share regions totaling only 621 square clicks.

Humanity almost ran dry on Ancient Earth. Global militaries set war aside and combined to form the Armada before making the jump to Kep Four. The hope was to geo-engineer and heal this planet's deteriorating state upon arrival, but filtration systems that once stood a click tall across Kep Four could not keep up, nor could automated water rejuvenation boats that once patrolled poisoned seas in vain.

Humanity pushed Kep Four's ecosystem. It was not deliberate. Residual warp signatures from early long jump prototype engine tests to get off this rock proved to have uncorrectable terrestrial side effects. This sped up Kep Four's approaching doom.

Testing the engines in a sterile environment to observe environmental interactions before trials should have been done. They were not. Sure, Kep Four was already deteriorating when humanity arrived, but, clearly, we did not learn from the mistakes of the past.

Toxicity followed. Nothing organic can maintain continued exposure without belonging to the brown. Carbon-based life tends to biodegrade quickly here. Bones of the dead... What used to be plants... Things that once swam in or thrived in the oceans... They are all part of what we breathe and muddle through in our terra boots when we walk the outdoors.

Seas covered in a half-pace worth of sediment prevent the sun from reaching it. Waving brown-coated waters supply a source for filtrating H2O, but the scenario also made Kep Four a dry globe. There is no rain. Anything and everything that has died outside are now dust in the winds we walk.

My brother, Comilo, is part of it. So is the small, hairy, monkey-like flagert that saved him psychologically. They surround me in the winds and lie in sediment covering the ground. I ponder them with each step and breath of every rotation. As much as Comilo loved me, what remains of him would take my life if I stopped to breathe him in.

Broken before my first breath, my heart sinks to know I will never see living waters. Turbulent in depths, waves here matched encasing clouds long before my birth cycle. They will continue until they are mud, dry, and gone after my life ends.

The Armada moved filtration systems to concentrate on the territory of Chimark as things continued getting worse.

Tens of thousands of them stand tall and run strong, but they cannot overthrow the planet's terrestrial decay.

The Suicide Fields are the most toxic areas on the planet. People go there to die when life exhausts them or depression overwhelms. With resources low, only loved ones will attempt to stop another who wants to end their lives this way. People can choose to die as they wish, and two-step guides on suicide are posted throughout districts of poverty.

> #1. *Head to The Suicide Field's event horizon of toxicity and corrosiveness.*

> #2. *Keep walking until your equipment fails or remove your protective gear and take a breath. You will not need a second.*

That is how I lost my brother, Comilo. Talking about him with others saddens me. Visiting him in memory files angers me. He took the loss of Father harder than even Mother. Depression almost ended his life through self-induced starvation, but the wild flagert he befriended psychologically saved him when we could not.

Comilo was doing better by half a cycle of befriending it. I was confident he would live a long life with me if I made it into the flight program, but that changed when Armada patrol units saw him with it one rotation. Their scientists showed up soon after with enforcers and took it away.

My brother received a cracked orbital and a concussion for his efforts to stop them. I heard the commotion and rounded an exterior corner by our place to help him, but an unseen blow to the side of my head knocked me out. I was only twelve cycles of age but remember the jar and carry a reminding scar on the right side of my head.

Comilo took the Suicide Fields's two-step process soon after. My jaw clinches without warning while thinking about it as mixed winds pelt me with grains of sand. I will never forget my brother or his love for animals. I will never forgive the Armada scum that drove him to his death.

Dr. Sellers approached me about joining the A.R.S. shortly after its high-standing members heard what happened to my brother. Our meeting led to me joining him in the fight—fueled by anger and a determination to make things right. I will not falter the movement until experiments are no longer performed on helpless flagerts and other animals.

My stride has slowed while reminiscing, but I shake it off and continue with more determination than I had thirty paces ago. The atmosphere is not harmful enough to the skin here to harm me without long-term exposure under Chimark's protective dome, which is better than the air in the Sigma Green District. The opposite is true for lung and eye tissues, which begin a slow decay upon contact.

I see no one on my path, as far as I can see into the brown. They dare not. Most follow the Armada's entry-level training slogan to the tee. It crosses my mind every time I venture outdoors—*No exception for protection.* I am not worried about it. Dr. Sellers keeps my gear in top shape. I believe in him enough to trust it.

I could have taken the underground corridors but favor making fast steps across barren land. Nobody will bother me here. The gale's howl pushes against my body and garments as if to halt my plan on this rotation. Struggling to see beyond fifty paces ensures solitude. At this distance in Chimark, everything fades from sight.

The cadet flight building is the only thing peeking. It comes further into view with every step, but the structure is too tall to see its upper levels. I reach the outer door and enter the building's exterior elevator. It closes, and I turn back to look through its panel. The path I walked to get here reveals nothing as the elevator car rises.

One thought bothers me about this rotation: *if anything goes wrong, it will spell the end of my conversations with Mother.* Concern takes over, making me more nervous than I already am. A breath's shudder binds me to carry her strength and clear my thoughts. Concealing my shaking heart is not an option. It is a must.

2–2

Sergeant Major

Noob cadets with unfamiliar faces are approaching from the opposite direction. I doubt they care any more about me than vice versa. I pass without a glance.

One turns his head to look. Others turn their pupils in their sockets. Why are they? Never mind. I know why they are staring. Forgot something in my haste.

I remove the ocular goggles and Farca as the first of two security doors leading to Hangar 9 grow near. I approach and wait for it to scan my bio signs, tapping my foot with impatience. The scanner is taking forever to...

Bio-scans bathe me in a stream of red lights.

"Finally."

Clearing me to enter, they deactivate, turn yellow, and power down. The door slides open to show me an empty corridor.

My posture relaxes, knowing I am alone. False conversation is the last thing I desire. I am not fond of fakery, even when on the verge of doing something the Armada considers a crime. The Armada and I do not see eye-to-eye on that. They should hail people like me for saving lives. It will be the downfall of my collaboration with them. My partnership with them is not sustainable the way Dr. Sellers's is. I joined only to help Mother, and she is gone.

Windows running alongside my path starkly remind us of Chimark's fortune. I look down at districts on the surface. Najasa is below on the right. The Sigma Green district is on my left under C.H.I. (the Chimark Holding Institute), but the brown separates us. Being privileged can provide tears when you grew up in the below, but, as always, I bury them and continue moving forward in life.

How does one shake the guilt of leaving others behind? I ask myself that all the time, floating high above surface-side civilians under a protective energy dome. The air up here is cleaner, with thirty percent better visibility and sixty percent less toxicity. Below us, the poor struggle to survive a culture where classes mean life and death ... and prejudice is strong.

An R&D hangar everyone is chatting about rests on my left. I cock my head with inquisitiveness. It is a thousand paces long and a quarter of that tall. Rumor has it the Armada is developing a prototype to get humanity off Kep Four and onto a suitable planet. I believe it is impossible. The chances of me dying in the next few taks are greater.

The jump to Kepler 442-b happened just over 4,000 cycles ago across 1,206 light cycles of space. Ten generations of people were born and died en route to Kep Four. No other Earth-like planets were in our quadrant of the galaxy. Other galaxies are beyond our technological reach for travel.

Few have knowledge of what is happening inside the classified hangar. Those possessing clearance cannot talk about it. All I know is what they have electro-stenciled on its exterior:

EXPEDITION: ANCHOR

The door at the opposite end of the corridor opens as I grow closer. Thankfully, I have not run into anyone looking to talk.

Sergeant Bentley enters the corridor ahead of me. I take a slow, deep breath. He is approaching. My lips part. Going the opposite direction would raise suspicion.

"Sergeant." I raise my hand to my chest, palm up, and turn it out to my side in our traditional military salute.

"Cadet Mason," says Sergeant Bentley with a return of the salute. "I've heard good things about you in the ranks. Still enjoying the training program?"

"Yes, Sergeant Major," I answer and enter parade rest. "And thank you, sir."

"Lay back, Cadet," he says.

My posture shifts. I am grateful to relax. Not that it is, but I find standing at parade rest for the Armada demoralizing. There is not much I like about anything here anymore.

"They caught Dolofónos," says Sergeant Bentley.

"Really?" I ask.

"Yes," answers Sergeant Bentley through snickers of disbelief.

"That's a good thing."

He nods his head with pride. "Took quite a few cycles to locate him. He was my bunkmate when we first enlisted. There was always something off about him. Went by Barron back then."

It is good news, and surprising, but I remain stoic.

"And the Uprisers?" I ask.

He nods with raised brows. "He was with a small group. We think he was trying to stay low, but he's being monitored at the lockdown clinic now. Prosecution is in a cycle."

My blood boils thinking about it. My eyes squint in frustration. "A cycle?"

"They want his Butchers before they end his life," answers Sergeant Bentley. "No way it'll work. He knows he's up for processing. He's not saying anything before he dies."

I remain silent, done with the conversation. I cannot, however, be openly disrespectful of the Armada or their decisions. Detainment for insubordination would be unacceptable during this rotation.

"Why flight school?" he asks. "From what I'm hearing, you could do anything you want with a few cycles of study."

I look at the door behind him, wishing to pass through it. "I just like hitting the black."

He looks me up and down. "Do what makes you happy. If I've learned anything in life, it's that. Have a good rotation, Mason."

I salute. "Thank you, Sergeant Major."

His appearance is hard yet friendly under dagger-hazel eyes, difficult to ignore. Many females in the Armada would be happy talking with him. He is attractive and highly sought after, but not my type. Sergeant Bentley is unequipped with what I need in a partner, but women with my mindset are nonexistent within the confines of the Armada.

He continues down the corridor, and I move to the secured door, daring not to look over my shoulder until its bio scans are complete.

"Cadet Mason," says the A.I. interface. "Clearance five, hata, detron. Access granted."

The door opens. I enter the lift and turn back, waiting for it to close. Sergeant Bentley is nearing the other end of the hall. He has a nice backside, but I think it is his eyes and personality that have others in the training program ogling him.

2–3
Hangar 9

The lift opens. I enter a hangar with multiple spacecraft tailor-built for cadets. More people are here than expected, but my focus is on a ship built around my body and capabilities. Dr. Sellers will have everything uploaded by the time I reach it.

The Plegma Nine is to my right and looks like a flying sphere of glass. They constructed its hull with a material known as hollow lead. While not the most durable stuff, the Plegma Nine is excellent for non-confrontational research in Kep Four's radioactive zones. I have always wanted to fly a bubble with a transparent hull. Its pilots are free from worry over blind spots beyond cockpit controls, seats, and other internal guts visible from the outside.

Two other vessels stand in the hangar. One is a primitive combustion-driven jet called a Lockheed Martin F-35 Lightning II. No one ever uses it, but they built one for each capital in honor of pilots of old. Armada engineers redesigned their engines for our atmosphere to be flown on the 79th rotation of each cycle ... piloted only by the highest-ranking flight instructors. It came from the most advanced schematics of Ancient Earth's airborne military combat going into World War III—ignited by the Russian/American conflict—which started the planet's decline.

My Beltric Class Six Starfighter is the only other vessel present. The rest are out on training missions, atmospheric rescue, or running S.T.O. (supervised training operations) to gain extra credits and expedite individual cadets' graduations, which take 10 cycles without.

I approach with eyes locked on my Beltric. It is going to help me save lives Armada scientists deem worthy of slaughter. Aggressive angles and gunmetal gray overtones visually define the vessel's hostile maneuverability. Less than 1% pass its flight test.

James Algash is working at the station next to my vessel. I met him when I signed up for the Armada internship program to get Mother out of Najasa. He was born into wealth, joining only because of his father's hierarchy standing in the ranks.

"Hey," says Algash. "Did you hear about Dolofónos?"

"I did," I answer.

I want to walk past him but cannot. He outranks me, oversees its terminal, and is the only one who can give me clearance to the Beltric Class Six. Being a cadet comes with its own downfalls.

Algash continues working at the control station as I ease closer to the starfighter.

"I hope they end his life sooner than later," he continues. "One less sociopathic leader to worry about."

All the fuss about Dolofónos is understandable. The man is an all-around horrible example of humanity and leader of the Uprisers running off the grid at 80,000 strong—killers and rapists at best. He formed their movement to preserve the remaining racial heritage in their bloodlines. Over time, the group grew radical and started a revolution against the Armada.

Algash stops working. "I bet you're hoping for a fast sentencing."

"Won't happen."

"What makes you say that?"

I push closer to the starfighter. "A little whisper told me."

"Send your whisperer my way," he says. "And you're nearly thirty teks too early. What's going on?"

I take a deep breath and pause for effect. "I was wondering if I can get early clearance for the Beltric."

"Negative on that one, Mason," he says, double-checking the schedule. "You're not cleared for a solo flight for another... Another fifty."

He is right. I am half a tak early. Thinking about it reminds me of the education I underwent in my youth.

I learned the history of time during our first rotations of education in our youth at five cycles of age, and how it differed compared to Ancient Earth. Millenniums ago, aionas were *'centuries,'* dekatee were *'decades,'* cycles were *'years,'* rotations were *'days,'* taks were *'hours,'* teks were *'minutes,'* and tiks were *'seconds.'* Kep Four rotates 401 times per cycle, and there are 31 taks per rotation. Within each tak is 100 teks, each comprising a matching 100 tiks.

"Could I sit in it for a bit?" I ask. "Pre-flight nerves, you know? I need to shake them."

"Again, with a negative. If anyone's calm in the black, it's you."

"Look..." I say, closing the distance between us. "This rotation's the anniversary of my mother's transition. I think I spent too much time with her in the memory files, and I... I don't know. I'm..."

"I get it," he says. "That's why I don't use those things. The memory files, that is." He taps his temple. "I prefer to keep everything right here. It hurts less that way, and I'm not lying to myself."

I brush my hand along the starfighter's cold, sandpapery hull. "So?"

He inputs security codes on the terminal and hands me a small, round device with a flat surface on one side of it. "Here's your integration jewel, but if anyone asks, I'm having you check the connection relays before you take it to the black.”

“Of course,” I say.

The cockpit entry raises and slides back. A ramp ascends from the floor, and I grab the integration jewel from him.

“Thank you.”

Algash is always kind and has been crushing on me for half a cycle. I am taking advantage of it, but there are no other options. Lives will perish if he stops me.

I need time to enter Dr. Sellers's uplink commands before takeoff and cannot leave before completing the process. Few would attempt something like this. Right or wrong, it is a significant risk for Armada members with families. That burden no longer falls upon me. I can put others before myself without the risk of Mother losing housing for my actions.

I walk up the starfighter's ramp with guilt. They may hold Algash responsible for my activities. A sacrifice for the greater good? I disregard it. I cannot let the possibility of remorse stand in my way.

The starfighter's door is sandpapery and icy slick like the rest of the vessel. Its ramp rises further when my body gets closer, and I toss my bag inside to enter and sit. The harness locks down tight when I pull it over my shoulder and click it in, pressing hard into my chest and abdomen.

2–4

Override

The mechanical seat contorts around me. Seared citrus odor itches my sinuses as its thorium core ignites. Integration jewels tingle my temple. It feels like a thousand bugs crawling through my head as the vessel links with my thoughts. I hate it, but never leave it in place long enough to bother me.

Integration jewels allow cerebral communication between pilots and their vessels while maintaining diagnostics with people like Algash working at their terminals. This ensures fewer flight errors and enables pilots to fly without manual controls while engaging safety protocols for gravitational forces—Gs, as we call them in salute to ancient aviators.

I open the starfighter's mainframe. My actions need to be quick. There are firewalls to bypass, but I remember the program regulations and sequences Dr. Sellers briefed me on a few rotations ago.

Regardless of complexity, I remember everything that interests me. Always have. Full spectrum H-SAM—a highly superior autobiographical memory with acute echoic properties—has its perks. It is a rare disorder that drives some mad before their brain shuts down and heart no longer beats. For me, it has been a blessing.

Algash is going through his system with squinting eyes, highlighting a puzzled expression. Things are not lining up correctly on his end. He does not know I am the catalyst for his confusion.

He turns from his terminal and back to it again. "We're losing cognitive readings down here, Mason. How's translation up there?"

I move through the hacking sequences to stay ahead of him. "Everything's fine on my end."

Something is not right. Algash should not be picking up improper synapsis translations from the jewel. They must have changed coding sequences earlier than Dr. Sellers expected. This could be bad, and, honestly, there is nothing I can do about it.

Armada protocols will forbid me to take off and stop me from covertly heading elsewhere under a masked flight. I cannot let that happen. I will not let them die.

"Hmph…" says Algash, pausing in thought. "I'm locking the Beltric down for inspection. You're on hold for now."

I snub his words and finish what I need to do on the ship's mainframe before disconnecting audio contact with him. There is no point in talking. He will know what I am trying to do when they run inspection.

The Beltric Class Six is coming with me regardless of what they think, but my original plan is out the window. I will no longer be bringing it back as if nothing happened.

"Protocol one," I command. "Three, one, seven, McKayla, nine, program, Mason, three, six, seven, coded one, four, nine, five." I pause for the O.S. (Operating System) to render changes. "Employ new command pathways."

I reach into the bag, activate the Song Hen, and stick it to the hull to play low tones of classical electronica as the starfighter's engines warm. It helps me focus, and it will not be long before the Planetary Sovereign decides my fate. Hangar doors high above become translucent and fade away. The only thing left between me and the sky is my inner fret.

Armada alarms trigger to sing sonnets of my capture. They are on to me. My controls strobe in and out. They are trying to shut down the starfighter, but Dr. Sellers's firewall is holding.

My body jolts when Algash bangs on my port window with barely heard shouts. I give him an apologetic look, raise the protective exterior shield over the window … and bank to the right upon ascension to avoid hurting him.

The look of betrayal, unforgettable.

"Cadet Mason," says Sergeant Bentley through cockpit audio feed. "You mind telling me what you're doing?"

I depart toward polluted heavens at the point of no return on a mission I cannot stop. Many will condemn me for this. Some will brand me a traitor. Others will call for my execution, a price gladly paid to improve something on this dying rock.

I guide the starfighter into low orbit through thoughts alone via the integration jewel. Brown below. Black above. The radiant H.U.D. (a heads-up display providing the vessels current and changing system readouts) behind retracted manual flight controls shows nothing of concern:

Two blasts ring my bow. My head whips to the fourth left center pane for a visual when a third grazes my stolen vessel to light my cockpit. They were only warning shots, but their nature will soon change.

Several patrol vessels—bulky, blue, and the Armada's policing units designed for arresting and hauling inmates—emerge from the brown, reinforcing notions of them being cautionary blasts and letting me know I am in as much trouble as I can be with the Armada. This was not the plan. All I can do now is finish what I have started.

Algash's voice echoes in my cockpit. "Over one hundred and eighty rotations together, Mason. Don't let the black be the last thing you see. Just turn it around."

"Can't do that," I say.

"Think about it, Mason. Do you really want to do this?"

I double-check the H.U.D. display and bank into the brown atmosphere below. They are following, but I will lose them surface side. Armada law once forbade firing between buildings in civilian-populated districts, that has changed since battles with the Uprisers spilled into the streets of Najasa. Still, it is my best option. I know the area well, and it will be stop number one on my way to the Sigma Green District.

My stomach rises a little when I drop the starfighter back through Kep Four's upper atmosphere. Black shifts to a blur of fire created by the air's friction and then to brown. The tops of failing buildings come into view—some destroyed and only reaching halfway up from former Armada battles with the Uprisers.

Personal shuttles and transport vehicles are going about daily routines near large buildings and housing units. I blaze the streets between them a few paces from the ground. Edifices fly by like drunken Jerleanian blurs rendered on my forward viewing pane.

"Cadet Mason," Algash's voice raises. "Last chance."

I recheck the feeds. They are still on my six and not following the protocols. They are persistent, if nothing else.

"Point of no return, Algash," I say. "Can't turn back now."

"Don't do it, Mason."

I lift the switch cover on my left. Behind it is a clear button. It flashes when depressed, and I slide into a helmet that straps itself on for manual flight. Its fit is snug and one I could fall asleep in under different circumstances.

Most fear overriding safety protocols for gravitational forces while flying a vessel of this class in manual, but I can handle the Gs. No way they are following me. Not if they want to remain conscious.

"Last warning," he calls again. "Stand down."

My H.U.D. flashes. I study the visual feed panes in the starfighter to see pursuers right behind me. Manual flight controls fold out from their retracted position. They will not be on my six for long. I think Algash knows that. If not, he is about to.

"Targeting systems locking from aft," says the A.I. interface.

Five pressure-sensitive clickables are on the right and left controls. From thumb to pinky-finger, the left sides are acceleration, breaking, yawn, and purge, which is rapid acceleration without warp. Right mirrors the left. Both have a fifth button for small warp jumps. The controls are simple: pull back to go up, push forward to dive, horizontal slides for strafing, back tilts for rolls, and forward tilts for vertical ascensions and plummets. A tight grip on all ten buttons at once activates eight thrusters beneath the ship for immediate vertical ascension, which most need to brace themselves for before attempting.

"Beltric locked," warns the A.I. interface system.

"Okay," I whisper, powering down the integration jewel to remove it from my temple. "It's time to burn the birds."

"Let her have it," says Algash.

I snatch the starfighter hard left between an Armada transport emerging from an avenue to my left and a worthless streetlight. A blast misses my vessel and slams into a building down the way. Debris bounces off my craft as I pass through the shot's aftermath.

It is time to mix it up on them. The Armada tested my body to 146 sustained Gs. I can probably handle more. It is a benefit of having H-SAM in combination with Doctor Utley's medications to heighten my abilities to handle such forces.

He has not explained the medicine's long-term effects. I do not think anyone knows. Dr. Utley calls it *X-1* and does not tell me about its properties. I am surely another test subject for them, but if it helps me do what I do, I will accept it. My life for hundreds is an acceptable statistic.

"See you later," I say. "I have a date at Sunrise Beach."

I cut acceleration and pull back, forcing my stolen starfighter's nose to rise to the sky while clamping all ten points tight. The Gs drop my stomach as the vessel comes to a complete stop. Its nose goes up. I tilt right to fall into a tight alleyway.

We call it a dead man's stop. No way they are doing it at 141 Gs. Flight suits can only protect the average pilot from so much. *X-1* and my condition allows me not to fall into that category.

"Full scans," says Algash. "Split up."

My pursuers are splitting up to cut me off. Two pass overhead and drop in front of me to cut off my path. Another pair coasts over my starfighter so I cannot pull up. Three are now behind me with more in route.

I pull the starfighter's nose up, bank left, then right, and hit a series of dead man's stops through several narrow alleyways. The skin on my face tightens from blood pressure each time I dare the maneuver. A sinking sensation flushes from my head to my eyes, chest, and stomach. My skin warms until it burns for a tik. Despite fading vision, normalcy will return after leaving the dead man's portion of flight.

Halfway through the alleyway, I turn the starfighter skyward. A kaleidoscope of Kep Four spins across my eyes as I corkscrew over a massive building hosting an array of bright lights to warn airborne vessels of its presence. The visual pirouettes with electronica as the starfighter slips into another alleyway. I pull back on the flight controls, and my stomach drops again with further fading of vision and burning. The sensation is something I find enjoyable.

Another patrol unit is behind me. Must have seen me in my corkscrew and moved into an intercepting position. I believe it is the last one near me, but the others will know my location again now. More aggressive than the last few, I hit a dead man's stop hard enough to send pressure through my internal organs and fall toward an alleyway on my left into an unkept zone abandoned by society.

My teeth grit as I level out. The patrol vessel tailing me attempts the same: its pilot breaks, the craft's nose goes up, and it drifts forward, slamming into the corner of a building at the alley's edge before spinning from sight. It is a good thing he did not try it in a Beltric Class Six. The pressure may have caused a crash worse that the pilot just experienced, or killed someone... presuming they are not dead already.

An open vessel garage beneath a private residence catches my attention. I dart the craft in and power it down. A moment of nothing passes. Time's tiptoeing is killing me. They must be close.

I sit in wonder about the severity of charges they will place on me for this. I was a part of the Armada's team to decipher ancient artifacts and have since flown recon a few times against the Uprisers. Hopefully, it will be enough to prevent them from processing me if captured. I am breaking their laws to save lives, but do not especially wish to have mine ended.

Someone is tapping into the Armada patrol audio feed. "Kuzio, to Algash. I overheard your situation from high orbit patrol. Sergeant Major Bentley asked me to assist. Do I have permission to intercept?"

"Granted," says Algash.

This is the last thing I want. Kuzio is the Armada's top combat flight instructor for the black wings, where only the best-of-the-best are invited to fly. He is the only person in the Armada that I am one-hundred percent sure can out fly me. This mission is getting messier by the tik.

Kuzio and I have never faced off in training or simulations, but I can handle more Gs than him. Hopefully, it evens things out. Kuzio is a reaper.

Impatience sets in. I can no longer sit here thinking about my new personal bounty hunter or failing this mission without pulling hairs from my head.

"Three," I say. "Two ... One."

I exit under heavy acceleration and go skyward to level out along the building tops as low as possible. My H.U.D. shows an interceptor banking for me three-quarters of a click out, quarter click elevated, and on my eight. It is Kuzio. There are no doubts.

He micro-warps in behind me, forcing me to dip back down between the building below. The chase is on. He follows me around an abandoned construction building, down an old dumping road, through a hanging bridge limp on its right side, and back into the district that this whole mess started in.

I try a dead man's stops again, but he pulls up and watches me from over the building. A series of several rights and he is still overhead. His circular path is wider than mine, but I am not losing him.

Shots rip through a portion of my Beltric Class Six.

"Alright," I say. "Lets do this."

I snatch the flight controls and spiral toward him and around his line of fire, banking a heavy G U-turn around him. This vessel does not have the same level of armament as his does. They only staged me for routine training during this rotation.

Kuzio's interceptor fires a steady stream of rounds my way as he pivots with my orbit around him. A heavy twist back in his direction, and I micro-warp across the horizon. My air reaper follows suit.

He will lose me without visual if Dr. Sellers's programming holds up. I trust it and continue into a low atmosphere revolution around Kep Four and accelerate until the starfighter tests my sustained limits. He is behind me but falls back quickly. Using my ability to handle so many Gs is working.

Kuzio falls from sight. I make a tough right bank and wrap the planet from pole-to-pole. This should leave my new enemy orbiting at a right angle from my path and leave me flying by myself. I continue until my area of interest grows near.

A risky idea crosses my mind. I will do it, but timing is crucial. My life will be otherwise in jeopardy while transitioning into the underground.

"Almost there," I say for confidence.

I make a break for it and plunge into the depths of a submerged passage for high-speed magna rail transports. It can be dangerous in here. The hovering magna rail cars can be up to 1.5 clicks long and are used for hauling equipment and supplies to various section of habitable places on Kep Four. Once used by civilians before they had to stay indoors most of the time, the Armada has seized and rebuilt them for their military and Expedition Anchor movement... and their speed is rapid. Does not matter. I am here now and over a click into in this dark tunnel with nothing ahead or behind me until lights from an approaching carrier come into view. A map of the underground rail system fills my panes with the transport's location flashing against mine as it approaches.

My brows raise. "That's inconvenient."

The map shows the nearest overhead exits in bright green, but the closest is over a click ahead. It will be a close call. I have no choice.

I clamp my ring fingers down tight and surge forward, hitting another dead man's stop, and lockdown both ring fingers again. The starfighter goes nose-up and shoots from the tunnel. A screech slips from me as the transport rail passes under the rear of my vessel, knocking its tail and sending me into the walls of the overhead exit.

"Warning," says the A.I. interface.

It jars me from left to right. Sparks light up my panes as I retake control and emerge from the vertical tunnel in a tumbling front spin. A sharp pull back on the flight controls stops my forward roll, and I level out.

"That was a close one," I say.

"Warning," continues the A.I. interface.

"I know. I know," I say, silencing it.

There are safer paths I could have taken, but the rail system all but guaranteed they would not follow. Magna rail transport schedules have been unpredictable since the Expedition Anchor project went underway. I am still alive to finish my rescue, and nothing else matters.

Brown fades to black. Stars come into view. I level out while setting jump duration to 0.9 and power to 0.51, launching me to my destination.

I break from the jump and spiral back into the melancholy atmosphere. Algash and the rest of the ships are most likely surfacing somewhere, drifting slowly, curious about my whereabouts and how to clarify matters to Sergeant

Bentley. I extend the signal range on incoming comms and listen.

"Anything on scans?" asks Algash. "Anybody got anything?"

All is quiet. I listen for a tik for someone to respond.

"Nothing here," says a pilot.

"Negative," another pilot answers. "I tried to keep up but passed out trying to bank with her. Woke up next to a smashed power grid in a damaged ship."

"You hurt?" asks Algash.

"Negative," answers the pilot. "Autopilot saved me, but I won't be able to get this thing back on my own."

"I'm going to assume we lost her," says Algash with a pause. "Is there an affirmative on that?"

"We're affirmative on that," answers the first pilot.

"Kuzio?"

"Back in high altitude and scanning," answers Kuzio. "I got nothing, but her Beltric has a black eye."

A breath of relief washes my body clean of repentance. I am on the lam for now but cannot let up. Me and other like-minded individuals have a strong dislike for the Armada's Kep Four Syndrome research policy, and we are about to dismantle one of its most abhorrent aspects.

I am wanted and on the run for no reason if I stop now. They can hand out what they wish for me once caught. I am going to complete this mission.

CHAPTER 4

Rescue

Mentioning the improperly named Sunrise Beach was a ruse. It may have been a "Sunrise Beach" before, but now it is simply an artificial body of water where swimming is forbidden. Either way, I want them looking for me on the wrong side of Kep Four.

I switch the starfighter to E-output drive—an untraceable low-energy propulsion system—two clicks away. This quiet approach will not stir up sediment deposits known to be heavy in the Sigma Green district. I lose 80% of power using it but no longer need speed. Stealth is the goal.

The starfighter's I.V.C.E. (Internal Visual Control Enhancers) are a blessing here. It lights obstacles within a half-click radius and renders them on my forward-viewing pane like a mercury 3D model. Contamination in Sigma Green is too thick to tell early rotations from late ones without it.

High-powered streetlights laboring with futile efforts to brighten the scene are worthless. They need to be replaced, but that will not happen in an area of poverty on a planet with nothing left to give. The poor will have to suffer.

Undercarriage video feeds show my stolen craft's landing gear touching down. The seat bumps against my rear. Spongy sediment deposits rise and cling to the starfighter's anchoring feet like dark snowflakes. Contamination here is worse than I remember.

Buildings within sight in the brown are less than a cycle away from failing to support those within them. Reinforced walls holding the brown at bay are a palm length in depth with corrosion. Only a small fraction of the wall's thickness remains. The air is eating them away one rotation at a time. Occupants must move or die within a few cycles, as the Armada will not invest in a lost cause.

The engine's thorium core settles into rest mode. The press of a button next to my seat brings the holo-programming feed up, and I command the starfighter's mask to activate when my bio signs are fifteen paces from its hull. I alone need to know where it is located.

My helmet rises into its holding position, and I place the Farca over my nose and mouth while pressing the integration jewel back to my temple, mentally engaging cockpit opening protocols. The starfighter's seal breaks as I press ocular goggles over each eye. My last layer of protection.

I exit the vessel in a strain to look beyond twenty paces and grab the bio mask from my bag. The hard ground's soft sediment cushions the impact when my feet hit it. I take a deep breath to check the Farca. The smell of burning flowers prickles against clear-headedness. The respirator is not tight enough. Its straps pull my hair to give a pinch as I tighten them down until I no longer smell the unmistakable scent of Kep Four's poisoning atmosphere.

Every step I take from the starfighter wrenches me with anxiety, but it is not fear. My actions define me. I glance back—the starfighter cloaks itself invisible to the naked eye.

4-2
Struggling Family

My target building comes into focus. I sneak around it with my feet stirring up an antagonistic death-cloud of lethal dust. The door I plan to access is nearby.

"Almost there."

A voice of unknown origin sends me ducking for cover behind an automatic G2E (Garbage-to-Energy converter). They compress waste into dense, marble-sized units used for energy extraction at matter conversion plants. They transport the waste to Gwadel Valley, which is a muddy, slime-pitted area of Kep Four littered with toxic waste and where they dispose of things after melting them down.

I listen for what may be those seeking my capture, hoping it is not the Uprisers, but hear nothing. A moment passes and silence shifts. A voice taps my eardrums. I want to look. I need to peek before panic fills me. Who is talking? Where is it coming from?

Curiosity is an ugly crutch of mine. The G2E finds itself in my line of vision as I glance around its edge. The sight both relieves and saddens me.

A mother in her forties walks down the untraveled roadway with two children: one girl and one boy. They look close to being seven cycles into their lives. Filthy clothing. Torn. Layered several times over to keep sediment at bay. They are different shades of gray when acquired from Armada clothing dispensaries and the only colors commoners are allowed to wear.

I have never seen an Armada soldier in those shades, off-duty or otherwise. Clothing separates the classes. I, however, did not mind wearing commoners' garbs before I started my Armada training program. People of significant wealth wear handmade clothing of the highest fashion from the best tailors. In the Armada, we have the freedom to wear whatever we want when off duty, as long as it does not resemble poverty linens and is not considered high fashion.

I remember walking with my uncle in similar attire to the mother and her two children in the street, but we survived, and we were happy. I am sure she wants a better life for her kids, but those lacking wealth with children are especially unfortunate. One cannot join the Armada with children.

The mother and her young ones pass by. She glances my way. Her eyes flare with equal measures of depression and embarrassment upon seeing my Armada flight uniform. I do not look down on her for life's challenges. Others would.

I step into the street and watch them. The little girl barely keeps up. She has an off gait, and her left arm, which is deformed and multi-jointed, is full of knots—a telltale sign that her mother was exposed to the brown during pregnancy.

The little girl trips, and her aged respirator falls off. She tears into a fit of coughing. My body flinches. I take off to help, but her mother places the mask back on her, holds it tight, and rushes her children away.

I stop to look as she runs with her son, turning sideways on her daughter's right to hold the mask on her little one as they go. The little girl struggles to keep up with her crippled stride. I watch until the brown swallows them.

Though out of sight, I cannot take my eyes off them. The path they took holds my attention. I stare into the point of the family's disappearance with watering eyes and swallow the planet's misery.

A door with a coded access panel on its right has my aim. It is my alleyway entry point. I am unsure if guards will be on the other side, but the payoff of saving lives is worth the risk. This is not my first walk in the park, but it is the first time things started off sideways.

I slide on my gloves, remove the bio mask from the bag, and drop the rest to the ground. The mask feels like a cloth sack when I pull it over my head, goggles, and Farca. It lowers my vision, but I will get scanned and identified without it.

My back goes to the door for one last Farca-purified breath of freedom before turning to the access panel. A metallic anti-sediment shield covers it. I lift it to input key codes as instructed by Dr. Sellers.

"Five, six, nine, one, three, five, seven, six, four, two, eight, one," I say aloud while entering the code.

It beeps. I crack the heavy door to aim an eye inside and find it clear of activity. There is no turning back.

4–3

Access

The first room I enter holds nothing more than a few shelves of unlabeled boxes and surgical experimentation equipment on them. Someone keeps the facility clean, polished, mopped, and free of dust. It is unabandoned, but Dr. Sellers said they are soon to change locations.

A small sphere in the corner matches others in the facility. They double as cameras and bio-scanners, but I have never seen them outside the Armada's capital cities. It is troubling. It means the Armada is not just cracking down on A.R.S. members like me. They are hazebent on catching us for what they consider hefty crimes.

Leading scientists working here will say they have no choice but to perform the experiments if I confront them.

They do, of course. Everyone has free will, and I am exercising mine.

Experimental processes in places like these are harsh. Flagerts are the most common animal targeted because they share a brain, heart, lungs, and circulatory system almost identical to humans. They subject the animals' lungs and blood to varying phases of the atmosphere's power to kill—from mild to concentrated levels greater than that of the Suicide Fields. The ones that survive have their blood filtered and suffer the process again.

This continues until they are too weak to remain alive. Then someone murders and dissects them. Scientists slice and examine the subjects' organs—anything they can do to find out why they thrive outdoors while we cannot.

"I know you're in here somewhere," I whisper to myself.

I take cautious steps through the room until it is behind me. The second section is the same. A tightness in my chest... I need a moment to think.

A spherical biosensor is motionless in the upper left corner. I am undetected, but delay will expose me. The mask and goggles have prevented facial recog systems from identifying me... yet. The suited hounds would have otherwise been on me by now.

If I am caught here, the Armada will stack it as a second crime along with taking the starfighter. I do not need another added to my list of those committed this rotation.

I peek into the next door. Two guards are looking through an observation window, staring into a lab. Whatever the men are watching, they are highly interested. I hope their distraction is robust enough not to notice me easing up on them.

My breaths halt as I smooth the door shut behind me. They are still looking through the window. I lower my hands into my pockets and remove a pair of coin-shaped synapsis disruptors. Sneaking up on the guards is arduous. At any moment, one of them could glance over their shoulder.

My steps are light until within arm's reach. I place a disruptor on each of their temples. They fall into each other upon contact, and I guide their descent to prevent heads from hitting the hard flooring at my feet.

I stand and inhale deeply to make up for not breathing the tiks I crept behind them. It is hard to breathe in the bio mask and Farca respirator. I can take them off now, but I do not. No time to put them back on if alarms go off.

The integration jewel on my temple buzzes twice. I close my eyes and focus on accepting the connection. Dr. Sellers's voice whispers into my mind.

"Are you in?" he asks.

"Yeah," I whisper.

"Be safe. I'll be watching from here if you need me."

"Thanks." I glance over my shoulder to ensure I am alone. "But I'm going to be in hot tar after this."

"I heard," says Dr. Sellers. "What happened?"

I shake my head in thought. "I think they moved varying security coding sequences for the starfighter up a few rotations."

"Maybe," he says. "Sorry, Mason."

My brows raise. "Do you want to cry about it or get this done?"

"Roll out."

I move to investigate the observation window. An old, frail scientist is preparing to administer something beyond my line of sight. His subject is electro-strapped to a table between us. People like him make me sick. They are disgusting players within the Armada, and their game is torture camouflaged as progress.

"Moving into the lab now," I say, double-checking to ensure the scientist is alone. "Ready on your end?"

"I'm with you," answers Dr. Sellers.

I grab the small cylindrical access rod from the guard lying at my feet and insert it into a matching hole next to the door. It unlocks with a click. I enter.

4–4
Confronting Evil

The frail scientist looks at me when I enter the lab, shaking in fear. I cannot say I blame him. I caught him red-handed, being a monster. He knows what people like me do when we enter places like this. I step forward, tunnel vision with eyes locked onto his, as he backs onto the restraining table.

I move toward him with slow strides. "You disgust me."

"How did you—?"

"Stop talking," I interrupt, reaching into my pocket to remove another synaptic disruptor, brandishing it for him as I approach.

"They'll just die out there regardless," he says.

"Maybe," I say with a nod. "As nature intended."

The old scientist, two heads taller than me, backs up, taking a spill over a small stool. He looks up, finger-pointing from the ground. "You'll be brought up on charges for this."

I look down to see the scientist's subject. A waist-high, bipedal, hairy flagert is in bindings and helpless to escape. The begging call for help in its eyes... I release the binding clamps and slide them off him. It jumps into my arms like a baby.

"The satellites will track the animals," continues the scientist. "They'll just get captured again. You know that."

"We're removing the trackers," I say.

"Not this time," says the frail scientist with the shake of his head. "Not this facility. We injected nano-trackers into their bloodstreams. They bond with red blood cells. Extracting them is fatal."

I pause. If the scientist is telling the truth, he is correct. It is impossible to remove nano-trackers from their bloodstream without killing the host.

"You're lying."

"No," he says. "We began implementing them nine rotations ago. That one's from the last group without."

I move to the control pane and activate it. My heart sinks when it renders. He is speaking the truth. The flagert in my arms is on the visual feed with procedure dates and time-stamps matching the moment.

"Do you see?" asks the frail scientist. "The satellites will track them down no matter what you do here."

I look at the ceiling, through it, and into the black beyond eyesight. "No. They won't."

The spherical cameras and bio-scanners in the upper corners of the room pivot and lock onto me. They are on the verge of identifying me.

"Great," I say.

I move to the observation window. Spheres in the upper corners of the lab pivot to face me. The frail scientist sees the loathing look in my eyes and searches beneath a white cloth on a nearby tray for something to defend himself with. He finds nothing.

"I tried to warn you," he says, fiddling with something in his hand. "I gave you the chance to walk away."

I set the flagert down and step to stand over him and the toppled stool. "What are you holding?"

His head shakes rapidly. "Nothing."

I kneel to wrestle it from his hands. His arm pops.

"Ahhh…" he screams, clutching his upper hand. "You broke my wrist."

I did not mean to hurt him. He is feeble. I would only hurt someone as a last resort, but I cannot undo it. Despite what he is, my veins course with woe over it as I open my hand to examine what he held. It is small, cubical, and has a latch lifted on it, revealing a flashing red button.

"A pocket flare?" I ask.

No response. I cannot blame him. These small cubical devices have pivoting tops with buttons underneath them. Once pressed, it sends a silent alarm throughout its assigned building and to Armada authorities. Some A.R.S. member would end his life for this, knowing theirs is over.

"You triggered a silent screening," I continue.

The remaining spheres zone in on me and buzz.

"Enter the code for an emergency release," I say. "Do it under meltdown protocols, so all the subjects' holding doors open."

He is going to fight me on this. Meltdown protocol is an Armada emergency procedure that unlocks and opens every passageway in a building or vessel and disables the need for security clearance, identification, or codes. Typically, only used when a building or large ship is on the verge of destruction. He will face charges of his own if he complies.

"But the atmosphere…" he says. "I can't just… They'd hold me for treason."

Overhead spheres flash with white pulses. I have little time before I am check-mated.

"Now," I shout.

"I'm sorry," stutters the frail scientist. "I… I just… I can't."

I turn the dial on the synaptic disruptor. "This one's not set for sleep."

The frail scientist trembles upon seeing it. He looks back and forth between the disruptor and me, reading my eyes.

My gaze shifts from the flagert to him. "Call my bluff."

He stands to input codes into a nearby panel. The subject-holding cells overtake the viewing pane. The doors are opening. Alarms wail throughout the facility.

"You'll face charges for this," he shouts.

"An acceptable martyr." I place the disruptor against his temple.

He falls unconscious, thinking I had it set on parameters to end his life. There are sympathizers like that, but ending lives is not my forte. He got lucky.

Dozens of animals making a break for freedom catch my attention through the lab window. Guards chase after them, but there are too many of the scientist's test subjects heading in unpredictable directions. A hidden grin forms behind my Farca watching their break for freedom.

I extend an arm to the flagert. "Come on."

It takes my hand.

4–5

Escape

We rush into the hallway. Brown swirls of death are visible through a door at the rear of the building, but the flagert needs to go in that direction. It is safer than where I am heading. They will kill him if he comes with me and I am caught.

The starfighter is my only chance of escaping with the Armada after me. Surely, they are on their way to arrest me.

I nudge the flagert while pointing down the long corridor. "Go."

He eases down it, stopping halfway to the door.

"Go," I repeat. "Go."

I spin to move but catch a guard trying to grab the flagert in the corner of my eye.

"Hey," I shout.

The guard locks onto me. His face is twisted, and he no longer cares about capturing the fleeing animals. He has a new target.

I eye the heavy-set guard and run, free of worries he can catch me. His physicality does not lend itself to speed. Too many Armada meals do not make one a sprinter.

Another guard appears from a side door to grab me, but I duck under his attempt and maintain pace. He slams into the wall on my left. A flesh-on-steel impact. A moan. Sounded like it hurt.

I cut back into the lab, surge through the experimental chamber, and hurdle the two guards I downed earlier under flashing lights and alarms.

"South of primary lab entrance," calls a guard.

I glance over my shoulder. Three others approach, closing the gap. My mind races. How many are there?

"You need to move," says Dr. Sellers.

"Yeah?" I ask. "What makes you think that?"

"Less than thirty tiks before they make you."

The spheres dismount from the upper corners of the room and hover after me, but I think I have lost the guards. My exit is in sight. I surge for it.

Another guard steps in my path from a side room with his arms wide for a tackle. I slide feet first through his legs and swipe them out from under him. Sometimes it is good to be small.

The guard gets to his hands and knees, catching a soccer kick to lift his head.

My left fist meets his jaw to knock him back down, and I run as he rises to chase.

"Cadet Mason," says the automated system, "serial number M5S14m36–ND, you have violated Armada law. Locate an Armada patrol station and turn yourself in immediately."

I remove the bio mask and reach into my vest pocket to remove a small, short-range, E.M.P. (Electro Magnetic Pulse) field generator—with heavy electric charge production, and stick it to the coded door as I exit into the brown.

The restrictive Farca causes my breathing to become labored as I run after fighting. I need to confirm the guards do not make it out in time. I look back in stride, knowing I will not make it up and into the starfighter in time if they exit the building.

"She's baking the doors," shouts a guard as he reaches to remove the short-range E.M.P. field generator.

I take back into my run.

ZAP

It most likely knocked him out. At the least, it fried the door and forced it closed. E.M.P. field generators have never failed me, but using one is going to add to my punishment when they catch up with me. Nobody can hide from the Armada forever.

My feet are quick enough to leave a brown cloud rising from the ground behind me. It covers my legs. Buildings pass by. I am close to the starfighter, which has not yet shown itself.

"Come on," I say.

The integration jewel tingles my temple, and the starfighter renders itself visible fifteen paces ahead.

"That a girl," I say.

I assigned a female gender to my stolen starfighter the first time I took her into the black three cycles ago. She is powerful, intelligent, and stimulating—all female.

My footing slips halfway up the starfighter's side, and I take a spill into the cushioning brown sediment below. I look over my shoulder. Guards have not made it out yet.

I squat down and jump for the open hatch frame. My fingers wrap around its edge to pull myself up and slither in. The positive pressure system blows hard from the cockpit's bottom to keep hostile air from entering as the hatch closes.

The pilot's seat contours to my rear. I pop off the goggles, accidentally dropping one of them. It falls into a slight recession between the manual flight control arms and readout panels. They built it for my body type, a prototype and the first of its kind, but interior design was not the Armada's priority for intern testing trials.

"That's..." I say. "That's just great."

I cannot pilot the starfighter in manual with it lodged there. The controlling arm will be stuck in a diving position if I do not use the integration jewel to fly it. I reach hard, but it is too far down. Short arms are never an advantage during times of crisis.

My ship moves with a light rock. At least, I think it did. It was subtle. I am unsure. My eyes widen, listening for a moment to hear nothing.

I reach back down for the goggles, stretching to the point of pain until I have it in my fingertips and pull it out.

The flight helmet lowers onto me as the hatch closes. It seals. I grip the controls for a sharp vertical lift and bank. Wait... Something is on my arm. A bug? I freeze as it crawls on me, dreading to look.

"Please don't be a goneth jumper," I say.

Goneth jumpers are one of three insects thriving out-doors. The six-legged creature is thumb-sized and non-venomous, with sharp barbs on its feet. They insert small amounts of Kep Four's sediment into the skin and clothing as they step.

I pivot to look. A hand on my arm forces me to jump, accidentally pulling the flight controls and spinning the starfighter into the side of a building. My right shoulder blade burns with pain when I bounce off the dashboard. I reach for the controls. Another impact sends me into the cockpit's port side. Everything spins.

"Engage autopilot and stop vessel," I say.

The starfighter slows to a halt. I shoot my eyes to the stern, unsure whether to run or face whoever is with me. The flagert I rescued peeks from behind the pilot's seat.

"What the haze are you doing here?" I ask.

I turn to see a guard opening the facility's baked door with onium rifles.

"Don't guess it matters now," I say.

I strap in and pull beyond the brown for the black with onium rounds flying past me. The guards cannot hit me at this altitude without luck. They are firing blindly.

It is time to finish my quest and figure out what to do with my new passenger. Flagerts are nicer than most humans, but I cannot keep him—not in the hole I have dug myself with the Armada. I will have to figure it out later.

CHAPTER 5

Cargo Cube

The flagert slinks from sight when we hit the black. I doubt his previous presence here. He is somewhere behind me, hiding from the stars and terrified.

I stop to check on him. He is as still as the surrounding shines. His grip wrenches into the seat's fabric. He must feel cornered up here. I feel bad for him. His eyes are shaking.

"It's okay, buddy," I say. "It's okay. I have you now. No one is going to hurt you."

Research suggests flagerts are intellectually equal with a child ten cycles of age. They are cunning and playful under the right circumstances, but this one is uncomfortable. I do not blame him.

"I'll have you out of here in a tek or two," I say, punching in coordinates for satellites and trackers orbiting the region. "Fire."

A multicolored beam zips from the starfighter, and the ship re-angles itself to face another distant satellite.

"Fire."

I repeat the process three times. Small flashes light distant patches of black as satellites fry from over-surge. It is better than destroying them. The Armada can repair the burned components within 30 rotations. It will make my sentence less harsh once they catch up with me.

I jump the starfighter to an unoccupied space on the planet and bank into the brown. My destination is two clicks away. I snug my vessel in a few feet from ground level before switching to E-output drive, coasting the rest of the way to my extraction point.

Fallen statues—separated sections of Mount Rushmore brought from Ancient Earth to Kep Four—dominate the scene. All four stood on individual pillars thousands of cycles before my life began, but time has taken its toll on them. Lack of upkeep, a diminishing population in the area that crept down to zero, and the atmosphere ate away their bases along with the people's morale.

The brown grows almost too thick to see through. A swirl of toxins float within it like petrol fumes from an open bucket. I have reached the edge of the Suicide Fields. No one else will be here. Even in protective gear, the area is not safe.

A cargo cube that is to be my taxi drifts into view.

"Dr. Sellers..." I whisper to no one. "Just on time, as usual."

The cargo cube eases to within five paces of my stolen starfighter and comes to a stop. Its exterior is dust-covered and battered with dents and rust from a dekatee of work. Sediment impedes me from seeing through its side windows.

I kill the starfighter's engine as it comes to a stop. My heart hurts to engage its mask, knowing I may never fly her again. I wonder how long I can avoid the Armada, but such thoughts are fleeting in comfort.

There is an emergency cat-5 suit pack situated under my seat. They come stored beneath the pilot's chairs in all Armada-issued vessels and are reflective silver for easy visibility in areas of dense pollution. They are the best suits made to venture into the suicide fields and offer an additional seventeen teks of time over all others—just long enough to think about your death before dying. I need it here.

The flagert watches curiously as I grab the suit, slide it over my feet, up my torso, and push my arms through its sleeves. A pull on the fastening cord seals its airtight construct. It vacuums to my body. I wait for it to confirm a full seal and pressurize before exiting.

Dr. Sellers opens the cargo cube's door in a matching suit and steps out as my hatch raises.

"That was close," he says.

I slide off the starfighter to scan the area for hidden Armada patrol units. "Can we hurry?"

The flagert jumps from the cockpit and lands in front of Dr. Sellers, screeching when it sees him. Its feet slip in sediment as it tries to backpedal. I rush to calm him, but he bolts past me and disappears into the brown, instinctively heading away from the Suicide Fields four times faster than I could take chase.

"What the haze was that about?" asks Dr. Sellers.

"Long story," I answer.

"Hmph," mutters Dr. Sellers.

He turns and enters the cargo cube.

I follow him in. "Another cube?"

"Deal with it," says Dr. Sellers.

Cargo cubes are less than five paces wide inside. As short as I am, I cannot stand upright in them. The smell of used equipment and unwashed clothes does not make it any better. As he said, I can deal with it. Dr. Sellers has rewritten its delivery path, and I will not be riding in it long.

I look around. There is nowhere to sit. They build cargo cubes for crates and other random goods, not people.

Its doors close behind me. It is ugly, empty, and dull. I sigh and sit in a corner to my right.

"What?" I sarcastically ask. "No S-Class?"

Dr. Sellers sits in the opposing corner three paces away and pulls up a digital flight guide on the viewing pane. The acceleration is tedious. It is fitting, I guess.

5-2
The Drinking Station

We reach our destination, and the door opens for us to exit. I step outside and glance back in the direction from where we came. It is an empty path at least five clicks from the nearest anything.

"Do you think he'll be alright?" I ask.

"The flagert?" he asks in return. "Why do you think they're targeted for research? They're resistant to the syndrome."

"But this close to the Suicide—"

"They're fast, Mason," he interrupts, stepping from the cargo cube with its flight log in hand. "I'm sure he cleared the area before it affected him."

I acknowledge his correctness, but my worry continues. I do not want the guilt of having him die because I dropped it off at death's edge. The flagert will make it out. At least, I hope he does.

"Over here," says Dr. Sellers.

I follow him to an S.C.P.T. (Science-Civil Personal Transport) vessel. Only doctors and scientists of the highest standing in the Armada receive them. Its doors pop out, slide back along its side, and roll up over the decklid when we near it. The vessel is nice: sleek, only a pace high, has an interior of Armada greens and whites with a dash full of instrument clusters trimmed in gold—a symbol of being at an Armada General's level in the medical field.

I move to the vehicle's side as he sits in the passenger seat and plugs the flight log into a rectangular device that scrubs electronics clean enough that information is irretrievable. In the A.R.S., we call it a wiper.

Dr. Sellers finishes, stands, and shuts his S.C.P.T., carrying the flight log with him. He motions to the building across the parking grounds. "Shall we?"

I study the hand-cut wooden letters on the establishment's outer wall:

THE DRI KING STATION

Despite its excellent old-world style, it is a dive. I have been there a dozen times with Dr. Sellers. Members of the Armada avoid it as much as they do the Suicide Fields. It is commoner ground, and we enter knowing it is the best of crappy choices to lie low for a bit and figure things out.

5–3
A Chat With Sellers

Its wood replica panel hangs by a thread with a missing letter in its name near the entrance. A protective overhead board flaps repeated taps to the wind's will as we approach. The rest of its exterior matches in dilapidation.

The shift from its unkept exterior is not as stark as one would think. Its interior aura matches its exterior upon walking through its doors. Unsavory characters of all types visit unswept floors to sit in chairs laced with cracks and unknown faded designs. The bar's top is a riddle of knife-carved insignias. Four carvings where I am sitting read:

The Armada can eat it

Death to the machine

Equalrightstolive

Contact3792-4-19foragoodtime

I move past tables of not-so-common commoners with Dr. Sellers. His Armada medical clothes stick out like a sore digit here. A tall man with broad shoulders, a long beard, and chipped teeth sees us and stands to head our way. I recognize him. Though, I do not know his name.

He reaches us and stops to block our path with crossed arms and a long beard.

"What are you doing here?" he asks.

"Trying to figure a way out of a jam," answers Dr. Sellers.

The man looks my way. "What'd she do this time?"

"Same old, same old," answers Dr. Sellers while cutting me a quick glance. "Got burned this time though."

The bearded man chuckles, pats our shoulders, and rubs my head as he passes between us. "Ask around if you need to lie low."

"Will do," I say, turning to watch him walk away.

The man exits. Doors reaching from ceiling to floor swing shut like an old Western saloon. The halo-filter in the archway keeping death at bay is fluttering as the doors swing. They will need replacing soon.

I admire what Ancient Earth once was but despise its conquerors. It was the first planet humanity lived upon before destroying its ability to harbor life. It was stunning, but that did not last with human involvement: wars, pollution, carbon build-up, and everything else leading to a runaway greenhouse effect ended its reign to protect life. I know of its beauty from images alone.

Moving took our ancestors hundreds of life cycles onboard generational starships to accomplish. It landed us on Kepler 442-b, which was the Kepler designated name filed on the cycle of its discovery. Most call it *Kep Four*.

"Come on, Mason," says Dr. Sellers.

I look at Dr. Sellers with a sigh and raised brows. "Why do we always sit at the bar?"

"Better to have our backs to everyone," answers Dr. Sellers.

"That's like..." I say, looking around. "That's the opposite of what I was thinking."

"We don't need anyone here thinking we're looking for anything on the underground market," says Dr. Sellers. "Let's just get this situation figured out."

I can agree with him on the underground market comment. That is where people go to purchase stolen or illegal items on Kep Four, such as Craga juice (a potent and illegal drink mixture of several drugs and 98 proof liquor). If you know the right people, you can gain access to unpermitted Armada firearms hidden within the shadiest areas in districts of poverty.

We take a seat and study the other patrons before talking. The Drinking Station is an interesting place. It is full of criminals and anti-Armada alike, but I would not say there are any real scumbags here. Most are committing crimes to survive and keep their families alive. They come here to talk and trade resources, but none share their names. We spoke to the man who stopped us before in the past, but we have never exchanged identities.

"You know..." I say, adjusting my seat. "I'm going to have to say things have gone better."

Dr. Sellers smirks. "You think so?"

I nod. "Just a tad. Yeah."

The look-a-like working the bar approaches. "What is to be on your palate tonight?"

I look it over carefully. They have bothered me since childhood. Especially models like this one. It is retro with sleek curvature and seamless joints that look human. Their glowing eyes for easy visual identification do not make them appear far enough from alive. This one was most likely intercepted by civilians or went dead in whatever valley of death they had it mining in.

"What is to be on your palate tonight?" it repeats.

"Water," answers Dr. Sellers.

"H2O. Certainly," it says, extending an arm. One of the fifteen fingers on its hand flows water into a glass. "And for you?"

"Same," I answer.

It pours from the unsanitized finger again. I gag, thinking I am about to drink it.

"Have a wonderful rotation," says the look-a-like, moving to a slobbering lady waving for service a few seats over from Dr. Sellers.

"That lady does not need another drink," I say.

Dr. Sellers looks her way. "No, she doesn't."

Not that her drinking habits are any business of mine. I watch the look-a-like's hands closely as it makes her next drink. A small squirt of powder from its palm mixes with the liquid. It is slipping her detox.

She jests with the look-alike ... like it is living and sips. Once ingested, she will be sober in less than ten teks.

"What's the plan?" asks Dr. Sellers.

I take a sip of water. "Not a clue. They made me this time."

His head lowers. "I know. What are we going to do about it?"

"They'll catch me eventually."

"That they will," he says, pinching the bridge of his nose in thought and rubbing it for a moment. "The penalty when you're caught will be harsher than if you were to—"

"Right," I interrupt. "But I'm not sure about turning myself in."

"The sooner you do it, the lesser the penalty," he says. "I mean, you could run for as many rotations as you can, but each rotation you don't turn yourself in..."

"I know." My palms brush instinctively over my face. "It's an extra cycle of incarceration for every rotation I don't surrender."

Dr. Sellers chugs his water and stands. "It's the best option, Mason."

He is correct as usual, like the time he told me not to drink randy root (a recreational narcotic that, depending on dosage, causes anything from a mild buzz to powerful hallucinations). I knew it would get me buzzed, but I failed to test my tolerance beforehand. That stuff made me hallucinate for quite the spell and ruined a few rotations of my life.

"How long do you think I'll get?" I ask.

"I don't know," answers Dr. Sellers. "You didn't kill anyone that you know of, but you destroyed Armada property. Go a few cycles without turning yourself in until they catch you, and they may execute you for it."

I think they will give me twenty cycles for my crimes. Perhaps worse. The funny thing is the fact that I harbor no worries about it. Am I depressed? Sure. Scared? No. It will probably improve my dating life if they do not lock me in solitude.

"All right," I say. "I'm going to do it."

"You're going to do what?" he asks.

"Right now," I continue.

"I'm not... How?"

His eyes follow as I stand to exit.

"How?" he asks.

I turn back with sarcasm. "I'm taking the starfighter back and telling them I'm sorry."

"Now, look..." says Dr. Sellers. "I'm closer to you than all others involved, Mason. The thought of you—"

"Hey..." I interrupt and wrap my arms around him. "Aren't I supposed to be the one upset?"

His body jumps a few times from subtle spasms laced tightly around internalized sobs.

"Sellers..." I say. "You know I'll say nothing about your involvement."

"I know," he says. "But do you have to do it right this tik? Can't you wait until—"

"I need to do it while I'm confident."

I head for the exit.

"Hey," he calls from behind.

I turn in time to catch a pair of 15-Fargon re-breathers right before they hit me in the chest. The small, egg-shaped canisters clip onto Farcas to clean and recirculate air, which makes them highly desirable in the underground market.

"Won't you need them?" I ask.

"I'll be fine," answers Dr. Sellers. "It's you I'm worried about."

I study him for a moment before nodding and walking from The Drinking Station. He is no doubt burning a hole in the back of my head, but I cannot stop to look back. I may not leave if I do. Part of me feels terrible about it. I am usually more talkative with him at The Drinking Station, and my sudden departure is unsettling for us both.

reach the cargo cube at the other end of the parking grounds and enter. It will be a ride back to the starfighter in solace, and I may reprogram it to take its time on the return. The desire to face trial is non-existent.

I am not looking forward to what may lie ahead, but I have earned it by being committed to a good cause. Time served with probation will not be on the table when I am brought forth. Several cycles of incarceration? Processing for execution? I have known the possibilities that loom with every rotation I have followed the A.R.S. path.

The thoughts fade as my trip back to the starfighter nears its end.

Dr. Sellers was generous in tossing me those 15-Fargon re-breathers. He will have to write them off as missing when he requests more from Armada supply. They will question how the re-breathers became lost, but Dr. Sellers is trusted amongst the ranks and should have no issues swaying them.

The cube slows, catching my attention. It must be navigating between the fallen monuments. There is no other reason for it to reduce speed. I pull up external feeds to see them one last time.

Fallen monuments of Ancient Earth's Rushmore come unclearly onto the cube's viewing pane and always feel larger than they are—the power of history. Uprisers have covered them in graffiti, and the sight of it cooks my blood. Red pinstripes run across the Monument's face in jagged lightning bolt patterns, diagonally from bottom right to top leftover black. Their twisted symbol of a white, human pelvic bone is in the center of each monument's forehead.

Dolofónos ordered his Uprisers there last cycle to issue a warning to current world leaders that they are no longer in control of society. They should heed it and take him seriously. Dolofónos is maniacal at best.

George Washington comes up on my left, laying on an ear. Thousands of cycles' worth of weather have battered the carving's curvature and overall shape of his face smooth. It has wholly eroded the tip of his nose. Corners of his left eyebrow and ear broke off during transport.

The cargo cube veers around Thomas Jefferson's monument lying dead center of my flight path. A fall from its mighty pillar generated too significant an effect for it to sustain its original form, and the impact that followed cracked it in two sections from ear to ear.

Theodore Roosevelt and Abraham Lincoln are on my right, though Roosevelt came to rest quite a distance from the others. We know little about Roosevelt, but, according to records, Lincoln was partially responsible for our mixed-ethnic society. I cannot believe they once stood cliffside on another planet.

Their fate will soon be ours.

The cargo cube continues until they are behind me... and stops. Its power core is failing. This happens on rare occasions when using outdated equipment that is no longer being tracked by the Armada for A.R.S. activities.

"That's just great," I mumble.

Its last sliver of power opens the door—a safety protocol to ensure no one is sealed within a cube. I exit and head toward the starfighter. Three point five clicks to trek and I am climbing inside of it.

6-2
Oxygen

I am feeling weak, like I need sleep, from not getting enough oxygen, but I cannot be tired from walking a mere three clicks. My respirator must be weakening. I take the deepest breath possible and hold it while unfastening the left filter and screwing on one of two 15-Fargon re-breathers Dr. Sellers tossed me.

My lungs are getting tight. I take a few more deep breaths to compose myself and remove the right side to install the remaining re-breather, but something is stopping me. I am having trouble lining up its threads. Panic sets in. I am getting frantic and lightheaded from holding my breath.

They finally line up, and I take a deep breath while screwing it tight. The first breath burns my lungs with the hot sensation of swallowing broken glass. Coughing ensues. I am dizzy. My knees hit the ground, then my hands. Crawling.

A single thought crosses my mind as my arms buckle, and I fall to my chest.

Who will find my body at the edge of the Suicide Fields?

My vision fades. A last effort to press on fails. I can no longer...

6-3
Death's awakening

My eyes open. Several teks or more must have passed. I stand to walk a crooked line back to the starfighter—my body is reacting to the air I took in. An itching sensation I cannot scratch through protective gear covers my body like a jagged jumpsuit.

The starfighter renders itself visible. Its hatch lifts as I near it, and I climb inside under an approaching countdown surrounding my freedom. Soon, I will not worry about being exposed to the atmosphere... but taking part in my fallen family's memory files will be a thing of the past.

My vessel's hatch lowers, releasing a small, airtight wave as the cockpit floods with positive atmospheric pressure. It creates compression on the body, but it is normal after sitting so long in a highly contaminated zone.

"Confirm full seal," I say.

"Beltric Class Six seal confirmed," says the A.I.

I remove the Farca. A deep gasp and lightheadedness blow through me. I must have taken in more of the brown than I thought. Oxygen floods the cockpit. I am relieved to breathe fresh air. Tense muscles in my body relax.

I power up the E-output drive and route a course over the fallen monuments straight to Hangar 9. Staying low to avoid being seen by lingering overhead searches until I am close to Chimark is best. Satellites relay inaccurate positions in that region, but it is mental comfort more than anything else.

Twenty cycles, if I get that, will be a long time without visiting mother. Such solitude drives people crazy. Following my recent behavior, certain individuals may consider me to be insane. I am not. Artistically determined in my personal life, outspoken, tactless, and wild after one too many Jerleanian shots, sure, but not crazy.

The last segment of the flight drags. Thoughts of solitude are outrunning the starfighter and not slowing. Depression sets further in. Maybe it is apprehension.

The Armada Alliance Capital of Chimark appears over the horizon. Coned peaks of black ferromagnetic city lifts, ones we call city-flyers, hover in ring position and point sky-ward while looming over a metropolis three clicks off the ground. I have been looking at them since my birth 22 cycles ago, but they still impress me floating in the lighter regions of brown. Above them floats a sky wishing to be bluer under all else in the universe.

Electromagnetic baseplates with vast amounts of metallic osmium possessing a gravity property of 22.5 line the bottom of each capital. The antigravity properties of Spletnumd-27, when mixed with melted osmium, release untold levels of power for vertical lift. It is how they keep capitals from falling to Kep Four and crushing districts below. City-flyers are similar in antigravity design and charge through lightning generators.

I have never dabbled into how antigravity mechanics work in relation to vessels, the City-flyers, or the capitals they support. I may not be wholly accurate in thinking about how they work. All I know is the term anti-gravity does not work to describe them properly.

City-flyers create artificial gravity above them to pull objects on a vertical trajectory. The more power, the more lift, but the working system is not technically ridding itself of the gravity below. Counter-gravity seems like a more appropriate description than antigravity.

"I'm going to miss seeing those," I say.

They are the prettiest things remaining on Kep Four. Trees have been gone since before I was born, but I have city-flyers to appreciate. Varying lightning storms tightly encasing them grow louder as I near them, but they are easy on the eyes.

Chimark and other capitals are self-contained with artificial plant life lining their edges for visual beauty, but like everything else natural looking on Kep Four, it is artificial. Nothing here beyond life, death, and the battle to stay alive is real. Those struggles come into perspective when a pair of floating prisons enters my visual range.

There are three holding systems. Each unit is disk-shaped and supported by a colossal cylinder of steel containing an elevator running through its center. The highest is for the least dangerous criminals, middle for mid-grade offenses, and the bottom tier is for anyone facing crimes worthy of processing. Rules there are deadly strict. The prison administers sharp punishments, ejecting prisoners from its sides if they get out of line.

I can only hope they place me in the all-female system. The Armada will lock Dolofónos up in C.H.I., closest to me on my left. It is where they keep the worst of the worst, and he is the nastiest of that. His followers are no different. They emulate their savage messiah.

They incarcerate many on Kep Four for stealing food and water. It is a crime. I understand, but some have no alternative. On the rotation I joined the Armada, an entire family got themselves deliberately arrested. After the authorities took them into custody, they separated the family for three cycles and placed each in a separate location with clean air and manufactured food—a fair trade for most parents.

The Armada takes in the children of arrested parents to be future cadets. It benefits the government; it is survival over freedom for families.

To most, getting locked away or executed and losing their children is a better choice than watching them starve to death. I have no children and cannot offer input on the mindset, but I understand it. For six cycles, the Armada has been my prison, and I placed myself in its grasp for Mother.

I open comms to communicate with approaching Armada crafts.

Sergeant Bentley's voice comes mid-sentence over my cockpit's comms. "...or we're going to initiate capital assault practices used when Armada vessels are involved."

I do not have to hear the first part of that sentence to know what is happening. What transpires for those who opt to ignore them is known. I am not foolish.

"Cadet Mason," says Sergeant Bentley. "You have one tek to comply before we—"

"I know the drill," I interrupt.

The effect of taking that partial breath near the Suicide Fields is lingering. I am still lightheaded, but, at least, it is taking the edge off my nerves. It is not a high or drunk sensation, but it is close to both.

"Bring her in," says Sergeant Bentley.

The reward for saving lives on Kep Four is getting a trip straight to trial. I made my decision and acted upon it. The consequences are mine to face.

Eighteen Bomba Class Ones are about to surround me. It is the standard Armada number for theft of a flight vessel.

I exhale. "And so, it ends."

They emerge from the capital's energy dome, which is explicitly coded to allow only Armada vessels to pass through. It destroys any unauthorized craft. I saw it happen once. Upon contact, the dome introduced the vessel to its end. Being shaken in random, one-pace patterns fifty-seven times a tik, tears anything not coded correctly apart.

The interceptors are sharp in design and three times the size of my starfighter. They look similar, and, although more agile, I am in the baby version of what my captors are piloting.

The Bomba class has more firepower than my stolen starfighter. Scat shots—a single burst from a large barrel releasing fifty-one balls of antimatter—are formidable. If I so much as flinch, they will fire one of their two scats, turning the surrounding black into an unescapable zone of destruction.

Even with the Beltric Class starfighter's mobility, I cannot make a run for it. Truth be told, I am not worried. I did what was right. Running away from what awaits me is not part of the plan.

Sergeant Bentley pops onto my forward viewing pane. "Hold your position, Cadet Mason."

The reality of what is happening sets in.

"Haze," I say, looking off to my left at nothing and wishing to be anywhere else.

"Why'd you have to do this on my rotation?" he asks.

"I couldn't watch it happen," I answer. "I couldn't just sit back anymore, and no one else was going to do anything about it."

I am unsurprised to see him leading the interceptors. The confidence he used to hold regarding my future is melting from his face. He will never trust me again, but he will not have to.

"You could've talked to someone before betraying the Armada," says Sergeant Bentley.

I sit up straight and lean to the pane. "Can I ask you something? Why's everyone on Kep Four so quick to stick their heads in the sand?"

"Come again?" he asks.

"Everyone lies to themselves and expects others to do the same."

"Afraid I'm still lost here," he says. "And we've only got a few tiks before you're silenced."

"Why bother saying I could've talked to someone?" I ask. "Would it have made a difference?"

"No. Those experiments are vital to make—"

"Then why say it?" I interrupt.

He gives a mean eye to intimidate me. I expect it from someone of his rank, even though he knows I am right about this world and what is happening on it. I give him a few tiks, but he does not reply to my question.

"Edifying answer, Sergeant," I say.

"Shut her down," he commands.

I power down the comm link between us. Everything goes black in the cockpit as they kill the starfighter's mainframe.

"No sounds," I mumble. "No lights. No way out."

They lock onto my starfighter, and it hums a dark vibrato inside, a tell-tell that someone has electronically grappled onto me. There is nothing I can do about it and no use in getting upset. All I can do is sit.

Trial awaits. The Armada does not give A.R.S. members a chance to gain representation. I will be no exception. I should have visited the Capital Museum a least once to see its exhibit of ancient Earth's relics and fossils. Only Armada members and those wealthy enough may visit. I just never thought about it.

Half the Bombas have locked onto my Beltric with localized gravity wells. The others are positioned to follow. Sergeant Bentley will be the next living soul I see, with escorting guards and a lecture for me waiting in his throat. After that, the Planetary Sovereign will decide my sentencing.

I do not believe they will execute me. After all, I have handled many tasks involving the A.R.O. (Artifact Recovery Operation) over my cycles with the Armada. Unless they put me in the Chimark Holding Institute with Dolofónos, I will be fine. If they place me there, I will request execution.

I have been sitting in a cell for six cycles. The buzz of electro-bars pulsating currents of energy from left to right no longer bothers me, nor does the hallow lead wall behind them separating me from the guards' walkway. The mind's power lies in its ability to adapt.

Wardens who decide executions in facilities they oversee never reveal their names to the inmates or the public. The one we have at A.H.C. (Armada Holding Center) allows its guards to move me every five rotations for the use of its exercise facilities, but I spend most of my time reading. A.H.C. holds former Armada members, and, as far as Kep Four prisons go, is a cushioned ride.

I have spent most of my time reading from its library delivery service. My favorite so far is a series about deciphering ancient languages and how to read hieroglyphs called *Cracking Words*. It left me thinking about the Egyptian pyramids, which were still standing when humanity left Ancient Earth.

The series told me nothing unknown but sparked new thoughts on how to approach languages since my time deciphering for the A.R.O. Should I ever work on the project again, I will try to access more of its secrets. Though humanity has never stumbled upon an intelligent alien species, there is undeniable proof of their existence. A.R.O. is that proof.

Humanity settled Kep Four thousands of cycles ago. A discovery followed a few thousand later, thus launching the Artifact Recovery Operation. That finding changed the way we looked at the universe.

They found remnants of an advanced civilization beneath Mt. Ragat, our tallest natural forming peak, and the discovery dated to 850,000 cycles before our documented existence. The unknown language coating its surface was the first of its kind and disconcerting. With it, our race was no longer the supreme beings of all in sight.

Those before me deciphered fragments of the inscriptions. It was not until the Armada learned of my H-SAM that they asked me to join the few others with it and help in its final translations. I buried myself in it until we had an official translation and solved the barriers holding us back.

Cracking the linguistic code was a heavy hand in getting me accepted into the Armada, who briefly hailed me for it but disapproved of glorification. I agree with them on that. One should never seek panegyrizing when working to benefit others. What I unlocked allowed the Armada to reverse engineer technology, but it does not make me special.

Following breakthroughs allowed Armada vessels to make small jumps in space without further destroying the ecosystem, but those of great magnitude remain impossible. They estimate another twelve cycles before we can build ships capable of jumping magnitudes greater than a fraction of the quadrant. It would be a crucial step forward.

There are no other habitable planets within our sector of The Milky Way. We can only hope Kep Four has twenty or more cycles left. If it does not, it will spell our end.

Most of those incarcerated with me are good examples of humanity, at least the few I converse with. Ninety percent of them have done nothing to warrant being jailed. We call these people passersby. They intentionally get themselves locked up, because they are at a point in life they can no longer feed themselves or their families. Prisoners holding passersby titles are innocent in my book.

The remaining ten percent here is a mixed assortment. Five percent committed crimes worthy of traditional imprisonment. The remaining five percent are dangerous in the lower holding disk and have coins flipped on their lives. One would think humanity could have moved beyond a murdering mindset by now, but there are still stragglers with poorly developed DNA, upbringings, and low intellects to stir chaos.

Opinions aside, facts remain: intelligent individuals tend to refrain from starting street fights or committing heinous crimes. Civilization banned violent and/or intellectually challenged people from reproducing through sterilization 800 cycles ago. They do it through chemicals in the food, but I do not know what it is. It has nearly paid off. We are closer to breeding out violence and random stupidity from the gene pool than ever.

However, Dolofónos has found a way around it with his Uprisers. We believe his five Butchers are giving the Uprisers a counter-agent ... and a highly addictive one at that.

I think about it for a tik and grab the latest shipment of digi-books they delivered. Nothing interests me in the stack. I grab one I am half finished with and continue it while exercising.

A cycle after turning myself in, I used a digi-book's internal chip as a launch point for a hack. It was not with evil intent, but I routed a visual feed into my cell for news updates. The Warden was not pleased. I spent many rotations after that swabbing the decks.

Two cycles went by before they allowed me to have digi-books again. My hair has grown long and drapes my shoulder, but I have not had a way to see it without mirrors. All that remains of what it used to be is my natural brunette color.

I finish the digi-book, *Language of the Gods and How to Speak It*, while doing bodyweight squats. My legs are shaking. Sweat burns my eyes to force a wince when I set it down to grab another, *Primitive Warp Theory... and Why it Failed.*

The cellblock beeps as I start the first chapter. Electro-bars shut down, darkening my cell with an accompanying quiet. Someone is coming. It is not a visitor. Inmates do not have that luxury.

The silver-haired warden steps into view with a few guards.

"Assume the position," he says.

I lay face down and place my hands behind my back at my waistline. It is standard when they come to drag me away for rec time, a privilege they took from me a quarter cycle ago. I did nothing to deserve it other than talking down to the warden.

"Open it," he says.

The sound of glass-on-glass fills my cell as it slides open. A guard moves to each of my sides and places organic cuffs on me. I grimace as they clamp my wrists.

"Tight enough?" I ask.

"Get her up," says the warden.

They pick me up. I turn to face the warden, squirming my wrist under the pressure generated by muscle tissue running throughout the bindings. Organic cuffs are not jagged, nor do they hold any sharp edges. They are soft, like a constricting serpent, and designed to operate similarly. The more you move, the tighter they constrict.

My nose wrinkles with the guard's overstretching cologne. "What's this about? I haven't done anything wrong since my first twenty rotations."

"Can't tell you," answers the warden. "These orders came straight from the Planetary Sovereign."

"The Sovereign?" I ask. "Wait. What did I do?"

He walks off. The guards guide me to follow behind him. This is bad. Terrible. There have been just a few dozen capital punishments during my life, and I might face one.

"Seriously," I say, locking my feet into place. "Are you listening to me? What did I do?"

A shove at my back stumbles me forward.

"Keep walking," says the shoving guard.

The Planetary Sovereign only meets with people when there is a heavy consequence to be faced unless a large-scale military movement is underway. Armada skirmishes with the Uprisers are the closest thing to war on Kep Four. It must be about me. They are going to be planning my execution once we reach the Planetary Conference Hall.

Sealed entrance and exit points open automatically as the warden nears them, allowing us to pass through without pause. Bio-scan security feeds inlaid into walls map our DNA. We enter a cylindrical lift unit.

It is empty inside and reminds me of the cargo cube I was in six cycles ago. I do, however, appreciate the change of scenery.

"Landing deck," says the warden.

He, nor the guards, smile. Ever. Cycles of following Armada law in mundane routines have washed their emotions clean. They are drones with heartbeats.

The lift's upward acceleration is quick enough to buckle knees. I barely brace myself in time to keep from falling. Deceleration is smooth to keep us from coming off the lift unit's floor and into the ceiling but gives the sensation of weightlessness.

It comes to a stop and allows us to exit. A StarBird comes into view awaiting us with its core warm and running. The sight of it brings relief and signals the improbability of my execution.

The vessels are significant in posture and bear the shape of an oval-like star, with spikes exploding from them to work as lightning rods. Should global unrest occur, they are great for hiding near the southern pole's storm. The powerful can then hide while giving battle orders.

I have never seen the inside of one in person. They reserve StarBirds for people higher seated than I am in the ranks, but something big is going on. They would not have sent it for me otherwise.

A panel on its side opens.

"In you go," says the warden.

"A holding room?" I ask.

"Still a prisoner, aren't you?"

The panel closes, leaving me in solitude.

7-2
Apparel

Wall-to-wall padding lines the round room with two plush chairs present. I take a seat and wait with nothing else to do, easing to the edge of the cylindrical wall and leaning against it.

"Hello, Miss Mason," asks an A.I. system. "Are you ready for appearance selection?"

"Appearance selection?" I ask. "Define."

"All individuals pardoned by the Planetary Sovereign are to be granted preferable changes to their appearance."

I stand, squinting a single brow in thought. "I'm being pardoned?"

"Undecided," answers the A.I. "Would you like changes made to your appearance?"

"Then why did the warden say I was still a prisoner?"

"Your pardon may be based on stipulations."

"At least they're not executing me. And stipulations?"

"Stipulations," answers the A.I. with hesitation. "A condition or requirement that is specified or demanded as part of an arrangement."

"I'm aware of the definition, but why?"

"Unknown."

"Well, you're informative," I say. "At least I'm not in a cell."

"You are in pre-conference styling station two," says the A.I. "Location, StarBird fourteen."

A 3D projection of me comes into view. It is indistinguishable from reality.

I investigate the image of myself for a moment. "So, that's what six cycles of hair growth look like?"

"Correct," answers A.I.

"It wasn't a question," I say. "Let's start with the hair. Give me a laser razor."

The want to have my bangs dull-green and white-tipped back is strong. Under cadet status when I was pre-full-fledged Armada, it was a tad rebellious in their eyes ... but allowed. However, this is a chance at freedom. So, I will conform to their policies as if a member.

I grab my hair in and pull it out to the sides, letting it slide through my fingers and fall to my shoulders as a small hole opens behind the projection in front of me. A laser razor materializes in the slot. I reach through the image to grab it.

"What are the settings for a military fade?" I ask.

"Setting seventeen," answers A.I.

I enter it into the pane. The laser razor moves around my head from back to front. The scent of burning hair floods the room. A warm sensation crosses my scalp.

Hair falls to the ground with rising scents for unseen fans to pull out and drag a cooling sensation across my skin. I check myself with tough eyes and move the razor to the side of my head. High and tight. The image before me appears as tough as any male cadet. I will take it.

"Clothing?" asks the A.I. "Skin decor?"

"No," I answer. "I've spent enough of my life hiding who I am. No décor to cover imperfection. Give me something that resembles my old Armada flight uniform. Black and formfitting. Throw in a trace of civilian gray."

"Armada law states custom designs in clothing options are—"

"I'm not a member of the Armada," I interrupt. "Just do it."

The projection displays an outfit. The blend is eighty percent Armada, twenty percent me. It is proper, yet a statement that I am a civilian representing my roots and accomplishments while serving both in and under the military's nose.

I nod in agreement with its design. "Fabricate."

"Processing," says the A.I.

Part of the cylindrical wall to my right opens. "Enter."

"Okay," I say, passing through and mumbling to myself as I go. "Entering suddenly appearing door."

The room's only five paces wide and home to twenty-something little, golden hovering machines. Materials are being lowered from the ceiling to feed them. They are fast. I have heard about them... researched them, but I have never seen them in person until now. This is how the ultra-wealthy live while the rest of us die in the streets.

They finish, form a joint effort to fold my garments, and hand them to me with thick-soled Armada terra boots resting on top of them. The feeding arms fold up neatly into their resting position on the ceiling, while the style bots move back into their little resting holes.

"That was faster than I envisioned," I say.

I slip from my A.H.C.-issued jumpsuit and slide into my new outfit. It is snug but will loosen up. At least, I hope it will. I can breathe and move comfortably. That is the most important factor here.

7–3
Exiting

The StarBird's door opens. I exit to look around. We are in the capital city of Chimark, levitating above the rest of Kep Four. Artificial sunlight brightens the scene.

My appearance catches the warden's attention.

"Interesting choice," he says. "You realize you're going in front of the Planetary Sovereign and his Council of Chiefs, correct?"

"What about it?" I ask.

"That outfit is a gray area in the guidelines."

"Then I'd say it's a perfect fit for my standing in the Armada. Wouldn't you?"

I walk on, leaving him to talk with my back if he wishes to continue. Several soldiers at the Armada Alliance Headquarters watch as I approach. I do not care what they are thinking. They are no more A.R.S. than I am Armada.

This is the largest building in Chimark and houses several important government halls, including the one where they hold Planetary Conferences. Everything legal from important decisions to execution sentencing takes place here. I press forward with tense steps.

The eying soldiers part ways as I enter, some with mocking expressions. It could be because I am a convicted member of the Animal Rights Sympathizers once plotting against Armada activities. Perhaps it is the size of my confidence, which is on par with the hall's 16-pace wood replica doors parting in front of me.

I pass through in bitter-sweet admiration of the engraved Armada emblem. It is a combination of Ancient Earth and Kep Four with stars in the backdrop and no frame. The symbol is of past and present, with a blank spot for what lies ahead.

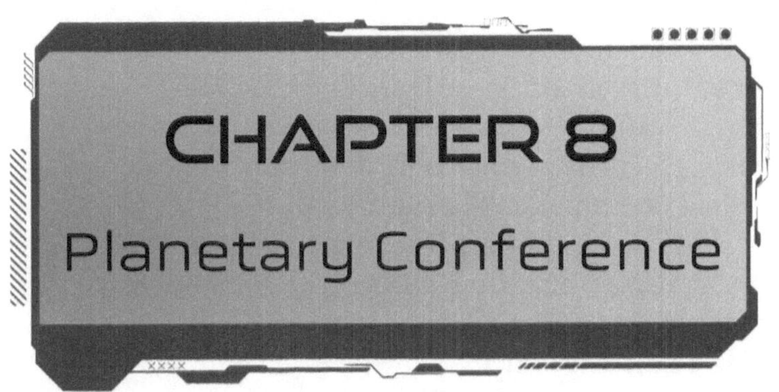

The 16-pace doors do not make a sound when they close behind me. A line of twenty soldiers split evenly on the left and right, form a path guiding me straight to a lift unit. The only place to go is between them.

My serial number takes shape on the floor two paces ahead of me:

$$M5S14m36-ND$$

An arrow materializes above it to guide me across reflective flooring toward the lift and between the soldiers. I look back at those watching me before turning to enter. The closest guard motions to the female soldier on my right, and she enters behind me.

We ride for a moment before the lift opens and allows us to exit into a small hallway. A pair of soldiers stand at each side of the lift's doors.

"McKayla M. Mason of Najasa district?" asks the soldier on my right.

I nod. "Yeah?"

The soldier removes a pen-sized Armada identity tracker from his waistline. "I need a full identity scan."

He scans my face, searching for signs of surgical alterations common amongst Uprisers. The tracker admits no lights or sounds. A thumbnail-sized image of my face and name projects from the device at its upper right.

"Next," commands the soldier.

I press my pointer fingers to my eyebrows and the tips of my thumbs under each eye to pull them open.

"Whenever you're ready," I say.

He scans my left eye, projecting its image from the device on its upper right. The same happens with my right eye until both are next to my facial image.

"Open," orders the soldier.

I open my mouth and place three fingers on each side to pull back my cheeks. He scans the inside of my mouth and dental records pop up next to the images of my face and eyes. A quick dip of the device under my tongue has my DNA on display next to everything else.

The Holo images come together and confirm my identity. Rarely is identity verification so in-depth, but it makes sense if I am about to share walls with the Planetary Sovereign. Nobody ranks higher than him.

The soldier motions me to the door. "You're cleared."

I am shuddering inside and can feel it at my wrist, trying to work its way into my hands. It takes a tik for me to move. This is an unusual feeling for me, but something serious is underfoot.

I glance at the guards, then quietly open the door and enter.

8-2
The Reason

Sergeant Bentley is moving to a spot-lit circle dead-center of the mighty conference hall. I think, maybe, it is about the rotation I took off with the starfighter. I cross my fingers for anything else but that. There are over a thousand people here—enough to cast a decision on an execution.

I need to settle my thoughts and stop being paranoid.

Stadium seating is not present the way it is at the BlazeBall events I have seen others watching on game feeds. The walls are straight up. They cut attendance seating inlets into the walls, resembling old-world theaters. Individual capital leaders sit with personal guards to watch as if at a Gelgorn opera (a high-level performance event with Kep Four's best vocalist entertaining those of wealth and high status in the Armada), but no one is singing.

The hall's flooring, walls, and ceiling are polished marble, with hints of fluctuating tans, greens, and whites swirling through them. Silver outlines the voluminous slabs in thin strips to form a pattern of rectangular shapes. Gold-tipped corners highlight a design unmatched in grandness.

The Planetary Sovereign is sitting high-center in the backdrop. He is less attractive than he appears over video panes lining the city during global updates. He and the others are wearing amplators (small sound amplification devices resembling a circular camera lens worn on the neck, just to the side of the vocal cords, that can reverberate words up to 500 paces clearly). I study the Planetary Sovereign's stoic expression as Sergeant Bentley reaches the spot-lit circle and stands at parade rest.

Dr. Utley, Kep Four's highest-rated doctor and physicist, is sitting on the Planetary Sovereign's right. He tested my ability to handle Gs before issuing training to focus my H-SAM. His disposition is dry. I remember him being boring but nimble-minded enough to keep my attention during conversations in the past.

Commander Helmwoke is the lady in charge of Armada military engagements controlling Dolofónos and his Uprisers. She is sitting on the Planetary Sovereign's left. All three are in their late 90s and three-quarters through the average life cycle, though I am sure their standing in society has them monitored for top health parameters.

Thousands have eyes locked on Sergeant Bentley. Those watching are in district leader uniforms, displaying themselves as higher-ups of various capitals with black-and-gold adorned sashes of thick cloth crossing their chests. Whatever is going on, it is important enough to gather them into a single location, which has not happened in my lifetime.

Dr. Wright, a slender, goofy-looking man with gigantic eyes narrower than most, walks up and bumps boots, introducing himself to Sergeant Bentley. It is informal, but a standard amongst Armada males. He receives a nod from the sergeant, and they turn to face the Planetary Sovereign.

I ease behind those on the lower level to remain from sight and listen. I want to know what is happening and why this meeting is taking place. It has been a long time since being around so many people, and I do not want to draw attention to myself.

Sergeant Bentley snaps to attention and raises his hand in their traditional military salute. Commander Helmwoke salutes back, and he returns to parade rest.

"Lay back, Sergeant," says the Sovereign.

Sergeant Bentley relaxes. "Is someone going to tell me what I'm doing here?"

"Go ahead, Doctor," replies the Sovereign.

The 200-pace hall's ceiling releases a photonic, three-dimensional display as believable as my image was in the StarBird's styling station. Two words are drifting in rotation to name the file:

EXPEDITION: ANCHOR

Our Milky Way galaxy comes to life under it. The Andromeda Galaxy forms next to them, identical in appearance to the Milky Way, and slides three-quarters across the conference hall before lowering toward the floor. An animated trajectory course plots itself from our galaxy to the outskirts of Andromeda.

"Okay," I whisper. "This is going to be interesting."

"It's a cut-and-dry operation," says Commander Helmwoke. "Just get there, do surveillance, come home safely, and report back."

Sergeant Bentley snickers. I do not think it was intentional.

"Problem?" asks Commander Helmwoke.

"Number one," answers Sergeant Bentley, "what the haze am I looking at there? Number two, cut-and-dry? It doesn't exist in the Armada."

"You want cut-and-dry, Sergeant?" asks the Sovereign. "I'll sum it up for you. Findings five cycles ago confirmed that Kep Four only had nine cycles remaining before its core goes solid. Our efforts to purify its atmosphere and warm the planet externally will no longer be sufficient once the magnetic field reaches zero activity. With only four cycles left, long-range found a habitable planet on the outskirts of the Andromeda galaxy. We're going for it."

The statement catches a group of tougher-looking men seated near Sergeant Bentley off guard. I do not recognize them, but their seating location means they are involved or about to be. Either way, they appear to be as ill-informed as I am.

Sergeant Bentley looks at the galaxies above him. "That's two-point-five million light cycles from here."

"Roughly," says Commander Helmwoke. "Your crew selections are as follows."

Sergeant Bentley shakes his head with uncertainty. "Are we planning on moving everyone across—"

"Not everyone gets to go, Sergeant," interrupts Commander Helmwoke. "Prisoners make up sixty-three percent of the surviving population, and they aren't going."

"Even so..." continues Sergeant Bentley. "How are we supposed to travel two-point—"

"It's time to stop talking, Sergeant," interrupts Commander Helmwoke.

Sergeant Bentley rolls his head before turning back to her and nodding.

"Tighten up, Sergeant Major," says Commander Helmwoke.

Sergeant Bentley grits his teeth, flexing the muscles in his jaw. He wants to fire back verbally, but that is unacceptable in the Armada. Repercussions are severe, and a response would prove foolish.

"First, there's Dr. Wright," continues Commander Helmwoke, "whom you've already met. He'll be the commanding overseer on Expedition Anchor and the only one above you on the totem pole. He'll have the same overseer capital leaders wear."

"An overseer?" I whisper.

I watch in awe as they bring it out to Dr. Wright. He clears his throat with nervousness. To be handed one is both an honor and a daunting responsibility.

The A.R.S. tried to get their hands on one for cycles.

Overseer bracelets run from one's wrist to the middle of their forearm, generating a three-dimensional projection from any visual feed recorder within two clicks. They relay closer signals first and are motion sensor responsive with threat detection prioritized, if not commanded otherwise; and deliberately the only things on Kep Four with long-range hacking capabilities. Should their wearers' lives be in danger, they can access everything made by the Armada and take over war-time protocols.

"Dr. Sellers," continues Commander Helmwoke, "our leading biologist and the one that developed the hop-serum to protect your bodies during flight, will also go with you. He'll be making the final decision on the target planet's habitableness."

Dr. Sellers is going? I have not seen or heard from him in six cycles. Armada law forbids communication when incarcerated. Another partial grin forms as a mirrored panel slides open in the wall at Sergeant Bentley's far left. Dr. Sellers emerges from it to take a place at his side. They share a nod, and the commander moves forward with her introductions.

8–3

The Big Guns

Commander Helmwoke motions to the lady operating the photonic projector. "If I could once again draw everyone's attention to the above images. I've compiled combat recordings for a general introduction to your squad. I want to make certain everyone understands why we chose who we did."

All eyes go skyward. It is stunning, like a satellite drifting without a destination through the cosmos.

"First on the list is Sgt. Skedelski," continues Commander Helmwoke.

An overhead projection of a waging battle against the Uprisers comes to life. Four soldiers are trying to upright a toppled armored military vehicle called a hover-trike, a mid-sized ground combat vehicle with limited lift and the ability to crawl along surfaces. It is pinning a soldier beneath it. Skedelski, a man with impossible height and mass, comes into view as his squad flees the vehicle's cover to return fire. He notices the pinned soldier, drops his weapon, and slams his mammoth frame into the side of the hover-trike, rocking it up enough to grab onto it from beneath.

His feet move earth as he lifts the vessel and topples it right-side-up, freeing the trapped soldier for others to pull to safety. The visual feed stops.

"For those of you that didn't follow the Galactic Combat games before they banned him," continues Commander Helmwoke. "Skedelski's hand-to-hand capabilities are brutishly sublime. He's loyal, strong as the dyoggs here on Kep Four, and makes for one haze of a hauler. He also suffers from a rare disorder known as congenital analgesia. However, there are no detectable physical abnormalities in his system. The disease has rendered him insensitive to pain."

Titanic and bruising in appearance, Skedelski stands from the group of tough-looking men to salute Sergeant Bentley. He towers a half-pace over the rest, and his shoulders stretch over a pace wide. He salutes and sits back down. I remember his reign in the Galactic Combat games. It was a brutal N.H.B. (No Holds Barred) hand-to-hand combat sport where anything goes in a single thirty tek round. Fights did not stop until someone was unconscious.

"Next," continues Commander Helmwoke. "We have Armada blood, Rhigas and Fister, the only cousins on the mission."

The projection switches to show Rhigas's lean, muscular arms putting a burned-colored gel onto a door wearing nothing but military fatigues, terra boots, and a tank-top flak jacket. He finishes and steps around a corner for cover, taking a seat cross-legged with his back against a wall. A tik passes. He peeks around the corner and rolls a marble-sized, metallic bead toward it. The small ball arcs a spark into the gel when it gets close, blowing the door open. A concussion wraps Rhigas, but he does not flinch.

Fister, sharing a striking resemblance to his cousin, gives Rhigas a nod and enters the breach with a flamethrower. The boric acid canister at the weapon's tip mixes into the fire, spreading green flames throughout the area.

"As you can see," continues Commander Helmwoke, "Rhigas is an explosive expert second to none; and his cousin's a self-proclaimed firebug with an addiction to incinerating devices. They'll be your heavy gunners and have extremely high ratings in the field. They should have your complete trust."

Rhigas and Fister are in their 30s and match the preferred Armada physique to a tee. They are lean and tight, with chiseled faces and sharp jawlines. While mixed like everyone else in the hall, they have some Asian ancestry trickling into their bloodline, showing through as epicanthic folds in their eyes. They bump boots from their seats.

"Next up," says Commander Helmwoke, "we have Sgt. Sapp and P.F.C. Morris."

The overhead projection transitions to show Sapp laser-marking a location during a skirmish. Heatwaves hit the area a few hundred yards from him, but the Uprisers continue advancing in black and red, forcing him to ignite combat thrusters throughout his suit.

Sapp goes over a collapsed building's final remaining wall to escape, turning back in mid-flight to mark the area with a laser. He lands next to rail-thin, tech-guru Morris. Dirty, breathing heavy, sweaty, and exhausted in appearance … both look to have been in battle for rotations.

Morris inputs code into a receiver on his wrist. A district city grid pops up with a flashing dot on the area Sapp marked.

"Target confirmed," says Morris.

A more powerful heatwave descends from an unseen ship to burn the area Sapp marked as he fled. All inside … cooked.

"Sapp will be second in command during ground operations," continues Commander Helmwoke. "Technical communications expert Morris will be with us in the unlikely event we encounter intelligent or advanced life out there."

Sgt. Sapp and P.F.C. Morris are older than the others seated with them, and I guess them to be middle-aged in their late 60s. They stand from the group, salute, and sit back down without a word.

"Corporals Bell and Chubb," says Commander Helmwoke, smiling and tapping the desk in front of her, "two I hand-selected myself, will accompany you. Corporal Bell is a water purification specialist, but he's a solid point man. Scout class Corporal Chubb has a twisted sense of humor and a chip on his shoulder, but he's earned it. Sorry to disappoint, but we don't have video feeds on them to share. Their operations are classified."

They stand to salute and sit back down. Bell is in his late 20s and has an attractive, symmetrical face that looks like it will crack if he smiles. Chubb is in his 40s and only a head taller than I am, making him the shortest of the bunch.

Sergeant Bentley clears his throat.

"Sergeant?" asks Commander Helmwoke.

"Excluding Bell," answers Sergeant Bentley, "I've never worked with any of these guys. I'm sure they're all fine soldiers, but—"

"If they were selected," interrupts the Sovereign, "it's because they're the best. That's your team, Sergeant. End of discussion."

"Yes, Sovereign," says Sergeant Bentley.

"Continue, Commander," says the Sovereign.

"Your last crew member will be former Armada Cadet Mason of Najasa, whom you are also familiar with," says Commander Helmwoke.

Sergeant Bentley turns his back to them for a moment before facing them again.

The last impression I left on him was a bad one. I do not know why they want me on Expedition Anchor. They also told him to recon and return, nothing else, yet they have put together a squad of combat soldiers. I wonder what cards they are keeping close to their chest.

The hall grows silent as Sergeant Bentley, onlookers, and the assigned crew glance around the hall upon hearing my name. I take a moment to gather my nerves. It is a lot to take in.

"Mason of Najasa?" asks the Sovereign. "Didn't she take out three satellites trying to protect those creatures she freed from being tracked? Who selected her?"

Dr. Wright steps up. "I did. She came highly recommended by Dr. Sellers."

The Planetary Sovereign's face contorts with confusion. He eyes Dr. Sellers and receives a nod of confirmation.

"And what led you to select an individual with her track record?" asks the Sovereign. "I find it disturbing that a man of your standing wouldn't only consider, but recommend such an extreme A.R.S. activist, an anarchist at that, to any mission, much less one of this importance."

"Because she's abstract in her brilliance, Sovereign," answers Dr. Sellers. "Mason's one of only three people on Kep Four with full-spectrum H-SAM and the only one of them with echoic properties extraordinary enough to back it. She's a linguistics expert beyond comprehension. Her ability to absorb information is radical."

The Sovereign's voice raises. "She's unpredictable, Doctor."

"With all due respect, Sovereign," says Dr. Sellers. "All I care about are the specifics surrounding her abilities. The fact she spent the better of her last ten cycles locked up is irrelevant. What's relevant, however, is how she ended up incarcerated."

The Planetary Sovereign's brows furrow. "Insubordination, destruction of Armada property, ignoring safety protocol, stealing a starfighter, complete and total disregard for her own life. Is that what we're talking about here?"

Dr. Sellers matches the Sovereign's tone. "She bested the Armada's patrol pilots, while under Sergeant Major Bentley's leadership here, whom you're assigning as head of the mission's ground team." He turns to face Sergeant Bentley. "No offense."

Sergeant Bentley's face shows no reaction beyond a hidden undertone of anger.

"The reason they incarcerated her," continues Dr. Sellers. "Is because she brought the starfighter back on her own accord, and to be frank, there isn't a pilot on Kep Four to hold a candle for her to work by in the black. H-SAM set aside, she's the best choice to helm flight controls."

"An extreme activist led by her heart more than her mind, Doctor," says the Sovereign.

A calm demeanor settles over Dr. Sellers. His posture relaxes. "That may very well be, Sovereign, but we know there's intelligent life elsewhere in the universe. Artifacts found on Kep Four, ones she helped decode, confirm that. Should we encounter and want the slightest chance of communicating with them, she's vital."

The hall is silent as the Sovereign turns to Dr. Wright and takes a deep breath. "What proof do you have she won't wreak havoc on the mission?"

"Hard proof?" asks Dr. Wright. "No more than I do that the ship won't disintegrate when it enters the Ein-Rosen bridge."

The group of tough-looking men no longer look harsh in disposition. Their eyes have widened. Bell raises his hand in concern for a tik and lowers it. Like the others, I find the possibility of disintegrating problematic.

"Very well," says the Sovereign, staring them down. "But any mishaps she has along the way are on you and Dr. Wright. You'll be personally responsible and charged accordingly for her actions. Are we clear?"

"Yes," answers Dr. Wright. "She's done her time. I'm sure she's settled over the past few cycles."

That is my queue. I discreetly move from behind the people in the back row, taking my time to reveal myself.

Commander Helmwoke looks over the crowd. "Can we get someone to locate Mason and—"

"I'm here," I say.

Thousands of eyes are upon me as I approach, no doubt gawking at me because of my past. They do not understand it. I do not care. It is no fault of mine that they lack empathy for the living.

The masses come into view. I spin while nearing the middle of the hall to see everybody. This is the most exciting thing I have done in six cycles, and I am not about to go back to sitting in prison for another six. They are getting whatever they want from me.

Dr. Sellers and Bentley are cutting me matching looks—lips parted with confused eyes cutting back and forth between one another, surprised to see me here. I bet they were expecting me to show up with my hair... well... on my head with dull Armada green and white highlights.

"Where do I sit?" I ask.

"Over there with the rest of the crew will be fine, Mason," says Commander Helmwoke.

I approach the selected crew's seating area to take a spot behind Skedelski. He is too big. I have to squeeze past him, placing my hand on his traps to lift back into the seat. He did not feel me. This is a scary man.

"You and your team will get briefed and brought up to speed over the next few rotations," says the Sovereign. "This meeting is over."

He taps a small gavel on the marble surface in front of him. A loud rumble with deep pulsations fills the hall. Skedelski and the others stand while I sit digesting every-thing. Capital leaders, higher-ups, and those on the lower floor mutter amongst themselves about Expedition Anchor as they funnel from the building.

I follow the last person out on ground level. A male and female guard are awaiting me, and their escort ensures I will not be free until the mission is over. None of us speak as the man in uniform motions me to walk behind him, and the female soldier follows me out.

We spent the last seven rotations training, mostly reading and Commander Helmwoke talking theories to a squad that already knew their jobs. But they have finally granted me a rotation out. The others carried on with their lives. Not me. I have been on lockdown since they released me from A.H.C.

Dr. Sellers contacted me earlier on this rotation. He heard I am getting free time under escorted supervision and says the selected squad is heading to an N.C.O. (Non-Civilian Operated) pub club. It does not sound like my cup of tea; then again, I will take anything over another eleven taks of confinement. Boredom makes me want to hit my head against these walls.

It is not plain. I like the layout, but I can no longer handle my detention. The Armada could at least trust me enough not to place a guard outside my door while I sleep. Then again, I labeled myself untrustworthy in their eyes.

BEEP—BEEP—BEEP

"Come in," I call through the door.

The soldier guarding me enters. "Be ready for escort in ten teks, if you're going at all."

I think about it as he steps out and shuts the door. Six cycles ago, an N.C.O. pub would have seemed boring, but now, trapped in this room, I need to escape. Might as well have a few drinks before the pub closes for the rotation. If they allow me to drink, that is.

I get ready and exit to meet him. He eyes my body and averts to act like he is not checking me out. It is a sign I have chosen the right outfit. Shimmery, fitting, and black and blue like forgotten skies, it hints at what little I have below the neckline.

I hope it is flattering enough to land me some female-on-female conversation without offending the Armada. I seldom dress like this, but before embarking on a journey with unfamiliar faces, engaging in a discussion with someone intellectually captivating would make for a delightful parting gesture.

"Okay," I say. "Let's party."

The guard smiles, and we head out. I figure he would be hitting on me if not on duty. Getting lucky is not something findable with me. Not for him. I would not slap him or anything, but he would hear harsh words dictating him not to my taste.

9–2

N.C.O.

Modern electric pop music is blaring in an immaculately decorated sports bar when I arrive—not at all what I expected. Knowing the Armada mentality and never holding an interest in entering an N.C.O. pub, I assumed it would be bland and quiet. Anytime someone had brought up anything in the past involving the Armada and its popular pastimes, I would always cut them off and change subjects. These were the consequences of living a reclusive A.R.S. lifestyle.

Dr. Sellers greets me at the door near the bottom of whatever he is drinking.

"How's it feel to be out?" he asks.

"You have no idea," I answer, studying my surroundings. "This place is louder than I thought it'd be."

"First time in an N.C.O.?" asks Dr. Sellers.

"Yeah," I answer.

He smiles. "Me too."

A sarcastic giggle escapes me. "Yeah, sure it is."

"Come here," he says, taking my hand and guiding me through the crowded pub. "You're going to get a kick out of this."

An oversized video-holo-dome housing a pair of large holographic androids, referred to as holo-droids, comes into view beyond a thick crowd.

Dr. Sellers grabs a glass from a table and hands it to me. "Still into Jerleanian?"

"I'll tell you in a tik," I say, grabbing it from him and shooting it in a single gulp. "Yes, I am, and you're offi-cially my hero."

"I can see that," he says. "You want another?"

I cut him a side-eyed look. A single brow raises. "Who do you think you're asking?"

He chuckles and waves me down a second drink.

High-hung ceilings catch my attention as I wait. Beautiful men and women with bodies and clothes designed as matching works of art dance between us and the ceiling in silver and gold-plated Spletnumd-27. Their gear matches what Morris and Sapp are wearing in the spheres ahead, but the dancers are wearing nothing under it. The outfits cover only what is necessary.

Flashes of light illuminate our surroundings as electrical discharges roll currents over us. I duck as they strobe the ceiling and overhead dancers while onlookers cheer.

I look around, searching for its source. "What was that noise?"

"You'll see," answers Dr. Sellers, pulling me closer to the domes.

I give one last look at the slender dancer spinning above me with red-dyed hair and matching bloomers beneath a black skirt. She is right up my street. I would love to pick her brain but doubt it will happen with her high overhead.

"Next round's starting," continues Dr. Sellers. "Hurry."

He rushes me toward the holo-dome. Holo-droids locked in a heated battle come into view as we approach them. Bell, Rhigas, Chubb, and Fister are standing near the dome's edges and cheering.

Sapp and Morris are at each side of the dome in modified training spheres, each wearing Spletnumd-27 metallic gauntlets, boots, belts, and vests. It suspends them in the air with the holo-droids mimicking their movements to perfection.

"Right... right hand, Sapp," shouts Chubb, stumbling with a drink in hand and fighting to remain upright. "Right."

I look at Sapp's sphere. He throws a right. I shoot my eyes back to the dome. The holo-droid matching his movements, staggering Morris's droid when the punch lands.

Chubb clinches his fist in celebration. "Yes."

"Okay," I shout over the crowd, "this place is more exciting than I thought it'd be. How come I've never seen these before?"

"The battle domes?" asks Dr. Sellers. "You've seen—"

"No," I interrupt. "The training spheres they're levitating in."

"The gear they're wearing is Spletnumd-27," answers Dr. Sellers over the crowd. "Just like the dancers above us. It interacts with the metallics in the training spheres. Droids do whatever they think with the integration jewels, but the Spletnumd-27 was just added to the domes a few cycles ago for a better combative feel."

I look back as Sapp's holo-droid slips left and bangs in a superb combination that sends Morris's stumbling and turning yellow. Morris is rocked in his training sphere, matching the droid's stumbling movements. He locks his face in a pain-felt grimace and closes one eye. Holo-dome fighting looks like it hurts.

"You should try it," says Dr. Sellers.

I shake my head slowly from left to right. "Noooo, thank you."

I am not a fighter. That is for sure. Agile? Yes, but there is no way in haze I am climbing into one of those things just to get knocked around. A headache is the last thing I need on my only night out.

Morris is struggling to remain upright and keep his balance in the training sphere. Once righting himself, he leans forward into a sprint. His holo-droid matches to rush Sapp's and slams his opponent's droid into the side of the holo-dome.

An electrical charge matching the one I saw earlier ripples around the dome, and Sapp shakes in his training sphere with small currents passing through his body. His holo-droid turns yellow to match Morris's after the impact—a colorful sign of visual damage and hit points remaining for each combatant's projected avatar.

Morris places Sapp's holo-droid in a headlock. It takes a step and leaps into the air with both feet out in front of it. Sapp's holo-droid goes airborne as well.

I look at Sapp's training sphere and giggle. His body, suspended belly down, matches the holo-droid as both of their arms flail.

"No, no, no," says Sapp.

Sapp crashes belly-first into the floor of his sphere. His holo-droid turns red and disappears. The match is over. A victory alarm rings out. The crowd roars, and Morris's winning holo-droid dances in celebration.

Sapp moans in pain from the floor as Morris dances in his sphere, guiding the holo-droid to match his jig. Everyone laughs and points at Sapp while he gets to his feet and unhooks the Spletnumd-27 gear, handing it to the next player in line.

"What happened, Sapp?" asks Fister.

"I wouldn't have let him do me like that," says Rhigas.

Sapp laughs. "You sure you guys are cousins and not twins?" He pushes between them. "I need a drink."

The mission team chants Morris's name as he exits his training spear and raises his fists overhead. He moves them up and down in rhythm with the group's chanting. Everyone but me cheers. I am anxious in this social setting due to prolonged isolation.

"Not bad for a tech-geek, Morris," shouts Rhigas.

Dr. Sellers motions me to follow. "Come on."

We tail the group across the N.C.O. pub. They hoist Morris to their shoulders and carry him to a hovering tabletop. The group talks loudly, but I cannot make out what they are saying over music and club banter.

They are watching BlazeBall on an elevated viewing pane. Looks like the game is just about to start. Players are setting up on the field. The camera pans around to each of their backs as they get into formation, eventually reaching one with the name *FISTER* across its upper shoulders.

"There's Bo," shouts Fister. "There's Bo."

He and Rhigas bump boots a few hard times. The others cheer her on. Chubb wobbles in his seat with a lazy left eye. He looks tipsy.

"Wait," I say. "What's happening?"

Dr. Sellers leans into my ear. "That's Fister's sister. She's a pro. Full time."

I know nothing about the game but hear it combines several old-fashioned sports with metallic padding and various neon-colored lights. It is also violent. The play starts.

Thrusters propel athletes on the field and through the air. I am not sure why, but a referee in teal green stripes calls a foul and throws a hovering claret disk to follow over Fister's sister's head.

"What?" shouts Fister, drawing back his drink to throw it.

Rhigas grabs the drink just in time. "You want me to get you some detox, Cuz?"

"Come on," answers Fister. "You know that call was—"

"I feel you," interrupts Rhigas. "But let's just enjoy the game. If I know Bo, she'll, uhm, accidentally knock that ref into the next cycle before the game is up."

Fister smiles. "Someone bring me another drink."

Fister's sister starts an argument with the referee. He gets in her face, and she shoves him to the ground. The ref gets up and tosses a glowing white disk over Bo's head to join the claret one.

"There ejecting her?" asks Fister. "Get the haze out of here."

The ref rewards the ball to the other team for the shove as Bo's teammates hold her back. My new squad reacts in erratic disapproval. It takes them a moment to settle down, and I couldn't understand anything they were saying with them all yelling at once.

"That didn't take long," says Bell.

"That's Bo for you," says Rhigas.

Chubb and Bell join the others in laughter as they escort her from the playing field.

"The berry didn't fall far from the swizzel branch tree," says Fister. "That's for sure."

Skedelski approaches with two trays of dark-amber beer cubes.

"Good job, Skedelski," says Bell. "Another successful artillery run, my man."

Nobody is talking to me. Few are talking with Dr. Sellers. We do not fit in. Not yet anyway. The squad members are all battle-bred Armada lifers. Their demeanor is unlike Dr. Sellers's calm nature, and I am a traitor to their chosen lifestyle.

Maybe it is why Doctors Utley and Wright are a no-show. Perhaps I am overthinking things. The squad acts as if they have a longstanding connection outside the Armada. There has not been time for them to absorb us into their group.

Sergeant Bentley approaches the table as the group rattles cubes in their glasses, breaking them apart into dark liquid beer, and places his hand on Dr. Sellers's shoulder. "You guys remember Dr. Sellers? Give him a cube. He's going to need it around you guys."

They laugh as Fister presses a button on the tabletop, commanding a robotic arm to fold out and slide a pair of icy mugs to Rhigas, who drops a few cubes into Dr. Sellers's glass.

"To Dr. Sellers," says Sergeant Bentley, "our assigned biologist and medical diagnostician."

The group clanks their glasses again and sends splashes of liquid onto the hovering table as they drink. Sergeant Bentley does not acknowledge me. I deserve it after getting him reprimanded at Hangar 9 six cycles ago.

"As of now," he announces. "We're one-hundred and thirty-two taks from meeting at the briefing chamber. Then we'll be boarding to depart."

"Why you al da ways uptight?" asks Chubb. "Can't we have a… have a night without all the mission… mission talk?"

While I cannot agree with him more, Chubb is drunk. Someone needs to slip him detox.

"It's okay, Chubb," says Sergeant Bentley. "You don't have to come to Andromeda with us if you don't want to."

"Oh." Chubb stands and looks up to make aggressive eye contact with Sergeant Bentley. His body ridges to a tense state. "Oh, I'm go'an. You okay… alright with dat, sweet cheeks?"

The group grows silent.

"Or…" Chubb stumbles and falls over his stool, picking himself back up to wobble. "Or are we go… go'an to have urselves an altercation?"

He takes a sip from what did not spill out of his beer mug to look tough but chokes on it, laboring to catch his breath. The group laughs and bumps boots, shoving each other around by the shoulders.

Sergeant Bentley's face tightens not to laugh. "Can we get some detox over here, please?"

An N.C.O. bartender walks over with a glass of detox cubes and hands it to Chubb.

"I'ma no… not dranking tis," he slurs.

The bartender raises his hand, snaps his fingers, and points at Chubb. "Then you're leaving."

The Armada patrol agent, looking over the pub, heads our way. Skedelski looks down at him and steps back to make room as he passes by.

"Fine," says Chubb, rattling the detox cubes into drinkable form. "I'll drank it, but I'ma am get drunk again."

The team cheers as he chugs the detox.

I am ready to go. I know where the rest of this rotation is heading, and I do not want to be part of it. No one is talking to me anyhow.

"Think I'm going to get out of here," I say.

"Already?" asks Dr. Sellers.

"Yeah," I answer. "Everything's fine, but the part of partying I try to avoid is incoming."

"Understood," says Dr. Sellers. "With that reasoning, I think I'll join you." He turns to the others. "We're going to head out. I'll see you guys in training."

He bumps boots with Sergeant Bentley and walks to the door with me. My escorting guard is happily waiting near the exit, as usual.

"See you soon?" I ask.

"Often and soon," answers Dr. Sellers, climbing into his S.C.P.T.

I smile as he pulls away, glad he put his name on the line to get me out of that cell and onto the mission.

"You ready?" asks my escort.

"Back to my new holding cell," I answer with a tone ripe of spurn. "Why not?"

I follow him to his transport without a word spoken. The situation could be better, but I am happy. It does not matter that there are no conversations left for me to have with others. All that is important to me ... is that I am mostly free.

It has been thirteen rotations since the N.C.O. pub night, and I am sure it took Chubb quite a while to recover. He drank detox, but I hear he made his way back to a drunken state. It could not have made a good impression on our squad commanders.

Sergeant Bentley does not exalt me. Chubb is no different. They do not trust me yet. I should be happy the Armada let me get out once with the boys, but I am not as free as I thought I was going to be. The squad has no choice but to accept me as part of the team. Their respect will have to be earned.

We are going to Andromeda together. There is no other choice but to get along, and we better do it quickly, because I am in a single-passenger prisoner transport tanker approaching the most advanced ship the Armada has built to date. Soon, we will depend on each other.

I have spent the better of my time since being released from A.H.C. getting escorted to and from the housing unit they were holding me in, one they did not give me the access code for. Soldiers have taken me to a flight simulator daily to prepare for Expedition Anchor, though I did not need to put in so much time in a flight simulator. Not one of the starfighter I stole and had so much experience piloting.

There it is. Athanasios is coming into view. Excitement floods through me.

"Holy..." I say.

It is dark with an ominous presence. The hull encasing it is a black body, absorbing all particles of light reaching it. I would not know where it was located without the thin silver trim at the sharper points of its edges. The ship itself is darker than the space behind it. I am not sure where some of it ends, and the black begins. Portions of it disappear into the cosmos.

A dozen engineering rings spaced hundreds of paces apart wrap it from front to back without contact, leaving the ship to look like it is jumping through a series of hoops. Each ring has a blue and tan rail system bonded to it. This allows its workstations to move 360° around its hull.

I watch with butterflies in my stomach. Workstations are scissoring to and from the rings so those working can reach Athanasios. Most of the workers operating them are doing last-tek checks, but a few are electro-stenciling letters onto its side:

ATHANA

Studying blueprints and schematics is not something I get anything out of doing. I would rather board it, feel it, taste it, touch it, and smell it. My curiosity is a curse that I cannot escape. I need to walk its floors.

"I'm at dock two in three with Mason," says the pilot.

"Confirmed," answers the controller. "Dock two in three."

I stare in astonishment. A ship of this scale is unheard of. I have come across a few in the Armada close to its size, but none were as impressive. It is a prototype, the first of its kind, and while it appears large enough to hold a few thousand people, this mission calls for only fifteen. The engine occupies most of the space in Athanasios. Any they build after this will be much more significant if our target world proves habitable.

Athanasios is a culmination of everything the Armada discovered after our think tank unlocked the language barrier between ourselves and those here 850,000 cycles before us. Upon getting deeper into the language, they found a storage bank they still cannot fully unlock but got it to release a lifetime of knowledge. It was no simple task.

I spent two cycles translating for them, eventually gathering complete schematics to build a negative mass starship using an Alcubierre drive system on a once unspoken scale. They named it Athanasios for its Greek origin description: *eternal life.*

The oddly shaped engines resemble a damp, pink, cloth-like tube that is kinked and burned in several places. It is most likely dormant at its center now. The design is outlandish, but its power is formidable by any standards. I cannot wait to step onto it and explore.

Element 214 had to be stabilized before its engines could work. This took cycles to accomplish, but Armada scientists found its properties when combined with element 191, both stable and remarkable. That discovery eventually led to Dr. Wright's division cracking the 6,000-cycle old Einstein-Rosen Bridge, often referred to as the Ein-Rosen equation.

The ship's bio-computer is the most advanced ever developed. It operates with a grossly manipulated form of E.C.B. (Escherichia Coli Bacteria) to process information. Without it, Athanasios could not keep up with calculations under full flight, much less through the wormhole the core should create to work alongside the Alcubierre drive.

"Docking," says the pilot.

I lean to the port window on my right for a better view. We are too close to witness the vessel in its entirety. Even this close, the absence of light refracting from its exterior hull makes it a difficult observation. The transport's bright forward lights look as if they disappear and never contact Athanasios's exterior. The colossal vessel's perfect black body exterior absorbs and re-emits all radiation, no matter the wavelength spectrum.

The pilot docks us. A low-impact collision followed by a few metal-on-metal clicks secures us to the docking port.

"And here you are," says the pilot.

I stand and watch the door slide open. A tubular walkway only a pace long connects to my destiny. I pass through it and let the transport door shut behind me in anticipation of Athanasios welcoming me into her mighty belly.

10–2
BlazeBall

Athanasios is not as big on the inside as I thought it would be. Sure, I have seen the schematics, but its interior is small for a vessel with external dimensions of this magnitude. It is a scout class version of what they are building in Kep Four's orbit now and over the subsequent cycle or two. I wish we could see the other vessels under construction on our way to Athanasios, but they are orbiting the planet in different locations.

It looks like most of my squad is here; at least, some of them are. I move through the ship's central corridor. Dr. Wright is talking with Dr. Utley and Sergeant Bentley in the forward. That is the area we will be in under flight.

The large section of the ship houses several seats assigned to each on board. The backrests display the name of each squad member. Gimbles support the seats for mobility. This allows them to remain in a designated position without moving during travel.

A U-shaped integration flight control hovers just above Dr. Wright's backrest. If he needs it, he will interact with Athanasios mentally through the superior integration jewel. His division was at the forefront of designing Athanasios, but I do not think he would be at ease flying a vessel of this caliber. That is what I am here for.

There are no windows. Projections of its surroundings against the forward's open wall are a suitable alternative. A multitude of lights and controls flash beneath it, near Dr. Sellers and Dr. Wright's seats.

An automated ladder in the back center of the forward leads up to the cockpit, which is anchored into the upper wall of the ship's forward and hard-wired directly into Athanasios's bio-frame. More than a replica. They have integrated the starfighter I stole into this vessel with the ability to disconnect and drop from her mother ship if needed.

"So sexy," I say, backing from the forward and down the nearest corridor.

I study its seamless diamond lining. It is nice, but I can look everything over later. I want to find my private quarters.

Why they chose not to assign our rooms beforehand and give me a tour is beyond me. Then again, I am the only one who has not been on the ship until this rotation. Prisoner until post-mission. It is what it is.

"I know my private quarters are around here somewhere," I mutter.

An open door to my right has a name next to it:

SKEDELSKI

I peek an eye into the room. Skedelski is trying to get comfortable in his bed, but that man is too big for it. He is too big for... Well, I am sure he is too big for a lot of things. I watch as he tries to figure out how he will lie on it. He stops when he notices me.

"I'm sorry," I say. "I was just walking by and saw you struggling. You didn't ask for a bigger bed?"

He shakes his head and flops to his back, allowing his legs to hang off, bent at the knees. "This will be okay."

"Alright then," I say.

I continue down the hall, thinking about how deep his voice is. His tone is so full of bass it nearly sounds artificial. It reverberates when he talks.

Taking in the newly built ship's scent is nostalgic and reminds me of the first time I climbed in the Beltric Class Six upon its completion. It is lovely, sterile, and smells like a freshly run ionization chamber. It is a far cry from a musty-scented prison cell.

Bell, Sapp, Rhigas, and Fister are in the rec area watching a holo-projection of a semi-pro BlazeBall match. I did not know it is BlazeBall season, but at least they get to watch it one last time before we debark.

"Excuse me," Skedelski says.

His voice makes me jump. I move over so he can turn sideways, duck under the door, and enter the rec area with them. Poor guy. Where he gets his shoes from is a question to ponder.

"Start without me?" asks Skedelski.

"We're watching the last push a few times," answers Rhigas. "Just flipped it back on."

"Me and my cousin cut out all the crap and left the good stuff," says Fister.

Skedelski pulls a pair of chairs together and takes a seat.

"You ready for this?" asks Rhigas.

Skedelski nods, Bell plays the feed, and I watch on, trying my best to learn the game by watching a single push.

"Are you watching another Blazeball game?" I ask, with no interest other than connecting with the squad.

They turn to look, noticing me for the first time, and turn back to the game footage. I would be lying if I said it does not bother me. We are about to spend a long time together, and I do not want to feel like a prisoner again.

My attention returns to the game, but I am not leaving yet.

Two squads are squaring off. Five men on the opposing team form a circle around a teammate holding a pair of glowing orbs on offense. The defensive squad positions themselves in a second circle around them. Everyone is wearing metallic shoulder pads, leg pads, and helmets. Cone-shaped baskets surround the playing field seven paces in the air, illuminated by varying colors of lights.

Skedelski comes into view on the holo-projection.

I turn to him. "You played BlazeBall?"

"We all did," answers Sapp. "Same team. Sixty strong."

It shows how much I know about them, but it explains their comradery. I did not follow the sport and have not researched the crew's files yet, aside from Sergeant Bentley's, which was a must with the whole, me-stealing-a-starfighter-out-from-under-him thing, and going to prison for it.

"Play," says Skedelski.

"Hold on," says Fister. "Watch. I'm zooming in on this part."

Fister zooms in on Skedelski and plays the recording.

The big man trips over untied straps that have come loose from his upper boot. The play starts, and the opposing team takes the orbs in two different directions as he kneels to wrap them.

Rhigas laughs and points. "He doesn't even know the play started."

The game moves underway in the backdrop as Skedelski wraps his boot. He looks up. Two blockers ahead of the orb carrier are heading his way. Bell and Rhigas are giving chase behind them.

Skedelski drives from the ground and slams into the two blockers, lifting and crushing them into the orb carrier behind them. He steers all three to the ground in a vulgar display of power.

"Holy firecats, Skedelski," says Sapp.

Holy firecats is right. They are an extinct feline of Kep Four that dwelled and ate near hot springs and semi-active volcanos. Extinct sixty cycles ago, they were vicious, just like Skedelski, who catches me off guard driving from a kneeling position and hitting the blockers. The way he crumbled them like paper is scary. The man treats steel like straw and titanium like rotten wood.

Skedelski stands from the downed men, takes a few steps back, and starts wrapping his boot again. His head tilts for a closer look at his hand. He has a broken finger that is pointing in the wrong direction. I turn away with a shiver.

"Oooo," the group shouts and bumps boots, shoving each other about in laughter.

It grosses me out. A gag reflex sends an acidic taste into my throat. It looks painful, but I keep watching.

Skedelski grabs it, bends it into place, and starts wrapping his boot again as Rhigas grabs the now-rolling orb and throws it high into the air in front of his cousin, who is on a fast break. Fister catches it and reaches an offensive trampoline, launching himself high for a monster dunk.

Sapp tackles another player just before his teammate throws the second orb to him. It rolls into a side barrier. Sapp picks it up and advances for a moment before stopping to survey the field. He throws it sixty paces to Morris, who catches it without looking and takes a shot at the high baskets—from what they marked *no man's land* on the ground—just before another player tackles him ... but he scores. Morris stands and does his personal celebration dance.

Bell trips a man running past him for no apparent reason. Then he trips another player.

A referee blows an electric whistle, throwing a glowing claret disk to hover over his head. He takes his helmet off, raises it in the air, and shouts with exhilaration as his teammates rush to his side.

"You realize you cost us two points tripping those guys, right?" says Sapp.

"But not enough to lose the game," answers Bell.

The feed stops and they go back into Armada jock mode, which I understand less about than BlazeBall.

"Did your sister play on your team?" I ask.

"Bo?" asks Fister. "No. My sister's all pro. We just squeezed in game time during the Armada unit semi-pro seasons."

"That's outstanding," I say. "Does your whole family play?"

"Just me and her."

"Was she good?" I ask.

"Fister's sister?" interjects Rhigas. "She's a bad dream on the field."

"A bad dream?" I ask.

"Blazeball talk," he answers, "but you'd know that if you were an Armada lifer and didn't spend the last six cycles staring at walls as a traitor, wouldn't you?"

I shake my head and walk away. My face is turning red. Lips instinctively press together to stop from retorting. Hopefully, this phase of my standing with them won't last. Skedelski does not seem to mind my presence. So, at least there is one person here being nice to me.

Locating my personal quarters on Athanasios is no quick task. The ship's layout is going to take getting used to. All the living areas should be on the same level, or at least in the same section of the ship. Then again, having us spread out ensures someone will be close to each area of the vessel in case of an emergency.

I climb onto an automatic ladder at the end of the hall. My quarters are somewhere in the lower decks. I know that, but they did not give me a tour or tell me about the assigned location before boarding like they did the others. My current standing did not allow me access.

My eyes go downward. "Descend."

It lowers me to the next level. This section of the ship is not too different from the last. I am pacing in circles here, but there are a few corridors left to walk. I will find it soon enough.

I turn right down another corridor near the ship's aft. A door at its far end catches my attention. I approach to read its label.

MUNITIONS ARMORY:
Master clearance required

"Hmph," I say. "That's awful interesting for a recon."

The Armada reinforced the door. There are two methods of entry—a coded lock with a DNA scanner and an overseer access port—neither of which I have clearance for. Whatever is in there, it is important to the mission. The only three people I know of who can access it are Dr. Wright with his overseer, Sergeant Bentley by code and scan, and someone named Delgado, who is listed as the munitions hold and equipment expert in Expedition Anchor's files.

"Delgado," I say, thinking aloud.

It cannot be the same Delgado I am thinking about. If so, it may be an awkward introduction when I meet her, but that was a long time ago. Forgive and forget.

I backpedal for a moment and turn to continue the search for my personal quarters, making a right at the junction I entered the dead-end corridor from. My name comes into view a few paces later:

MASON

"Ah," I say. "Finally."

An awaiting receiver reads my palm. A tik later, and a strand of my DNA is spinning above my wrist in three-dimensional, holographic fashion. The door breaks down from bottom to top into smaller and smaller twisting cubes. They come to rest against the ceiling.

I peek my head in and look up. My eyes stay glued to them as I enter and back away. "Close door."

Another display of dancing cubes entertains the imagination as it reforms itself. I stick my hand where the door is forming and they build around it, leaving an unfinished circle. The little black cubes awaiting their turn in line stop spinning to hover in place, and I pinch one.

It is cold, hard as a diamond, and releases vibrations nearly too subtle to be felt. I pull my hand out and it restarts but stops again when I place my hand back into the hole. I pull it out to watch it finish sealing and go solid in wonder. It is as hard as any other door when I knock on it.

I take a few steps back, trying to figure out the science behind it. This is new technology that the Armada must have developed during my last six cycles of incarceration. I stare for a tek and speculate if it is exclusive to Athanasios.

A tan room one would expect to be in a mid-level overnight in Najasa priced at only 50 credits a tak comes into view. There is a bed, guest chair, small table, and holo-info projector for entertainment on the wall at the foot of my bed. Not that surfing video webs are on anyone's minds when checking into overnights for companionship.

A depressed sigh escapes me as I move to the linen holder and open it. I cannot hold back the smile when I look inside. Someone finally fulfilled one of my requests.

They have prepared everything I asked for in my wardrobe selection. I did not think they would do it, but I feel a haze of a lot better knowing they did. Even though I did not expect it, they provided me with color schemes that matched what I had chosen in the linen generator on the StarBird the rotation of my release.

There will also be no frag moths to worry about. Much like the moths of Ancient Earth, frags love nothing more than to become a nuisance by eating holes in your favorite linens and clothes. My brother, Comilo, used to feed them to his womosa bat regularly, and it loved them.

The chair in the corner looks comfortable, and I move to test it out. Its softness surprises me, and I bounce up and down before snuggling into it. This will be my reading space, should I have any free time on the mission.

The holo-info projector powers on to display a scene of mayhem:

EMERGENCY ARMADA UPDATE: Uprisers have attacked a prisoner convoy and overran its escort patrols.

It must have been an ambush. Followers of Dolofónos use weapons, equipment, and vessels converted to an untraceable state. They are strong in numbers at about 80,000 members, but that number could be more.

Another warning circles the projection:

Uprisers are lashing out against the capture of Dolofónos under the capital city of Galhet and demanding his release. Authorities urge residents to stay indoors until they clear the area and remove debris.

I know where this is going. The Uprisers will not stop until the Armada releases Dolofónos, and he will not be. Not a chance. This is going to become a war at some point, and we will not be in-the-know once we make the jump to Andromeda.

Heavy thuds coming from the room next to me interrupt my train of thought. Curiosity takes over and all but forces me to place an ear against the wall. My neighbor is Skedelski's size or stomping in anger. One or the other.

"Open door," I say.

I make room for the rising cubes, place one foot into the corridor, a hand on the frame, and an eye around the corner to peek at my neighbor's door but pull back when its opening process begins.

"Close door," I say.

It is not closing.

"Uhm…" I look up. "Close please."

Thumping footsteps grow closer. I take a step back. It reforms once I am clear of the cubes' paths. A pearl white toe-portion of a robotic foot takes a step into view behind the final spinning cubes as they rotate into position. I did not expect A.I.-powered machinery to be on such an important journey. Not when a moral decision needs to be made about relocating humanity.

The thumping fades quieter with each step until it is faint. A tik passes. I can no longer hear it.

"Open door," I say.

The door opens, and I look in the direction it went to see nothing before exiting into the quarters' corridor.

11-2
Thumping feet

I follow the sound down and around a corner in a fast walk. They get louder as I gain on whatever I am following. A cargo lift is closing ahead of me on the left, and it is going up.

An automated ladder on the right catches my interest before I reach the cargo lift. I grab hold. Its standard green powder-coated steel is cold on my palms when I place my hands and feet onto it—colder than the one I was on earlier. Then again, the other one was closer to Athanasios's core.

"Ascend," I say.

It rises to guide me through momentary blackness between 3rd- and 4th-level passages in pursuit of robotic footsteps. I stop it to listen at each level and hear nothing. One last ascension brings the thuds back into earshot.

"Stop," I say, climbing off.

Left and right sides of the corridor look the same when I reach the upper level, but the thumping... It is resonating from the port side. I know which way to go.

As I turn left down the corridor, it... No... A person comes into view. It is the same Delgado, the one I read about in Expedition Anchor's files. This is unexpected.

She gave me my first ass-beating racing against her and others in the onium-cycle division when I joined the Armada's training program. I was over-confident and did not have enough revolutions on the infinity track. She denied me an off-season rematch when I asked for one and left me steaming over it for several rotations.

"The infamous Delgado," I say under my breath with an exhale.

I used to love the sport, but, as if racing indoors on a figure eight shaped infinity track at high speeds was not dangerous enough, onium-cycle racers like us do it on two wheels with no roll cage. When crashes happen, there were always injuries.

The onium-cycles themselves are ground-based vessels comprising nothing more than two wheels, an engine, and a seat. Fast and nimble, the handlebars control both wheels, which can pivot through twenty-five percent of its mounting system for lateral movements. They are dangerous and fun to ride by those who seek a thrill.

She was its champion before my incarceration but would not have been if she had not bumped my cycles the way she did. It was a dirty move, but I shall say nothing and know I can take her if we ever hit the track again.

I snicker under my breath, thinking about the good rotations behind me and study her. A lot has changed. What happened to her since then is something I will have to find out over rotations to come.

Delgado is taller in M.E.R.P. legs than she was the last time I saw her. I do not know what accident left her mechanically enabled since then, but she is still beautiful. A lot has happened on Kep Four since my six-cycle stint at the A.H.C. prison facility.

Her robotic legs are thick and powerful in appearance. A solid, metallic housing hides hydraulics with a high-gloss white powder coat. They encase her body from the waist down with impulse-disks shaped in the fashion of small plates at her hips, knees, and ankles. Their weight must be immense to thud as they do, which requires power to move with such grace.

She turns left into a dining hold, and I glimpse the side of her face. Her cheekbones are sharp. Her nose matches a perfect face with a neckline holding a head of equal perfection beneath bobbed hair. She is as flawless on this rotation as she was cycles ago.

"Nice legs, Delgado," Sergeant Bentley's voice slips from the dining hold.

I slow and ease myself to the hold's entrance, stopping to eavesdrop, as she laughs at his remark.

"Do you have any idea how many times I've already heard that this cycle?" she asks.

"It's all I got," answers Sergeant Bentley. "Looks like you're getting used to them."

"Sure am. You should come out and dance with me sometime."

"Real men don't dance," says Sergeant Bentley through a chuckle.

"You can't be a hermit forever," says Delgado. "Everyone has to move forward at some point."

They stop talking. Sergeant Bentley must be uncomfortable with the subject. I am sure it is about his fallen wife.

I have read about her in his mission files and feel gravely about his loss.

"So..." Delgado breaks the silence. "About that dance..."

"Why do you think I got all dressed up?" asks Sergeant Bentley, most likely in fatigues. "How'd you end up on this potential trip of death?"

"Looks like the Armada wants you at maximum payload," she answers. "I've been loading it the last four rotations and told them, if there's room for one more, that you'd need someone to oversee the munitions hold and repair any weapon over surges that come up."

"That's it?" asks Bentley.

"Here I stand," answers Delgado.

"Good," he says. "I'm glad you're here."

Her feet thud a few times. "Same."

"You're still sexy, by the way," says Sergeant Bentley.

"Is it the legs?" she asks.

He snickers. "Let me hear about this payload."

"It's substantial," she says. "Anti-tank mines, anti-personnel mines, remote detonators, magazine-fed grenade launchers, onium rifles, pulse spread shotguns, flashlights, full spectrum eye-wear, stun, flash, smoke and concussion grenades, shadow knives, phase combat suits—"

"That's it?" interrupts Sergeant Bentley. "Interesting payload for a reconnaissance operation."

"Tell me about it," she says. "Guess someone wants to keep you safe. And the Andromeda galaxy? No telling what we'll run into out there, or what kind of technology."

"You care to test those new legs to the forward with me?" asks Sergeant Bentley.

I rush back down the hallway as they exit and hop onto the automated ladder.

"Descend," I say.

I reach my assigned level, head back to my private quarters, and enter, thinking about the connection Sergeant Bentley and Delgado share. I cannot blame him. She is stunning, but he is not ready. At least, I would not be.

My private quarters are not easing this racing mind. We will depart in ten taks, which means I need to be in the cockpit and ready in nine. I would like to sleep for eight of it. I must hurry.

"Lock door," I say.

I enter the bathroom attached to my room. A mirror scrolls from its cylindrical encasement above the sink when I enter. Bags under my eyes are not flattering.

"Hmph," I say. "That's unfortunate."

I waste no time getting naked, climbing under the covers, and closing my eyes. Beauty sleep sounds like it is not a real thing, but I am convinced otherwise. I activate my Song Hen and drift off to electronica. Sleep is the best remedy for the extra luggage my face is currently toting. Time passes—sleepier by the tik. Everything around me fades, and I am gone.

A series of rapid beeps at my door awakens me. Someone is blowing up my entry pad. I scramble to throw on my undergarments, socks, and clothes, moving to the access with my terra boots in hand.

"Open," I say.

The door opens. It is Sapp.

"Are you joining us, or what?" he asks.

I slide on a boot. "What time is it?"

"Time for you to come," he answers. "Now."

He heads down the corridor. I have no choice but to follow and do it now. If it was anyone else, I would have told them to give me a tek. That is not an option here. Sapp is second in command under Sergeant Bentley.

His steps are fast. I can barely keep up with him with these short legs of mine. I hop on one leg behind him to put on the other terra boot. Sapp pulls away from me as we near the lift.

I enter with him waiting for me and kneel to strap my boots. The lift rises, and I finish when the door opens. He exits without me.

Dr. Wright is in the middle of delivering a speech when I arrive. The crew cuts me a dirty glance. Skedelski throws me a nod, but Sergeant Bentley shakes his head in disappointment.

"There are no simplicities at play here," says Dr. Wright. "So, I'll just out and say it. The planet we're traveling to is two-point-six-three million light cycles from here. No one has ever attempted a jump of this magnitude, and you cannot be the first to fail. The first to fail would be the last. If everything goes right, we'll be finding ourselves a new home. If it doesn't, we die along with the rest of humanity. Any questions?"

The group is silent. A few shake their heads.

"Good," continues Dr. Wright. "Sergeant Major..."

Sergeant Bentley steps in front of his team. "I'm going to need everyone sharper than they've ever been. Here and now. When we reach our destination. The whole nine paces. Are we clear?"

"Yes, Sergeant Major," says the squad.

Sergeant Bentley cuts me a look. He tenses, burying what he really wants to say. "Nothing beyond your job." He turns to the others. "Doctor Wright, we're ready for final system checks."

Dr. Sellers exits. Doctors Wright and Utley move to a separate part of the cabin to go over whatever is needed before departure. I am not sure what that is, but I know they are competent and doing what is necessary. I have faith in this team.

Sergeant Bentley looks over a checklist as Bell and Sapp move to their assigned seats. "Before we get seated..." He halts them. "Bell. Sapp. Double-check all fire stations throughout Athanasios."

"Yes, Sergeant Major," they respond in sync and exit the forward.

"Skedelski and Rhigas," continues Sergeant Bentley. "Check the cargo holds. Make sure every electro-strap's secured. Triple check."

Rhigas motions to Skedelski, and they walk from the cabin together.

Fister cuts Rhigas a smile. "First pick? Looks like you're teacher's pet, Cuz."

Rhigas smirks, shooting him a pointer-finger bird, and exits.

"You'd better pay up," says Fister. "Thirty credits."

"Fister, Chubb, Morris," continues Sergeant Bentley. "Walk the ship, split up, and take separate levels. Secure all doors along the way."

The men acknowledge and exit.

"I'm hitting the bathroom," says Chubb. "Catch you guys in a tek."

Sergeant Bentley watches him exit. I doubt Chubb is his favorite person. Nor am I.

"What about me?" I ask.

"Climb in the cockpit," answers Sergeant Bentley. "Sit and wait until you're needed for departure."

I climb in and leave the cockpit hatch open to watch the others. Sergeant Bentley walks to the captain's chair as I ponder when he will think differently of me, other than as someone who once ruined his rotation. He looks for a harness.

Dr. Wright notices him. "Sergeant Major, the seats generate a small magnetic field that interacts with your suit. They're tailored to us."

"Okay," says Sergeant Bentley. "Where's the input?"

"There are none," answers Dr. Wright. "Didn't you read about—"

"No," interrupts Sergeant Bentley. "I didn't read about the seats."

"Why not?"

"Look, there was a lot to cram in the little time we had. How do I activate it?"

Dr. Wright forces a disappointed smile. "Each seat works under voice command and only responds to its assigned crew member. Activate and release are the commands you're looking for."

Sergeant Bentley moves in front of his seat. "Activate?"

The chair sucks him down when he answers, slamming his back into it. I slither further into the Beltric Class Six cockpit to hide my urge to laugh. I cannot help it. The look on his face... It is as if he thought the ship was destabilizing. I place a hand over my mouth.

"It takes some getting used to," says Dr. Wright.

A snicker escapes between my fingers.

"Close the cockpit already, Mason," says Sergeant Bentley.

"Yes, Sergeant Major," I say, climbing in and shutting the cockpit door behind me.

12-2
Dominoes

I reach to my left and throw the power on in the cockpit. Visual panes come to life: one top center, one in front, one below them, and one to the left and right of each. Nine in total. A 360 degree view displays as I capture Armada auditory airwaves involving Expedition Anchor.

There is a lot of clutter in the audio. I need to single out the tugs. There are two of them. Athanasios's topside is tethered to one tug. The other tug tethers the bottom.

"There we go," I say, dialing them in. "Got it."

"Easy does it," says tug one operator. "I can hardly see its outer extremities."

"Dr. Wright to tugs," says Dr. Wright. "How's it going out there?"

"We're looking good," answers tug operator two.

Dr. Wright is nervous. He would not have asked otherwise. We are all on edge, hiding it or not. In a tak, we will either be in a new world or dead along with the rest of humanity.

I cut my eyes to the panes as Athanasios glides through retracting workstations. It blends with the emptiness of space, and the electro-stenciling comes into view, reflecting off one of the engineering rings.

ATHANASIOS

I sigh with relief and set my Song Hen behind disengaged manual flight controls to enjoy the show. Then, it hits me... The name Mason will go down in history as the first person to pilot a vessel through a wormhole. Whoever the first female aviator was, I am sure this was how she felt. Surely, people will not forget my name over time like hers.

I open comms with the tug operators. "Mason to tug fifteen zero nine."

"Go ahead, Mason," answers tug one operator.

"Permission to guide Athanasios out manually."

"That's a negative, Mason. Ending transmission."

The feed between us stops. I sit back for a moment in wait, watching the external panes. The star around Kep Four's dying brown hue is picturesque, and this may be my last chance to take it in.

"Athanasios," says the launch coordinator. "You're clear for full disembarkment. Sit tight and we'll have you out of there in no time."

Tugs chugging along to pull Athanasios from its engineering rings have me bursting at the seams to get things underway. I watch on, wishing to pilot us out manually. Why am I sitting here? I should ask Dr. Wright. He is in command of the mission.

I crack open the cockpit door and step halfway out.

"Dr. Wright," I say.

He answers without looking back. "Go ahead, Mason."

"Permission to—"

A heavy jolt rocks the ship. My right knee buckles.

"What was that?" I ask.

"Someone talk to me," calls Dr. Wright.

Athanasios sways. My body swings around the cockpit's exterior. I tighten my grip on the entrance door's frame to stabilize myself. Whatever is happening, it is unplanned. Dr. Wright staggers into the forward viewing pane as I climb back to my controls and close the cockpit door. The Uprisers may be upon us.

"External feeds," I say.

My flight panes transition to show tug one repositioning itself after a hard jolt. The tether anchoring them to Athanasios has slack in it, and they are drifting back toward it.

"What was that?" asks tug one operator.

"Oh, man..." says the second tug operator.

I look at the starboard pane. "That can't be good."

An engineering ring drifts and rotates out of position. It sails alongside Athanasios and hits the ring next to it, creating a domino effect as they bump each other out of position with us pushing through.

My cockpit floods with red warning lights. An alarm joins them. My eyes widen. Workers manning the repair stations eject to safety and away from their assisting droids. Small and large hand tools alike drift with them through space as they flee danger.

I silence the alarm and check our surroundings. "Armada voice clearance, Mason, five, Sinote, one, four, McKayla, three, six, engage Athanasios power core."

Athanasios powers up. The ship's voice fills my cockpit. "Athanasios online."

"Establish manual flight controls," I say.

"Manual flight controls established," says Athanasios.

"Alright," Sergeant Bentley's voice echoes over the comms. "Somebody talk to me."

"I'm pulling up feeds now," says Dr. Wright.

I don't have time to explain it to him right now.

"Silence all but tug feeds," I say.

"Audio rerouted," says Athanasios.

"Mason to tug vessel one five zero nine," I say.

"Mason," answers tug one's operator. "We have a major—"

"Break from Athanasios," I interrupt.

"Come again?" he asks.

My viewing panes show multiple rings closing in on us.

"Disengage from transport," I continue.

"I'm not breaking protocol," he says.

"Release the ship."

"I can't do that, Mason."

This man is not paying attention to what is happening or calculating the tug's speed and power against Athanasios's mass in this equation. I end all communications. I cannot converse with someone being willfully dense.

"Alright," I say. "Have it your way. End transmission." I strap in. "Set engines to full orbiting propulsion."

"Orbiting propulsion set to full output," says Athanasios.

My upper starboard pane shows an engineering ring is about to hit. "Open full Athanasios comms."

I bank to lower port and accelerate. It forces me to lift in my seat, then to the right.

"All comms are now open," says the A.I.

"Mason to all personal," I say. "TOCSIN. TOCSIN. Hold on!"

Bio-inertia stabilizers online (the system used in the Armada's flight vessels to prevent both terminal acceleration and deceleration. Its application is a combination of internal gravity generators and an organic/biological locking system that counter-matches forces of inertia while stabilizing biological cells in both organic and non-organic materials)... I had no time to think. Reactionary impulses took hold.

"Oh, haze," I mutter.

I may have just caused everybody onboard to be thrown to the floor, but what is done ... is done. Getting dropped from the mission is the last thing I desire, but there is zero time. We must fly before destroying humanity's only hope for survival. I cannot worry about those onboard not being secured in their flight seats. The Armada's official distress call, formerly Mayday on Ancient Earth, was called out as soon as possible.

Focus heightens. I maneuver Athanasios through floating engineering rings as if A.I. were guiding it. The small tugs are struggling to stay ahead of me, but no favors can afford to be given this tak. Headache or not, they will make it.

"Sorry, tug one five zero nine," I say.

"For wha—"

I bump the last tug out of the way as it exits the rings. Athanasios makes it the rest of the way out, and I level off for a stop. My back hits the pilot's seat with force.

"Right," I say to myself under heavy breaths. "Bio-inertia stabilizers next time, Mason."

I disengage manual flight controls and crack the cockpit door open to peek out. Bentley and Dr. Wright are sitting in their seats with puzzled expressions. I cannot blame them. They are probably bent out of shape by my lack of warning. Maybe not. I just saved Athanasios.

They are going to bring up my lack of warning and the non-use of bio-inertia stabilizers. This is the system used in the Armada's flight vessels to prevent both terminal acceleration and deceleration. Its application is a combination of internal gravity generators and an organic/biological locking system that counter-matches forces of inertia while stabilizing biological cells in both organic and non-organic materials. They will not be happy about my lack of its use.

I just saved humanity. Well, I kind of saved it. Athanasios is an important part of the process.

The first person I see upon opening the cockpit door and stepping halfway out is Sergeant Bentley.

He goes to stand and cannot. "Release." He rises to his feet and walks across the forward cabin. The rest of the crew is trickling into the forward with panicked looks on their faces. All eyes go on me ... as if I am insane. It seems to be the standard.

"What was that about?" asks Sapp.

"The engineering rings," I say with a pause, not wanting to be the center of further scrutiny. "They—"

Flight control interrupts comms. "Flight control to Athanasios. Is everyone in good shape up there?"

"We are," answers Dr. Wright. "What happened?"

Flight control pauses. The crew periodically becomes deadlocked onto me with unforgiving eyes. Especially Rhigas. Maybe coming here was not such a good long-term idea.

"Pardon the delay, Dr. Wright," says flight control. "Lot of comm activity at the moment. To answer your question, a droid malfunctioned and reengaged its workstation. It telescoped back to Athanasios and got clipped by the ship. Moved its engineering ring into the one next to it and so on. We got quite a mess out here."

"Are we to keep schedule?" asks Dr. Wright.

"Affirmative," answers flight control. "Stay on schedule. We'll get this cleaned up."

"We're clear on that, flight control."

"And, Dr. Wright,"

"Go ahead."

"You have one haze of a pilot up there. Flight control out."

Dr. Wright turns to me. "Nice flying, Mason."

"Thank you, sir," I smile.

The crew takes their eyes off me. Tension leaves the room. It feels good being here with the others for the first time. Whether or not the rest accept it, I can contribute.

Chubb walks into the cabin. He is holding a white cloth to his upper left forehead with a little blood showing through it. "What do you think you're doing flying without stabilizers and going manual while we're still in the rings? And don't tell me that was a tug pull."

I do not respond.

"Chubb," says Dr. Wright.

"Have you talked to her?" continues Chubb, turning to me full of anger. "I'm standing there trying to drain my bladder and next thing I know, I have to dry off and stop my head from bleeding. Do you know what it's like to be in the middle of relieving yourself and floating into a ceiling?"

Skedelski's eyes switch back and forth between Chubb and me. His lips part. I think he wants to say something, but he does not talk very much.

"Nobody else's going to say anything to Mason?" asks Chubb, looking to his squad for answers.

"You sure you weren't drunk again?" asks Fister.

Chubb scowls. "And you think that's funny?"

He looks to Sergeant Bentley for answers, whose red face and tight-pressed lips signal he is having a hard time holding in laughter.

Rhigas slips out a snicker. "You have to admit, it was at least a little funny."

A few of the guys start into light laughter. Then Delgado. I think I am the only one that finds no humor in it. Guilt. Seeing him makes me realize that I could have seriously hurt someone.

Chubb's face flushes a bitter red, but I hope he is not too mad. I did not...

I jump as he punches the wall next to him and storms out. The team laughs again. Chubb turns back to face them, and they try to compose themselves. Not a drop of laughter escapes me.

"Alright," says Sergeant Bentley. "We're a go in seven."

The team acknowledges.

"You catch that, Chubb?" asks Sergeant Bentley.

"To haze with the lot of you," shouts Chubb.

The crew smirks and heads to their stations.

I ease back into the cockpit. A single thought dances in my head when I sit to wait. *In less than fifteen, I am going to be the first pilot in history to make this kind of jump... and I am doing it to save humanity.*

The Planetary Sovereign's image is in the corner of all Athanasios's panes and viewing screens. A proud look blankets an optimistically worried expression. It is not just our lives that are in jeopardy. And the rest of the world is no doubt watching over planetary update feeds.

Silence is in abundance. Conversation is nonexistent. Hope is high.

My cockpit's sixth pane gives way to Kep Four filling all of what I can see. I watch as I reflect on something I have considered throughout our training—all that is left of Mother is down there, and I may never return to take part in her memory files again.

Upon closing my eyes, I place my palm on the center pane to cover part of Kep Four's image. "I'm going to miss you, Mother."

The team has taken their seats and is prepared to jump. I am ready to make history, and humanity is desperate for a new home. I listen over comms from the closed cockpit as my squad talks.

Dr. Wright walks into the forward with a tray of injectors. "Time for the hop-serum, ladies and gents. Compliments of the Armada."

One by one, the crew grabs them from the tray, injects themselves in the wrist, and puts them back.

I open the door to climb down and get mine. Skedelski's hand comes into view with the serum.

"McKayla," says Skedelski.

He cuts me a contagious smile. His eyes are soft and reveal a loving heart with gentle sparkles. A tender aura surrounds this man.

"Thanks, Skedelski," I say through a grin.

I inject myself and put the empty injector back in his hand. He shuts the cockpit and walks away. Skedelski is my favorite among the mission's fresh faces.

"Everything's a go here," says Dr. Wright.

"When you're ready," confirms flight control.

"Enter stage one," says the Sovereign.

"On you, Mason," says Dr. Wright. "Ease us into position."

Bio-inertia stabilizers activate and confirm on my panes with artificial gravity wells ready. I guide Athanasios a few thousand clicks from the nearest orbiting Armada anything and start phase one of the Alcubierre drive system. Four arms topped with trapezoid-shaped drive segments extend from the front and rear sections of Athanasios, stopping sixty paces from its hull.

"Engage A B and maintain," I say.

They latch themselves into place.

"Lock drive rings," I continue.

The trapezoid sections atop the extended arms telescope toward one another and connect to form solid rings around Athanasios. The vessel hums when the Alcubierre drive system comes to life.

"Drive rings locked," says Athanasios.

"Ready here," I say.

"Confirmed," says Dr. Wright. "We're three before a go."

I kill the feed. My eyes close without effort as I relax. Critical moments like this leave no room for stress, and nothing can penetrate me in this cockpit.

"While you're not the first to lead humanity into a new world," says the Sovereign. "You are the first to do it under these circumstances. Make us proud."

"Thank you, Sovereign," says Dr. Wright.

"Good luck, ladies and gentlemen," says the Sovereign. "Godspeed. End transmission."

The feed stops.

Godspeed. It means to have a prosperous journey or success. There is debate about when and where the term was coined, but we know it originated before NASA succumbed to the rise of private-sector endeavors, all of which eventually succumbed to the Armada. Either way, it brings comfort to hear.

"Take it from here, Sergeant Major," says Dr. Wright.

"Mason," says Sergeant Bentley. "On mine."

I raise Athanasios's power levels to 98.6 percent. "Waiting on you."

Gravity well anchors are struggling to hold us in place. It stresses the vessel to do this. I cannot hold it here for long.

The opaque exterior of the ship lights up in my viewing panes. An exquisite swirl of blue and ultraviolet purple wraps Athanasios in its entirety. The vessel hums louder with every passing moment.

"Engaging bio feed," says Dr. Utley.

Silhouettes of each crew member come into view at the corners of my panes and, if working correctly, do the same at the sides of the team's seats and the left shoulders of their suits.

"Deep breaths, everyone," says Sergeant Bentley. "Light it up, Mason."

I switch my center pane to show the Alcubierre drive system. There is not much to see externally. A pyramid-shaped shield covers it.

"Armada voice clearance," I say. "Mason, five, Sinote, one, four, McKayla, three, six. grant Alcubierre drive system access."

"Access granted," says Athanasios.

A pyramid-shaped key lowers from the cockpit ceiling as a matching receiver opens next to it. I insert the key overhead. Three panels slide back to reveal a matching number of switches. One by one, I activate them.

A cloud engulfs Athanasios, causing it to rumble and display fluctuating colors from the darker side of the spectrum. A portal is opening in front of us—two paces off the hull. Subtle vibrations turn into angry shakes. The cockpit harness digs into my shoulders and sternum.

My voice shakes with the ship. "I can't hold this for long,"

"We're just about there, Mason," shakes Dr. Wright's voice like everyone else's. "Everything looking good in there?"

"Yes, sir," I say, staring into the portal.

"How are we looking, Utley?" asks Sergeant Bentley.

"Everyone's focused," he answers. "Blood pressure's up, but it's expected with the serum. We're fine for departure."

"Mason," says Sergeant Bentley. "We're a go for jump."

I power to one hundred percent for a tik of painful shakes and release the artificial gravity well, slamming the throttle forward. The shaking stops and Athanasios pulls me back into my seat with force.

We enter the portal, and a brightness too much to look at overwhelms the panes. I close my eyes and look to my left. The back of my eyelids are bright red for a moment before the hue dims.

I open them to see the rear of Athanasios enveloped with a haze of fluctuating colors. It dissipates in less than a tik. I look to the other panes, and my vision slurs to leave dozens of the same pane in view as if multiple exposures are happening in my retinas.

A second flash floods the cockpit. Disorientation sets in. I turn my head from left to right, hoping to shake the dizzy feeling. My head drops and... I cannot...

13-2
First Look

I regain consciousness in the darkness.

"Mother?" I say in confusion.

I do not know where I am. My hands instinctively feel the area without thought as I search for answers. Cold hard surfaces... Flight controls.

"Athanasios..." I say.

Something happened. Power is down. I see nothing but black. The wormhole must have interfered with Athanasios when we exited the Ein-Rosen bridge.

"Hello," I say. "Anyone else shut down?"

The silence is deafening, and I am stuck in perfect darkness without windows in the cockpit. I search with blind hands, looking for the manual release to the cockpit door. A cold metallic panel guides me to it.

"Can anyone hear—"

Inertia sucker punches and pins me to the door. My head hits its corner. Blood runs down my cheek like tears, itching my jaw as the door's edge digs into the side of my skull. I struggle to reposition and lay my cheek flush against it.

The viewing panes flicker back to life, but Athanasios's engines are still down. Streaks of white come into view. We were not out of the wormhole when I woke. We just exited it, and I should have stayed in my seat because we are stuck in a flat spin and drifting. Bright blue stars and other stuff I cannot make out flash across horizontal visual panes from left to right. Clockwise beneath us. Counter-clockwise above.

We are spinning too fast. I can deal with these Gs, but the others... I do not know. Flight controls are beyond reach, and I cannot get to them. I am not strong enough. The gradational forces of inertia are making me lightheaded.

"Armada voice clearance, Mason," I say, "five, Sinote, one, four, McKayla, three, six, engage Athanasios power core."

The mighty ship powers back up. "Athanasios online."

"Activate bio-Inertia stabilizers."

"Bio-Inertia stabilizers online," says Athanasios.

I am no longer pinned, but we are still spinning. The controls... I reach for them and start the orbital maneuvering systems for correction. They kick in at full capacity until the spinning slows. I pull myself from the door to open it as it stops, peeking my head out.

Sergeant Bentley and a few others are regaining consciousness.

"Crew status?" asks Sergeant Bentley.

"Serum holding," answers a groggy Dr. Utley. "All vitals stable."

Athanasios powers down again.

Sergeant Bentley activates his wrist light. "Everyone alright?"

Bell and Rhigas are still in their chairs but just waking.

"Armada voice clearance, Mason," I repeat, "five, Sinote, one, four, McKayla, three, six, engage Athanasios power core."

It powers back up. "Athanasios online."

"Troubleshoot systems and correct," I say.

"Troubleshooting and defragmenting to optimize," says Athanasios.

Sergeant Bentley looks around, seeing I am the only one up and about. "Care to update me, Mason?"

"Yes, Sergeant Major," I answer. "Athanasios went offline in the Ein-Rosen bridge."

"What happened to us?" he asks.

"Too many Gs," I answer. "We were in a flat spin."

"And you maintained consciousness?"

I shrug my shoulders. "We're still here."

"And that's why she's with us," interjects Dr. Sellers.

Sergeant Bentley nods and turns his attention back to me. "Remind me to thank you before we—"

His eyes widen in captivation, and he looks to the forward viewing pane. The others look and become fixated on the forward as well. Delgado and Skedelski are the last to awaken and stand from their seats and follow suit.

I turn to look: a massive, Ancient Earth-like planet is in the forward view. Two blue suns burning at 25,000 Kelvin are circling each other far from the orbiting planet in a long-standing dance of death. Surely, one rotation billions of cycles from now, they'll collide.

"Look at that," says Dr. Sellers.

"Wow," I say. "Those are beautiful stars."

Our target planet is four times larger than Kep Four. There are no polluted skies. White clouds hover over a large green continent surrounded by clean oceans, and a blueish-white planetary ring system—most likely formed from a captured body of ice broken up by tidal forces—orbits the planet, highlighting an already stunning natural rarity. I have never seen such beauty in person. White clouds... I want to lie on them.

A single continent takes up nearly a third of the planet's surface. I study its landmass with nearly watering eyes. "Langaea." I slap my palms together for a good sting.

Dr. Utley jumps. "Do not... please don't do that again."

"It's amazing," says Dr. Wright. "Would you like to take a gaze at what I've been wanting to see for as long as I can remember? Let's see where we came from."

He punches in a few codes and steps back to watch the forward view. It goes black and fades back to life.

The Milky Way's image is hard to accept. It is clearer than anything imaginable: part spiral galaxy, part polar ring galaxy like NGC-660, with a thin, fading, warped ring wrapping it in uneven patterns from top to bottom like a bending wave of light.

"Is that really our Milky Way?" asks Sapp.

"I can assure you it is," answers Dr. Wright. "The images of the Milky Way galaxy you're used to seeing are actually images of Andromeda, where we are now."

My eyes are watering. "It's magnificent."

"Astonishing." Sapp shakes his head. "What's the amber dust ring around it?"

"Remnants of other things in the cosmos it's been dancing with for millions of cycles," answers Dr. Wright.

The crew looks on. They are just as mesmerized as I am. Not a soul in history has seen the Milky Way before. There has never been a satellite out far enough to capture an image.

"Let's not waste another tek," says Sergeant Bentley. "Our people back home don't have a rotation to lose."

"Atmospheric readings just came in," says Dr. Sellers with raised brows and a smile as big as I have seen on him. "It's breathable. Damn near perfect."

"Get ready for descent." Sergeant Bentley walks across the cabin. "Skedelski, start unhooking the basics and ready ground transport. Delgado, load us up."

"Yes, Sergeant Major," says the squad.

I watch as he exits with the others.

Dr. Sellers breaks away from them and approaches me. "How you holding up?"

"Like brown rain," I answer.

"Troubleshooting and defragmentation complete," says Athanasios. "Main bio-feed lines rerouted to—"

"I got it," I say. "Thank you."

"Would you like updates on—"

"No."

"At least it's up and running again," says Dr. Sellers.

"Yeah," I say, rubbing the side of my head.

Dr. Sellers leans in to look at the wound.

"Hey," I say. "I've been wanting to say thank you but haven't had the chance."

"What for?" asks Dr. Sellers.

"For this," I say, looking around. "I went from incarceration to Expedition Anchor."

He steps back and gives me a wink. "Good to have you in eyesight again."

Fister walks toward a lush, faraway tree line. He fires wildly into it. Sergeant Bentley, Sapp, and Bell grab him. A scuffle ensues. They fall to the ground as Delgado steps from Argos with an open mouth under worried eyes. Fister punches Sergeant Bentley, but the others pin his arms to subdue him.

"Mason?" asks Dr. Sellers, bending down in front of me for eye-to-eye contact with his hand on my shoulder. "Are you okay?"

"I don't know," I answer.

He looks back and forth between my eyes. "You stopped moving and responding."

"My head feels funny," I say. "I think I'm fine, but I saw something."

"Saw what?"

"Fister," I answer, still running it through my head. "He was... He was shooting into these strange trees. Then Sergeant Bentley, Sapp, and Bell tackled him and held him down."

"Your head's not too bad," says Dr. Sellers. "And you don't appear to have a concussion. Maybe it was a hypnagogic hallucination. A few people with H-SAM have had them. Dream states activating while you're awake."

"It wasn't a hallucination," I say. "But it wasn't a dream, either."

"Okay then," he says, studying my eyes. "I wouldn't get too worked up about it just yet. I'll get Dr. Utley to run some scans."

"Don't worry about it," I say. "I'm fine."

"You're sure you're, okay?"

I nod.

"Your call," he says. "Let someone know if that keeps happening."

I force a smile, knowing he is wrong, and exit the forward. It was no dream. There was no hallucination. I need a distraction to get my mind off it ... before it becomes all I think about.

They are going to be awhile getting ready to descend, and I will not sit here and do nothing. I have done enough of that for the last six cycles to last me the rest of my life. Perhaps a nap is in order if they want me for nothing else.

I make my way back to my quarters and lie down but cannot sleep thinking about things to come. We are circling a new world. And we are doing it 2.5 million light cycles from where we were just a little while ago.

I study the baker-channel access panel on the wall. They are all over the place, more than other ships I have been in. Engineers and maintenance personnel use them for repairs, amongst other things. I am curious to enter one on a future rotation and snoop around, but they are hot inside.

The holo-info projection system catches my attention. There will be nothing to watch if I activate it. We are in Andromeda, and no signals reach us.

Once I tap into its O.S., I can assess its available tools and resources.

"Hard-wired," I say. "Through and through."

I just need to find the right drive to snoop a bit. Or do I?

"Hmmm," I think.

I would rather hack around than go sneaking about for the correct drive to access member files, which I may end up not finding. My time is too valuable to waste.

I drop to a single knee and dig my fingers into the seams at each side of the panel under the holo-info projection system. I give it a few good tugs. It pops off, and I fall to my back with it.

Bio-lines are behind the panel. Lots of them. The only airborne communication on Athanasios is that of comms. Nobody knew what to expect once we entered the Ein-Rosen bridge.

This is why Dr. Wright's division requested bio-lines on Athanasios to be lined with lead and rubber for reassurance. It is a good thing he made the call. Even with their extra layers of protection, whatever happened to our vessel when we crossed the bridge nearly knocked us out of commission.

It has another upside beyond layered protection. At least, an upside for me. It is easier to hack into this way. Disconnecting and rerouting bio-lines is less painstaking than it would be to hack something as advanced as Athanasios.

"A few feeds here..." I say, pulling bio-lines from one spot to reinsert into another. "A few receptors there..." I splice into Athanasios's main feed. "And a snip here."

I will complete my hard hack in the time it takes to watch an episode of Galactic Failures (a comedy show with plenty of slips, falls, and pranks) on The Citizen Streaming Channel, which is the only channel on Kep Four that airs live BlazeBall events and regular programs alike along with breaking planetary news. I nestle bio-lines out of the way to push the panel back into position. No one should be able to tell what I have done unless they give a long eye to inspect behind the panel.

My knees are stiff. I stand to find them cold, with poor circulation from not being the most active person. Maybe I smoked too many torran-sticks during my younger cycles. While not harmful to the lungs, the underground vice is popular in districts of poverty. The Armada does not approve of them.

Hacking used to be easy from afar a hundred cycles ago. Wireless signals were as simple to intercept as a child catching glowing meck-bugs with a laber net (small hand-held nets on poles used to catch meck-bugs in the brown as children once did with butterflies on Ancient Earth). When signal interception ran rapid, the Armada switched everything back to a 3,000-cycle-old hardline system for their exotic capital leader vessels. Athanasios is a little different with its E-Coli bio-lines and lead coating, but the principle is the same.

"Let's see," I say, thinking aloud. "Mason, private quarters, scan, clearance, combine mutual rank Armada mission Expedition Anchor and link with Athanasios flight clearance Mason for hardline feeds."

The upper corners of the room start a golden scan grid running over me from head to toe. The inlaid O.S. activates.

"McKayla Mason cleared for hardline access," says Athanasios.

Who to peek upon? Rhigas? No. I do not wish to watch him act tough or adjust his package. Chubb is a nasal worm infected dyogg turd. Not that I have eaten dyogg, but they are the largest and most powerful form of livestock on Kep Four and raised in capital cities for their tender meat. Upper-class citizens and high-ranking Armada members alone eat these large animals. No one else is permitted. Most would not want to. Worms occasionally infect their nasal passages, resulting in lung infections and necessitating the euthanization of the animal and others in proximity of it. It is non-contractable to humans. Even so, why would I eat something like that?

No. Not Rhigas. Someone more more... My head bobs in thought. I know who.

"Access personal records, Skedelski," I say.

A list scrolls through the air in front of me. Most are military engagements, information on his congenital analgesia disorder, and footage of his destroying opponents in the Galactic Combat games. Only one catches my eye:

THE BIG KID

I smirk at the title. "Start memory file."

14-2
The Big Kid

A one-pace wide holo-projection renders itself before me, revealing an adorable girl about twelve cycles old. She wears new civilian clothing and is in the mud near a leaking water filtration main, getting them dirty for the first time. Several boys stand over her. It looks like they have pushed her down. A few of them make fun of her.

"Oh, my..." one mocks with high-pitched, girlish inflection while walking around with his right arm up and flopping. "I hope I don't get sand in my freaky arm."

"Why are you crying?" another asks. "You're not even human."

She looks at her right arm, moving it in examination. It is robotic from the elbow down.

"I wasn't born this way," she says through cries. "The explosion—"

"Shut up, droid," interrupts the first boy.

I cannot believe people. To treat this poor little girl in such a way is heartbreaking. The M.E.R.P. program for amputees was founded fifty-six cycles ago. Thirty-one cycles have come and gone since the Armada sanctioned it for disfigured youth, but these kids remain a nasty display of discrimination.

A boy nearly twice the size of the others approaches her from behind and extends a hand. She takes it. He pulls her up without effort.

"What are you doing?" asks the boy's pack leader. "Mr. Too-Dumb-To-Talk-To-Anyone?"

The file shifts to reveal Young Skedelski. He is far from dumb but misunderstood because he does not talk much. Sounds are difficult for him, but I read his training file. The man is intelligent.

I continue watching as he turns to walk away with the little girl.

"They will come clean," says Young Skedelski. "Your clothes, I mean. Are you okay?"

The little girl nods, and a glob of mud slams into the back of her head. She stumbles a few steps forward, turning to face them. Her eyes squint when she sees another glob of mud in the air headed her way.

Young Skedelski steps between her and the other boys with his back to them. Ball after ball of mud hits the back of his head, shirt, and pants as he talks to her.

"Are you still alright?" he asks with a voice full of bass at a young age.

"Yes," she answers. "I am now. I just need to clean this out." She looks at her robotic forearm. "Thank you."

"We have one dummy and one freak here," says the boys' leader. "Together they're dumb freaks.

The little girl's head lowers as the group laughs. Her lip quivers. Young Skedelski turns and steps to the little punks.

"Think I'm scared of you?" asks the first boy.

"I do," answers Young Skedelski.

"Don't fight," says the little girl. "Please."

Young Skedelski turns back to her. She shakes her head.

My fists clench as I watch the halo-projector. "Kick his ass, Skedelski."

The biggest punk in the group steps forward. "Hey,"

Young Skedelski turns back, dead into a sucker punch. His head whips a little, but not much. He smiles at the boy who hit him, and the group of troublemakers runs off together. The memory file stops.

"Aww..." I say.

I have a good feeling about Skedelski. I could see the two of us becoming close friends, and I could use a friend. Maybe he can use another.

I stare at the inlaid projector, wondering who to investigate next. Sergeant Bentley comes to mind. He is still wary of me, but maybe learning more about his life outside of the Armada can help me figure out how to win him over.

"Access Sergeant Major Bentley," I say.

A list comes up. I scroll the air in front of me. Everything here is different versions of the same thing—Armada mission this, Armada mission that, Another Armada mission, and so forth. The man does not get out much.

Okay, I am done looking. Wait. No. Just a few more, and I will stop.

I flip files twice more before stopping. "Bingo."

A personal memory file is all but daring me to open it:

The rotation my world stopped.

I am not sure if I am going to watch the file. It is the only one regarding his wife, and I do not want to see the man have sex. Not without popcorn balls.

"Screw it," I say. "Start memory file. The rotation my world stopped."

14-3
Laura

Another holo-projection renders itself before me. A younger Sergeant Bentley is sitting in the front seat of an Armada staffing vessel next to an attractive lady. I can only assume this is Laura. They share a smile.

Delgado is in the back seat wearing a Farca, watching them as he speaks to the lady next to him.

"Laura," says Sergeant Bently.

"Yes," cuts Laura. "I'll be there for your pinning ceremony tomorrow."

He smiles. "Better be. We're getting married in a few rotations. You start standing me up now and we are going to have issues."

Dense pollution conceals the surrounding area as they kiss goodbye. It is a sweet side of Sergeant Bentley I have never seen before.

"Come on, Laura," says Delgado. "Stop trading DNA on my time or take him to an overnight or something."

They stop kissing and put on Farcas. His smile sparkles through his eyes. Oncoming transport vessel lights come into faint view in the backdrop as she exits the vehicle. Delgado holds her breath and hops out. She has magnificently toned legs under a dress and is a little intoxicated—apparently heading back from an N.C.O. pub. She gives Laura a hug and hops in the front seat of the car next to Sergeant Bentley.

"Look at you," says Laura, "riding off with my best friend."

They share subtle laughs as the vessel's lights grow closer in the other lane. Another vehicle comes from a side street and flies just in front of it. A near miss.

Laura turns to look as a pursuing patrol vessel comes from the same side street and slams into the oncoming transport with its sirens blaring and patrol strobes flashing.

"Oh, no..." I say, covering my mouth and watching the memory file with a sinking heart.

The large transport vessel fishtails it off course. There is no time for her to move.

"Laura!" shouts Sergeant Bentley.

It strikes her and simultaneously T-bones Sergeant Bentley's Armada vessel as Delgado winces away from a violent impact in the passenger's seat. I flinch with her. I do not want to look.

My eyes water, listening to the struggling breaths and labored words of a dying man as he cries out for Laura in a weakened state. Everything beyond the sounds of escaping gas and a still buzzing E-output drive fades away as Sergeant Bentley's transport fails to keep running.

I do not need to look to know that the crash took Delgado's legs or anything else. I know what is happening. He is stuck in his seat trying to get free. I can hear that, but I am scared to face the image of his wife if she is in view, and I am terrified to see what Sergeant Bentley is going through.

"Stop memory file and power down," I say.

The feed stops. I turn back and stare into the spot where the scene displayed itself. A sniffle escapes me.

"Set a probe launch reminder alarm," I say. "Maximum volume. Minimum warning time."

"Reminder confirmed active," says Athanasios.

I wipe my eyes, move to my bed, and lie down to let my emotions rock me to sleep.

The alarm sounds out and jostles me awake. My private quarters reverberate with sound in a capacity I did not expect. It is rattling my eardrums to the point of fracture.

I cover my ears. "Silence alarm."

The alarm goes quiet.

"Don't use maximum volume output on that," I say to remind myself. "Got it."

"Maximum volume disabled," says Athanasios.

"No," I say. "Never mind. That's fine. No more Maximum volume."

"We have already disabled the maximum volume."

I shake my head and stretch my arms to wake. Tension in my back lets loose. My neck releases matching pops when I tilt my head to the right and left. A slow-building, much-needed yawn escapes from deep within my gut.

"I need Stimulant 5," I say.

An automated atomic generator processes my waking drink and brings it to life in its cylindrical center hold. I move to it, eager to sip. Feels like dirty ice water hitting the inside of my cheeks. The flavor is bland at best.

"This is cold," I say.

"Yes," says Athanasios. "Energy replication is at a minimum for Expedition Anchor."

"And the lack of flavor?"

"Energy replication is at a minimum for Expedition Anchor."

"Great," I say, crankier than normal upon waking. "That's just great. Thanks."

"You are welcome, Mason," says Athanasios.

"I was being..." I say, chugging the Stimulant 5 to exit. "Never mind. Open door."

I wait for the door to open and enter a corridor that is cold and empty. Everybody else is prepping. I enter the forward and climb straight into the cockpit on the verge of being late and leave the door open.

Dr. Wright puzzles at his station with a mouth slightly agape and searching eyes. Something is on his mind, but I am not sure what it is. I have never seen him express concern. It makes me uneasy seeing him like this.

Sergeant Bentley approaches him. "What's wrong?"

"I don't know," answers Dr. Wright. "Half our systems are still down. I've known since we exited the Ein-Rosen bridge, but I can't run surface scans like this. Not clean ones. I think we should launch a data probe before you make your descent."

"Agreed," says Sergeant Bentley. "I'll see what Morris can do to get it straightened out."

Dr. Wright enters a code. I turn to the controls for a last check to ensure we are not in a degrading orbit and exit the cockpit.

"We're locked in," I say.

"Roger that," says Sergeant Bentley. "Double check system communications between the shuttles and Athanasios."

"Shouldn't I do a physical inspection of—"

"Negative," interrupts Sergeant Bentley. "Already taken care of."

"But if I—"

"System communications," he cuts me off again. "That's an order, Mason."

I nod and climb back into the cockpit.

"Mason..." continues Sergeant Bentley.

I turn to face him. "Yes, Sergeant Major?"

"Number one," he says, "you should learn to trust your team. Morris is a brilliant communication man, and he'll do us right on inspections. We're lucky to have him. Number two, good job coming out of the Ein-Rosen."

I smirk proudly and sit in the cockpit flight chair, leaving the door open. It was nice to hear a compliment from him.

Sergeant Bentley turns to Dr. Wright. "Let's get that probe in there and see what we get."

"Already on it," says Dr. Wright.

I run automated communication link checks between Athanasios and the individual shuttles, shifting in my seat to watch Sergeant Bentley and the doctor as it runs. A probe visible on the forward viewing pane catches my attention when it launches from the ship and races to the planet. It punches from sight into its upper atmosphere.

Sergeant Bentley and Dr. Wright watch the monitoring system. Why does their posture look tense? What has them concerned? I cannot see the readings at their station from here.

"How's the probe's signal holding up?" asks Sergeant Bentley.

"It's already getting weak," answers Dr. Wright.

The forward view flashes white and goes dark.

"What happened?" asks Sergeant Bentley.

"Couldn't tell you," says Dr. Wright, checking the station against the readings. "Some kind of static discharge in the atmosphere." He works to correct it until a blurred image appears on the viewing pane. "There we are."

"You're welcome," says Morris over comms.

Sergeant Bentley snickers.

A massive structure comes into view on the planet, but it is unclear. The disturbance must be severe. There is no other way it is stopping Athanasios from getting anything less than pristine images at this distance.

"Can you enhance it?" asks Sergeant Bentley.

"No," answers Dr. Wright. "That's it. Looks like a... I don't know yet. Something big."

"Could it be a natural formation?" asks Sergeant Bentley.

Dr. Wright leans closer to the image. "It's hard to tell."

He points to a section of the viewing pane and zooms in. The image becomes further distorted, but there is clearly an overgrown structure visible.

"Nothing natural forms with that kind of symmetry," says Dr. Wright. "Set up an enhancement perimeter when you get down there. Might give us a clearer image of what we are looking at here."

"Agreed," says Sergeant Bentley. "I'll inform the crew."

He walks from the forward and leaves Dr. Wright to study the planet's surface. I move to exit the cockpit when it beeps. It is time.

"That was fast." I close the scan, exit the cockpit, and head to the cargo hold.

15–2
Shuttles

I enter to find the away team suited up. Delgado and Bell are climbing into the smallest of the three transport shuttles. Sergeant Bentley approaches the doctors as the others climb into the remaining transports. A vehicle with four tracks is inside the largest of the vessels—a military green ground-crawler designed especially for Expedition Anchor called an Argos.

Dr. Sellers puts Eye-Cams in the left eye of each squad member. The clear, dish-shaped micro-panes contour to the iris and record/transmit their P.O.V. to active receivers onboard Athanasios. They have been in use for aionas of cycles, but these are the best the Armada offers. They are pricey. A three-cycle salary, however, will land you one from the underground market if you want it bad enough.

"Any word on scans?" asks Sergeant Bentley.

"I've just about got comms worked out," answers Morris. "But you're going to fly manually for now."

"Shouldn't be a problem," says Sergeant Bentley. "Why manually?"

"There is an electrical storm moving in right now," answers Morris. "Manual will keep transports from reading your surroundings through it and possibly miscalculating. Never seen a storm quite like this circling a planet. The upper atmosphere's going to be rough."

Sergeant Bentley studies him. "How rough?"

"Unusually so," answers Morris. "I suggest you push through as fast as you can without burning up transports."

Morris enters and hands Dr. Wright an arm band. "Finished."

"Thank you, Morris," says Dr. Wright. "That was fast."

Morris winks at the smack of his lips.

Dr. Wright clamps the band onto his right arm. Lights strobe across it in full spectrum.

"One vital band and the overseer was not enough for you, Doctor?" asks Sergeant Bentley.

"This is an intensifier Morris worked up," answers Dr. Wright.

"It's going to help get the signals through the atmosphere," interjects Morris. "You might be on your own awhile when you reach the surface. I need to stay up here and see what I'm up against to get it dialed in."

"Understood," says Sergeant Bentley.

"Good luck down there, Sergeant Major," says Morris, turning to Dr. Wright. "I'll be in comms station two, where the signal's strongest until I get this worked out. That's right around the corner … if you need a proper doctor at any point?"

"Very funny, Morris," says Dr. Utley.

Sergeant Bentley enters the largest shuttle. It closes behind him, and I hurry back to the cockpit before they depart. It is the best seat in the house.

15-3

First Entry

Back in no time, I race up the automated ladder, rush to the forward, and enter the cockpit, talking before I am all the way in. "Recover the last communication link checks between Athanasios and the individual shuttles. Leave them open." The records appear on the center pane. "Activate links with my override codes."

"Secondary pilot protocols initiated," says Athanasios. "Which vessel are you linking with?"

"All of them," I answer.

"It is not recommended that—"

"Override," I interrupt and switch audio feeds to contact ground team. "Mason to ground team. Everyone loaded and ready to go?"

"We are a go in five zero six, Mason," answers Sergeant Bentley.

"Okay. Ready when you're ready," I say, activating my cockpit's panes and communicating with Athanasios again. "Transfer Athanasios's visual recordings to cockpit." The panes in front of me power up with feeds. "Isolate cargo bay and forward on first and secondary panes. Isolate all currently running shuttles to the remaining four."

My requested visual feeds fill the panes.

The cargo bay slowly opens. Metallic brackets clamping the shuttles down release their grasp, allowing them to hover in place a few hands from the floor. Space fills much of the cargo room's visual when the bay fully opens, high-lighted by a beautiful planet we are soon to be the first humans to explore.

"Alright, Mason," says Sergeant Bentley. "We're launching."

"Right here with you, Sergeant Major."

I watch the shuttles drift from the open bay door, through the magno-barrier holding black's empty vacuum at bay, and into open space wishing I were going with them. I understand why I am not. They need me here, but the excitement they must feel entering the unknown...

"Switch internal Athanasios visual recordings to external," I say. "Nearest planet side."

I can see them now. They are just outside the hull. My head bobs with energy, watching the shuttles bank toward the planet. My panes zoom in automatically as they move away from us.

I would bite my nails right now, watching them near the upper atmosphere, if I had any. Anticipation is heavy. Then it happens. The three shuttles burst into the upper atmo-sphere. Friction lights up their protective under-plating like a gaznote egg cracked in Kep Four's Kelvo region of deserts (the hottest place on Kep Four with temperatures reaching

161 degrees when thermal activity is high). I miss gaznote eggs. They are artificial but cracked and eaten like any other. Its texture is firm when cooked and the flavor is over-salted. In Najasa and other districts of poverty, they were popular when I was young.

"Open Athanasios cockpit audio to ground team transport shuttles," I say. "Overlapping feeds."

Audio comes in to match what I am getting from the panes. Fister is at the flight controls. It is louder than I expected. Violet-colored lightning is abundantly visible outside his shuttle's windows.

"I'm on audio now," I say.

"Good," says Fister. "Because it looks like the upper atmosphere's everything that we thought it would be."

Sergeant Bentley helms the larger shuttle through subtle vibrations as it pushes through. A thick bolt of lightning passes right in front of him. "I think you understated the atmosphere, Fister."

"Agreed," says Fister.

"Everyone stay in manual," says Sergeant Bentley. "How are you looking, Delgado?"

She turns her head and blushes before checking her bearings.

"I think someone has a crush," I whisper to myself.

"Looking good," she says. "Just enjoying the—"

Her shuttle lights up brightly. I lose sight of her. My pulse waves.

Delgado is driving Argos on the surface of the planet below. She turns sharply with Rhigas hanging on the back when a rocky object bangs into the side of it and fragments upon contact. A second impact nearly tips it over. Fister's cousin is thrown, tumbling to the ground by the impact.

"Rhigas!" shouts Fister.

Delgado struggles to level out the vehicle. It comes up on two tracks again. She gets it under control and circles around to head back.

Rhigas stands to his feet. Something grabs and tosses him some twenty paces across the field. I cannot make it out, but more are running toward him in the distance as he stands.

"Stop Argos," says Sergeant Bentley.

It comes to a halt. They hop off.

"Lock and load," continues Sergeant Bentley. "Aim low."

15–4
Landing

I look around to see the cockpit's panes fading into view. Another vision… I do not want them to find out.

"Moving past stage two drop descent," echoes Sergeant Bentley. "Initiate landing sequence."

I watch as their shuttles near the surface. "I'm right here with you guys."

They circle for a moment in search of the best place to land.

"Got a visual on an open area," says Delgado. "About 1.5 clicks due southeast."

"Looks good," says Sergeant Bently. "Follow us in, Fister."

"Right behind you," he answers.

"Area confirmed clear on all visuals," I say. "Clear for landing sequence."

I study their landing speed and engine thrust to ensure all is going smoothly. They touch down. Exhaust systems blow uncut grass to lean away from them. Insects scatter to flee the scene.

They power down the vessels and exit, each looking down at the tall grass beneath them. None of us have ever set foot on fertile ground. I cannot imagine how it must feel beneath their feet.

Most cannot stop looking around at the new world. Delgado moves to the front of her shuttle. Her Eye-Cam reveals a darker burned patch on my video feeds.

"Glad that didn't get any worse," she says.

"Speaking of which," says Sergeant Bentley, "You mind telling me what happened up there, Mason?"

"What do you mean, Sergeant Major?" I ask knowingly.

"You stopped responding when we hit the atmosphere."

"My comms must have temporarily disabled during drop descent," I answer.

"Checking on her now," says Morris.

Morris opens the cockpit. Dr. Wright is standing behind him. The entire ground team is visible through my pane feeds. I look around.

"Another hypnagogic hallucination?" asks Dr. Sellers.

"Another?" asks Sergeant Bentley.

"She had one earlier."

"No," I say.

"Mason," says Dr. Sellers.

I look at Dr. Wright and back at the panes. "Fine. Okay. Yes. I had another one."

"Wright to Dr. Utley."

"Wait," I say. "I don't need to—"

"Utley here," he cuts in from Athanasios's med lab.

"I'm sending Mason to you now," says Dr. Wright. "Check her over when she gets there. She'll explain."

"Loud and clear," says Dr. Utley.

"Head straight there," says Dr. Wright. "That's an order. If the ground team would have needed you during descent and you hadn't been there... Don't keep stuff like that to yourself."

"Yes, sir," I say.

Morris pats the cockpit and steps down.

"Take care of yourself, Mason," says Delgado.

The ground team goes about their rotation one by one. Time ticks a few teks. I have but one question on my mind as I exit the cockpit: '*What the haze is wrong with me?*' I give Dr. Wright a look of confirmation and head for the med lab.

Dr. Utley intercepts me as I exit the forward. A sigh escapes me, but I guess he is best for the examination. After all, he is the one who conducted all my memory and virtual brain dissection for H-SAM progression back at the Armada.

"You ready?" asks Dr. Utley.

"Sure," I answer sarcastically. "I love having my head examined."

"Good. Let's go then."

I follow him. Vertical corridor reinforcement bars pass quickly as we make our way to the Med Bay. It is a brisk walk to keep up with him.

"Dr. Sellers tells me you had a hypnagogic hallucination or two," says Dr. Utley. "Has this ever happened before?"

"No." I round a corner with him. "First time. Well, second counting the first one this rotation."

"I see. We'll get you checked out here shortly."

The Med Bay comes into view. Its door slides open, and we enter.

15-5
Examine

Dr. Utley moves me to the back of the Med Bay and seats me in a chair. It is hard like the Armada. There is nowhere else to sit beside the hover gurneys (medical gurneys that drift over a small robotic ball that keeps them suspended), and I am not that ill yet.

Dr. Utley grabs three neural mapping nodes. "What made you lose the old hair style?"

"Why not?" I ask in return. "Why the glasses when you can just get your eyes fixed?"

"Why not?" he reflects my answer back to me.

I snicker. He is funnier than people give him credit for. Dry but funny.

He places a neural mapping node at my temples and a third at the base of my skull. Placed on three specific points on shaved portions of the head, they work with neural scanners to generate readings and predictions of neurological conditions. Highly accurate.

"Hold still for me." He grabs a neural scanner and raises it to the node on my left temple.

"Aren't you going to link them?" I ask.

"I did that the moment I knew you were coming," he says, moving to my other temple. "Hmph."

"Hmph, what?"

He moves to the node at my skull's base. "It is peculiar."

Unease fills me. "How so?"

He stops and makes his way to the other side of the Med Bay before setting the scanner on an inset, disk-shaped, input uploader. I wait patiently in the chair, studying the station he works at. Armada green and stainless silver line its sharp design.

The Med Bay station is at the forefront of our medical technology and can do just about anything one should need with simple commands.

"Full breakdown and analysis," says Dr. Utley.

My brain rotates in front of him. It is weird looking at my own thinker.

I try to hide my worries. "Am I going crazy or what?"

"Not according to this," answers Dr. Utley.

"What's it telling you?" I ask.

"Well..." he says, splitting the images into five sections to spread them out and rotate them for more in-depth examination. "Here's how it works. Your lower brain causes REM sleep, your middle brain adds emotions, and your upper brain makes sense of it all. The link between volume decline and increase in seriousness of hallucinations work in a combination of all three."

"And?" I ask.

"And you have unusual recent activity in the right prefrontal cortex that is incompletely attached to the region homolog to Broca's area. It's common with H-SAM, but yours is only in the left secondary supramarginal gyrus and transverse Heschl's gyrus. You have something going on there. I've seen nothing like it."

I tense up. "Speculate?"

He turns back to the projection of my brain. "I'm going to have to study these for a while to figure that out for you, but I don't think it is anything life-threatening."

"That's a good thing," I say.

"Yes, but you have considerable activity pulsating in the axial, sagittal, and coronal planes as well."

"It wasn't like that when you ran my initial tests at the Armada, right?"

"Not even close," he answers and turns to face me. "This is new."

I swallow hard. "Okay."

"There's no damage," he reassures. "I wouldn't give it too much thought yet. How much sleep have you been getting?"

"Not as much as I should be."

"You know people with H-SAM tend to sleep more than others. Get some sleep and don't distract yourself with digital interfaces. Doctor's orders."

"Am I good to go for now?" I ask.

He removes the neural mapping nodes from my head. "Whenever you feel like it."

"Thanks." I move for the door.

"Mason..."

"Yeah?" I ask, turning to face him.

"Report back to me if this continues after you get caught up on sleep."

"I will," I say. "Promise."

Dr. Utley goes back to examining my brain as I exit. "Good."

I walk the corridors glad to be out of the Med Bay but am stuck up here with Dr. Wright. He is not much for conversation, not that there is anything wrong with him. A distraction is needed, anything to get my mind off the possibility of...

The thought of losing control over my thought process or brain activity is nerve-rattling. Athanasios's security feed lab is my current go-to. It is only a few paces away.

I enter to find Morris with audio enhancements up and running strong. Visual transmissions are also syncing well. I can watch and hear everything from here. It is perfect.

Fluids, nutrition, and time to kill are all here. I figure if they do not want me doing anything beyond being their pilot, I might as well have some real-time entertainment going on in this oversized security hub. It is massive. The security feed lab, that is. It is a good 18-paces wide. Thirty-two security panes wrap the observer station in a partial horseshoe pattern.

It is not the Armada standard. Three different shades of silver coat the room. Its walls are the lighter of the three. The chairs in here are the darkest shade, and the control panel is sterling.

"Armada voice clearance," I say. "Mason, five, Sinote, one, four, McKayla, three, six, display all visual security feeds intercepting both Athanasios and ground team, split screens if necessary. Include Eye-Cams, bioscience ground team feeds, shuttle cams, and anything else with visual feed outputs."

The panes come to life with feeds.

"Visual security feeds routed," says Athanasios.

I drop a couple of nutrition packs inelegantly on the table. "Intercept all communications and reroute to my location."

"Communications systems rerouted."

There. Now I have everything involved in Expedition Anchor that outputs a visual recording routed here—both surface and topside. I take a seat and place a popcorn ball in my lap.

In the past, I never had an urge for popcorn balls. They are blue and crunchy, like thin pieces of glass when you bite into them, only they do not cut you. I still find it an odd sensation.

16–2

Campsite

Ground team settles a small camp on the exotic new world. Trees are unreal down there, and not because the only trees I have seen in person before were indoors. Some have canopies like plush carpets of greens and purples. Others look like they are about to cry, hanging unsatisfied amongst their surrounding beauty. The grass is thick. I hope to set foot on it soon, especially the areas with suede texture.

Mountaintops far in the backdrop are green to their highest peaks and littered with trees as if the oxygen is richer with the increase in altitude. The planetary ring system is faint from the surface with both stars high in the sky. A group of winged mammals fly toward summits hidden by clouds in the extreme distance. I think they are enormous in stature, though it is hard to tell from so far away.

Ground team is wrapping up the last of their tests for the rotation. Dr. Sellers passes an H.C.S. (hand-held CAT scan) around Chubb's head while the others prepare to lie down for the evening. I am sure he will be fine, but something must have happened while I was getting my head examined.

Dr. Wright walks to the forward view. He watches the same feed as the one on my 19th pane.

"How's he looking now?" asks Dr. Wright.

"All done," answers Dr. Sellers. "He might be a little light-headed for the next half-tak."

"Good to hear," replies Dr. Wright. "Keep me updated."

Dr. Sellers checks his readings again. "Will do."

Sergeant Bentley walks to Dr. Sellers and stops. "How's it going?"

"I cleared the concussion," answers Dr. Sellers. "He'll be fine."

Chubb stands. "Thanks, Doc."

"Don't worry about it," says Dr. Sellers. "It's nice being Dr. Wright's wingman from down here. Gives me something extra to do."

Sergeant Bentley approaches Chubb, bumps him shoulder to shoulder, and leans in for a joking whisper. "How you feeling, sweet cheeks?"

"I'm good," answers Chubb through snickers. "But you're a little too close for comfort right now." Chubb pushes him playfully away.

I shake my head and smile as they part ways. Comradery is high, and that is a good thing. We are all each other has.

"Mason to Dr. Wright," I say.

"Fire away, Mason," he answers.

"What happened to Chubb?" I ask.

"He tripped over something unloading and smacked his head on the side of Argos, but he's fine. Anything else?"

"No," I answer, returning my focus to the security panes. "Thank you."

Tele-tents are righting themselves in the background. They are always interesting to watch erecting. The tele in tele-tents is short for telescopic. They start off a small box that comes up to roughly one's waistline when stationary. Upon activation, a series of tubes within them extend to expand until they are a foot taller than someone like Sergeant Bentley. They are only about three paces wide but make up for it by being twice that in length. The flooring, walls, and ceilings all roll out like scrolls from tubes housing them on six sides.

Dr. Sellers holds up a capsule containing an odd-looking creature. It has qualities of both mammal and insect: a fuzzy torso, ten lengthy barbed legs shaped like sticks, improvised leaves for camouflage, and wings to match it all.

Dr. Sellers photographs it with a cube cam smaller than my thumb. "You still getting these up there?"

"Copy that," answers Dr. Wright.

"Perfect," says Dr. Sellers while studying the creature. "We'll need to develop an entirely new digipedia for this place."

"I'm sure we do," says Dr. Wright. "But let's focus on getting back on course for now."

"Loud and clear. Sellers out."

"One more thing," says Dr. Wright.

"Go ahead."

"The upper atmosphere's showing some pretty radical changes incoming."

Dr. Sellers looks up. "Another storm?"

"No," answers Dr. Wright. "I don't think so, but we could lose communication while it passes. Not sure what to make of it yet. I'll reach out to Morris and see what he thinks."

"Roger that. I'll keep an ear open. Sellers out."

Sergeant Bentley approaches and looks at the capsule. "What do we call this little guy?"

"There's not a name for anything here yet," answers Dr. Sellers, "but this little guy, as you called him, comprises all the elements that we expected things on this planet to be composed of. Its DNA's just arranged differently. I guess you can call it whatever you'd like."

"Ugly," says Sergeant Bentley. "That's what we'll call that one. Does it bite?"

Dr. Sellers smirks. "Not a single attempt. It's actually quite docile."

"Good," says Sergeant Bentley. "Keep it in the capsule. I'm turning in for the night." He turns to the rest of his team. "Let's shut down and hit the rack."

Everyone nods and enters their sleeping quarters.

"I feel good here," says Sapp.

"Me too," says Rhigas.

"Why?" asks Fister. "Are you sipping Craga juice again?"

"I wish," answers Rhigas.

"It is the planet's rotational speed," interjects Dr. Sellers. "It's big and its mass has a decent amount of gravity, but it is not as dense as our home world, and it's spinning at twice the rate. You're lighter here than you were on Athanasios or Kep Four."

A thump echoes from the nearby cluster of sad-looking trees. The sound of breaking branches follows to fill the scene. Dr. Sellers steps forward to read the area with his bio-scanner, though I am not sure how well it will work at that distance.

The technology Dr. Sellers uses is programmed to detect all known forms of life in our recorded history through LR-DNA mapping. However, since we are not on Kep Four anymore, I do not know if it will map a new lifeform unless he is within five paces.

"What do you see?" asks Sergeant Bentley.

"Nothing," answers Dr. Sellers.

"How come I don't think that's right?"

Ground team emerges from their sleeping units. A squawk echoes across the field from above. Their heads go up with curiosity to see what is going on. A bird-like animal gawks as it flies overhead.

Its size becomes clear as it nears. Another with a twelve-pace wingspan flies behind it. The crew looks up in amazement as hundreds join it in the magnificent fading blue sky.

"What the..." says Delgado.

Dr. Sellers's eyes widen. "Would you look at that?"

"Those colors," says Delgado.

I zoom in on her Eye-Cam feed. Their wings split into two at the tips and every feather is a different, ever-changing color. They are shifting as they move, flap, and turn through the sky to catch different spectrums and intensity levels of light. There are so many of them—hundreds strong—and they are beautiful with the twin blue stars behind them.

Flyers are new to me. I watch as they change course and descend on a flight path toward the ground team's campsite. Their curiosity about us must match ours about them.

The group of airborne mammals level off fifty paces from the planet's surface. They pass over the ground team's head, and I am jealous not to be down there with them for the spectacle. Dr. Sellers holds his arms up as they fly by, laughing with happy excitement.

One swoops down close to Chubb. He flinches, grabs, and readies his onium rifle.

"Son of a..." he says.

The others laugh. A giggle seeps from me. Chubb is stuck in a looping state of flinches as each flap over his head.

"Making friends with the wildlife already?" asks Fister.

"You think that's funny?" asks Chubb. "These things could be dangerous. We don't know what's on this—"

Others swoop to within arm's reach of Sergeant Bentley.

Chubb raises his weapon. "Watch out."

Another swoops to within a few paces from Chubb. He falls to his back, accidentally firing a three-round burst into the air.

"Secure that weapon," says Sergeant Bentley.

"They're just curious," says Dr. Sellers.

"How the haze could you know that?" asks Chubb.

Two of the rounds pass a second flock far away, but a third strikes a flyer. I gasp and cover my mouth when feathers burst from it and the once-perfect animal falls in a spiraling collapse of smoke and death toward the planet below. The lower flock of flyers scatter when the rifle blasts.

"What's wrong with you?" asks Dr. Sellers.

"I didn't mean to," says Chubb with a skyward gaze. "I swear, I didn't mean to."

Large flyers, one hundred strong from the second flock, turn and head straight for the ground team. They are fast. Bell and the others dive to the ground and cover up as the flyers bombard them.

"Chubb," repeats Sergeant Bentley.

Chubb drops his onium rifle and takes cover with the others.

Angry flyers reach the camp. The ground team dives for cover as the large angry birds pick up and drop several pieces of testing equipment Dr. Sellers has set out. They flip his table into the air and toss about lighter supply crates as they pass by. Two slam into the side of a tele-tent and stand with angry screeches, approaching members of the squad nearest them.

"Get inside," shouts Sapp.

Those close to their tele-tents enter for cover. The doors shut right behind them with the flyers biting and clawing at the hard tele-tents. More shrieks...

The angry flyers turn their attention toward those near Argos, running toward them on powerful clawed legs. Delgado, Fister, Sergeant Bentley, and Rhigas climb into Argos and shut its doors while Dr. Sellers and Chubb lay flush on the planet's tall grass.

"What do we do?" asks Chubb. "What do we do?"

"Don't move," answers Dr. Sellers. "Lie still."

A flyer attempts to grab a heavier crate but tumbles to the ground next to Chubb. It rights itself and takes a few steps toward him. Chubb crawls backward as it advances to release a hateful screech from its two-pace stature.

"Hey, hey, hey," says Chubb.

The flyer takes to the sky. Those in Argos watch as the two on the ground near them looks its way and take off after it. The flapping wings of others drown out Chubb's panicked breaths as they tear the camp apart. A full tek passes before they stop and take to the horizon.

Delgado, Fister, Sergeant Bentley, and Rhigas exit Argos.

"We're clear," says Sergeant Bentley. "They're leaving."

Sapp and the others come out of tele-tents and examine the scene: they find equipment scattered across the field for hundreds of paces, tables overturned, and claw marks on the tele-tents. Some of it is destroyed beyond repair. Other frag-ments are still being carried across the sky with the flyers—keepsakes for their vengeful attack.

Dr. Sellers stands with furled brows and stiff body lan-guage. The way he looks at Chubb... I would not want those partially squinted, cold, loathing eyes upon me.

Chubb avoids looking at him as he stands with the rest of the ground team. Sergeant Bentley walks up to him and opens his mouth to say something, then stops and walks away to leave him alone in self-disappointment.

Chubb shakes his head. "I... I thought they were going to attack."

"Everyone, get to, or back to, your tele-tents," says Sergeant Bentley.

"It's still daylight, Sergeant Major," says Bell.

"And we're calling it a day before nightfall. Set alarms for eleven taks out. No one is to exit their tents. Is that understood?"

Ground team acknowledges.

"We don't know what's on this planet," continues Sergeant Bentley. "Our safety's greater in there than it is out here. We'll clean this up first light."

Dr. Sellers steps over to a piece of his destroyed equip-ment, grabs it, and tosses it into the toppled table, breaking it.

I watch them get ready to lie down for a bit, getting up and heading back to my private quarters. My eyes are heavy.

Resting is necessary for me to be fully awake when they awaken next rotation to roll out. I will be drop-kicked in the head before missing what happens next on the new planet we hope to call home.

B right and early, I am up, Stimulant 5 in hand, and sitting in the security feed room staring at the panes. I have made my rounds and checked in with Doctors Wright and Utley. Morris, who has been too busy with schematics and comms to chat or get to know anyone, said that he has everything covered on his end.

They have not a thing for me to do. Dr. Utley has not left the medical lab much since our arrival. He devotes most of his attention to the ground team and how the atmosphere is affecting their vital systems. I find him much more interesting than Dr. Wright, but I know in my heart he does not differ from the frail scientist I rescued the flagert from on Kep Four. To people like him, all life but humanity's is expendable for the sake of progression.

I get it off my mind to ensure I can tolerate his presence and focus on the team below. Sergeant Bentley is next to last in emerging from his tele-tent.

"At least I'm not the only one slow out of bed in the mornings," says Fister.

Delgado exits her tele-tent and shares a smile with Sergeant Bentley.

Did I miss the good stuff? A little romance? No. Not yet. I am betting they will get around to it at some point. Maybe

I should have stayed up and watched the feeds last night, just in case?

Sergeant Bentley moves to the rest of the team. They are standing in a circle sharing whispered conversations, something about getting visitors while they slept.

"What's going on?" asks Sergeant Bentley.

The team looks at him and steps aside, revealing a set of small, human-like footprints. They are everywhere. Dozens of them.

"Get everything packed up," continues Sergeant Bentley. "We're moving toward the structure."

They pack up the collapsing tele-tents. My attention goes to Athanasios's feeds.

Dr. Utley is in the medical bay looking over the ground team's vital signs. He enters something into his pane-shaped data-logger, leaving me curious about what it was. Dr. Wright is walking from the primary control station Sergeant Bentley would be at if he were on board.

Morris approaches him. "Dr. Wright, I've almost got a handle on the upper atmospheric disturbances."

"Comms?" asks Dr. Wright.

"Still stable. I've isolated the elements causing initial disturbances."

"Excellent," says Dr. Wright.

My attention goes back to the surface-side panes.

17–2
Skedelski's Finger

Sergeant Bentley, Sapp, and Dr. Sellers load into Argos. Delgado hops in and takes control of Argos. They push through tall grass and away from their campsite in route for the structure spotted from Athanasios. We will soon find out what it is.

They near a large stone-type object protruding from the planet's surface. It reminds me of pyramids I have seen images of that once stood on Ancient Earth, only it is more rectangular than anything else. Its top reaches high over trees toward gray and white clouds.

Bell is walking point through a vast clearing filled with shin-high blades of wispy alien grass tipped with yellow pollen. Rhigas and Fister are behind him, whispering amongst themselves about nothing important. Skedelski walks behind them, easily carrying a ridiculous amount of equipment. Pollen clings to their legs as they walk.

Argos rolls silently behind them with its four tank-like tracks, crushing flora as it goes. Chubb mans its topside turret. I am not sure if he is the best one for the position after the campsite incident, but that is not my call. I will say nothing about it.

A highly reflective sphere-shaped hover cam glides above the vehicle, surveying the area ahead as they reach the clearing's end to push through a segment of trees. Bark covers them, thick and jagged, with deep trenches I could hide a finger in. They are too tall to get a good visual on their canopies from any of my video feeds. One would think them to go up forever.

Ground team continues into another clearing near the immense stone structure. The area surrounding it is unlike anything on our dark, dying home-world. Crops of alien vegetation come into view resembling off-colored tomatoes tinted pink and oval-shaped vegetables. At least, I think they are vegetables. Someone has farmed them out to grow in tilled patches of land.

"That doesn't look naturally formed," I say.

"No," says Dr. Sellers. "It doesn't."

"Clear the comms, Mason," says Sergeant Bentley.

"Yes, Sergeant Major," I say, closing comms on my end.

A makeshift pen of wood and dried mud neatly holds a group of small, pig-like animals with ill-proportionally tiny heads and a single eye. A few chicken-like things with four legs and oversized beaks scamper by. They release an atypical sound resembling nails dragged across sanded glass when the ground team comes into view. Our faces squint.

"Well," says Sergeant Bentley, "this is disconcerting."

"Actually," says Dr. Sellers, "I find it quite fascinating."

Sergeant Bentley and Dr. Sellers stand from their seats in Argos as a strange, soccer ball-sized dragonfly lands on Skedelski's weapon, forcing him to release a bass-toned giggle as it crawls toward his hand.

Everyone stares. Its transparent wings move with silky bends once relaxed on his finger.

"I think he likes you," says Fister.

Skedelski removes a glove with his teeth.

Dr. Sellers has an enchanted expression about him. His eyes sparkle with curiosity. "May I?"

"Sure," answers Sergeant Bentley. "Knock yourself out." He smiles, watching Dr. Sellers's inquisitiveness exiting Argos.

Delgado shakes her head with a grin as he exits.

Sergeant Bentley turns her way. "Must be a biologist thing."

Dr. Sellers raises his bio-scanner and locks onto it. The device sends a purple beam across the insect as Skedelski touches the top center of its head with his finger. The mammoth insect is larger than his hand and acts as if to enjoy the attention. It pushes the top of its small head into his finger like a feline would into its owner.

Dr. Sellers clicks his cube-cam to capture a few pictures. "Friendly little guy, isn't he?"

The insect turns its face into Skedelski's finger, bites it, and flies away.

"Or ... maybe not."

Skedelski puts his glove back on, but Dr. Sellers pulls it off to look at the wound.

"He bit you," Dr. Sellers continues as the team walks over.

"What's going on?" asks Sergeant Bentley.

"It bit Skedelski."

"How bad is it?"

"Small bite." Dr. Sellers skims through his readings. "The scan didn't reveal any known elements or combinations that could prove hazardous."

"Poisonous?"

Dr. Sellers cocks his head, reading the bio-scanner. "No."

"Alright," says Sergeant Bentley, turning to face everyone. "No more petting the wildlife."

Skedelski slides his glove back on. Dr. Sellers and Sergeant Bentley climb back into Argos, and they move out.

17–3

First Encounter

My eyes cut to another pane when Morris exits the comms room. He makes his way down a few corridors and enters the forward.

"Morris to Sergeant Major Bentley. You still getting a good signal down there?"

"Roger that, Morris," answers Sergeant Bentley.

"I got a gentleman by the name of Dr. Wright up here who wants to know how it is going if you got a moment."

Dr. Wright steps to his console.

"Doctor," says Sergeant Bentley, "have you been watching all this?"

"No," answers Dr. Wright. "I've been trying to keep up with everything Athanasios is picking up about the astro-region out here. We're going to need a new star map."

"I believe you, but you'd have a hard time accepting what's around this structure if you were here."

"Try me."

"It's incredible," says Sergeant Bentley. "Beautiful really. There's these—"

A banshee-type scream tears through the feed. Ground team shouts.

Dr. Wright activates the forward's video feeds. "Sergeant Bentley?"

A humanoid with a half-palm length, silky, flowing silver highlighted hair over a brown undercoat bounces off Rhigas and knocks him to the ground. It is not tall, my height at best, but its movements are that of a cat's agility. It stands on two legs and moves like us, making a break for it, but the ground team has it surrounded. Animal skin loincloths wrapped around its waist flap behind it.

Rhigas stands from the ground with a scratch on his face, raising his firearm. They better not shoot it.

"Wait," shouts Dr. Sellers. "Don't hurt it."

The humanoid looks at Bell for a quick moment and charges him. Ground team members run after it from behind. Bell squints his eyes and braces himself for the attack, but the humanoid digs both feet into the ground in front of him and flips backward over those running behind it.

It lands clumsily on the ground before getting up to sprint away. The hairy humanoid makes it about thirty paces before a terra-net wraps it, sending the humanoid crashing to the lush terrain.

"Sergeant Major," calls Dr. Wright. "Everything okay?"

"Affirmative," he responds. "But we got attacked by a humanoid lifeform. Intelligence unknown."

"Nobody was attacked," says Dr. Sellers. "It was scared and trying to—"

"Sellers…" cuts Sergeant Bentley.

Dr. Sellers gets quiet.

"Anyone hurt?" asks Dr. Wright.

"Startled is all," answers Sergeant Bentley. "Rhigas got a scratch, nothing big."

"And the creature?"

"Captured."

"Get it back to Athanasios," says Dr. Wright. "Send Dr. Sellers with it."

Ground team approaches the humanoid as it struggles to get free. Dr. Sellers pushes past them. His concern for its safety is unquestionable.

"Easy," he says. "Easy, fellow. Easy."

The humanoid looks at Dr. Sellers. Its gentle eyes catch him off guard, fearfully pleading for freedom.

"What am I looking at here?" asks Sergeant Bentley.

Dr. Sellers shakes his head and holds up his scanning device, but the humanoid becomes further terrified when it omits the purple beams.

"Whoa, buddy," says Dr. Sellers.

A deafening roar echoes from an unknown area, sending alien life-forms flying into the sky from treetops. Everyone looks its way. The young, captured humanoid looks toward the roar and returns the call.

17–4
Bloodshed

Roars from unknown lifeforms and locations captivate the ground team with uncertainties.

"Load it up and fall back a few clicks to get ready for nightfall," says Sergeant Bentley.

Another humanoid, grown and female, comes running from the side of a far-flung, hardened mud structure and looks their way. She is roughly the size of an adult human and wears coverings on her top and bottom. Her garments resemble what the captured younger is wearing, but the designs are different and colorful, like what we think Ancient Earth's pre-tech ancestors would have worn.

The small, captured humanoid releases a haunting scream when it sees her. My watching eyes water without warning as the female screams in fear for the smaller one's life upon seeing it in the cage. She must be its mother. Her steps are fast in its direction, sprinting as any mother would for a child.

I hope they surrender it to her.

"Fall back," says Sergeant Bentley. "Double-time. Move, move, move."

Skedelski and the others on foot hop onto the side of Argos. Delgado rips across the field in Argos, barreling around crops and small structures outlining the area as the mother humanoid releases another roar. Something different. A call for help.

Another humanoid does the same and the roars repeat from different callers throughout the area until they pass the vehicle. Humanoids emerge from random places. A few come from openings in the ground and take after the Argos on foot. Delgado dodges them.

The mother runs after them, reaching out an arm with a scream doubling as a plea.

The group is almost free when more humanoids emerge and force Delgado to turn again. Rhigas is hanging on the back of Argos when a large rocky object bangs into the side of it. A second impact nearly tips it over. Rhigas is thrown to the ground.

"Rhigas," shouts Fister.

Delgado struggles to level it out as Rhigas stands to his feet. A humanoid grabs and tosses him ten paces across the field. More humanoids run toward him in the distance as he stands.

"Stop Argos," says Sergeant Bentley.

It comes to a halt, and they hop off.

"Lock and load," Sergeant Bentley continues. "Non-lethal. Aim low."

The ground team configures their weapons and powers them up. Bell and Sapp are the first to ready, spreading out enough for Delgado to move Argos Between them in tactical formation. They advance with slow steps.

"Oh, no," I say, running my fingers through my hair.

Anxiety curses through me. Aim low—Armada code for no-kill live fire. This is bad.

Ground team moves in military fashion toward Rhigas, shooting out the humanoid's legs as they move. Dr. Sellers is panicking but does not know how to prevent the creatures from getting hurt. They drop from gunshots but return to their feet with limped runs ... still trying to attack.

Rhigas stands and points his rifle toward the ground team.

"Hey," shouts Fister.

"Whoa," says Bell.

Rhigas fires toward them, and they dive for cover, looking behind themselves from the ground. The silver-haired humanoid he was firing at stands behind Skedelski. It reaches for him and grabs his shoulders.

Skedelski's body jerks as the creature spins him around to look him in the eyes. It snatches back part of his suit, chomping into his upper chest with human-like teeth but powerful jaws. It pulls its head back, removing a plug from him.

The big man powers it into the air and drives it into the ground, but it remains latched onto him. He stands with it, pries it off, and tosses it to the ground as another approaches. A hard right hand from Skedelski echoes the field and collapses it into a comatose state at his feet, no doubt breaking bones in its face. A solid left crumples another onto its own shins like a wet cloth.

Nothing with a heartbeat can take a shot from Skedelski.

He turns and looks for Rhigas, but a creature bites him in the same area the first did. Skedelski steps back and trips over the one at his feet.

Another blast from an onium rifle laces into the humanoid's back. It screams, lets Skedelski go, and races to attack the rest of the crew. He grabs it by the ankle from the ground, stands, and does a single spin before throwing it toward Sapp and Bell. Several blasts from their rifles drop it.

I move my hands to cover my mouth. Eyes watering. This is not right.

"Rhigas," shouts Fister, surrounded and firing at approaching attackers on all sides.

Sergeant Bentley stops shooting and looks to see Rhigas. He is being attacked by a pair of adult humanoids and not faring well. He does not have Skedelski's power, and they are ripping him to shreds.

"Fister," calls Sergeant Bentley. "Aim high on Rhigas."

Fister switches his weapon's mode of fire and unloads on the two humanoids attacking Rhigas, ripping them apart.

"Noooo..." shouts Dr. Sellers.

The humanoids attacking his cousin's lifeless body drop to the grass below, but dozens more are closing in on them. Soon, they will get bowled over. They circle back-to-back around their transport vehicle as Delgado eases it toward their fallen partner, engaging the aggressors.

Delgado halts Argos. "We're stuck unless we get out of here or Chubb opens up on them."

Chubb powers up the turret atop Argos. "Say the word."

"Hold, Chubb," says Sergeant Bentley. "Fister, switch back. No more live fire."

Chubb hops from the turret and off the side of Argos, landing on its tracks and studying the field.

"I'm getting Rhigas," says Fister.

"Negative," says Sergeant Bentley, firing a few rounds.

Fister shakes his head in anger and switches his weapon mode and fires, but the humanoids are resistant to energy-based weapon fire. Ground team has difficulty holding them off. The aggressors are gaining ground.

The mother humanoid drops into one of the primitive structures for cover, peeks over, and looks helplessly into the eyes of her child. The young, captured humanoid watches her from within the tight netting behind the cage on Argos. Their connection is profound, and the sadness in his eyes melts into me as he tries to escape. The mother humanoid cannot take it anymore. She makes the break for it, but Chubb fires a few rounds her way. She ducks back for cover as Dr. Sellers reaches out from Argos and raises Chubb's rifle to throw off his shots.

Popping her head up, she runs toward her child once more, but a male humanoid tackles her to protect her from herself.

Chubb head-butts Dr. Sellers, knocking him to the ground. "Never do that again." He rejoins a battle to hold their ground, and the humanoids eventually succumb to the damage.

Another female emerges from the structure in the backdrop. Her scream is that of harrow as she runs toward one of the two fallen males.

Ground team rushes to Rhigas's but cannot reach him.

Sapp looks off to the side. Skedelski squares off with three humanoids waving clubs at him.

"Skedelski," shouts Sapp.

The big man looks his way.

"Get Rhigas," continues Sapp. "We're falling back."

The humanoids hit Skedelski in the back and head with clubs while he looks at his fallen teammate. He ignores the blows and runs toward Rhigas, knocking four of the humanoids out along the way. Others are lying in the field in severe pain. So many are in pain. Lives lost.

Rhigas's stomach has suffered a tear. He is fighting for his life as Skedelski picks him up and runs back to Argos.

More female humanoids emerge from the structure, running to their fallen families in the field. They drop to the ground next to the fallen and cry out in emotional pain, cradling the wounded bodies to their chests.

I am broken, deep below sorrow as I watch.

The mother humanoid is struggling to break free from the one holding her down. Profound emotion pours from her as she struggles beneath the male humanoid. She looks at her child and calls out through broken cries. "PRU'CET!!!"

Ground team hears the call, the word, the language, and look her way.

Skedelski reaches Argos with Rhigas and sets him in the back compartment.

"Load up," says Sergeant Bentley. "Get us out of here, Delgado."

They load up, most hanging from its side on the foot-rails above its tracks. Delgado takes off, leaving behind a wake of injured and heartbroken humanoids. The mother breaks free as they pull away. She is the only one still running after Argos as her people assist wounded humanoids in the backdrop. She releases a haunting scream as she reaches out, physically begging for them to stop.

Ground team watches from the vehicle, each lost in the heartache they have unintentionally unleashed. The young humanoid's arm reaches from the cage at their side, crying through its shouts.

"Azata!" shouts the mother, reaching hopelessly for her child as she runs. "Azata! Glenoda!" She chases Argos until it is almost out of sight and drops to her knees.

"Pru'Cet..." She calls. "Pru'Cet..."

She roles to the ground in emotional agony. Her cries fade until they are no longer heard.

Dr. Sellers looks toward the tree-tops and wipes his eyes as they ride from sight.

I kick the security panel a few times out of impulse with a tear-streamed face.

"Bentley to Morris."

"Go ahead, Sergeant Major."

"Have Mason block out our coordinates and remote pilot one of the medical vessels to within two clicks of our current."

I reopen comms on my end. "Mason to Sergeant Major. I'll come to you."

"And get Dr. Utley and Wright ready. Have them waiting in the shuttle bay when it gets there."

"On my way to Utley now," says Dr. Wright.

"Everything alright down there?" asks Morris.

Sergeant Bentley rides over the bumpy terrain without responding.

I kick the security feed station one last time and tear from the room for the cockpit.

CHAPTER 18

Trauma

The starfighter cockpit lights up when I enter. There is no time for delicacy. Rhigas's chances of living slip with every tik that passes.

"Armada voice clearance, Mason, five, Sinote, one, four, McKayla, three, six, open shuttle bay."

"Shuttle bay opening," says Athanasios.

"Activate remote flight to transport shuttle four."

"Remote flight link active."

Video feeds from transport shuttle four fill my panes. I grab the flight controls and exit it from the shuttle bay with the door still raising. A series of sparks fall to the shuttle bay floor as I scrape the bottom of the rising door on my way out.

I bank it left and down for the blue. Upper atmospheric resistance sends fire around all my panes, but I am pushing through quickly and burning it up if need be. I must get Rhigas back to the doctors before it is too late.

Red becomes white. Then blue. The lush planet comes into view.

"Lock onto Argos and track," I say.

"Argos located," says A.I. interface. "Tracking in progress."

A red square pops onto the front windshield to track Argos. All I can see in it are the tops of trees. The red square moves toward the tree line as I descend.

"Mason to Sergeant Major," I say, just as Argos emerges into a field headed toward the campsite. "I see you. I'm coming in."

"Make it quick, Mason," says Fister. "My cousin's hurt bad."

They are heading due east as I approach from the south. The gap between us closes. I turn the vessel's nose right and drift the transport shuttle in sideways to land next to them as Delgado stops Argos.

I raise the transport's hatch and wait.

Fister and Bell exit Argos with Rhigas's lifeless body and load it into Transport shuttle four.

Dr. Sellers climbs in and motions to Skedelski. "You're coming with us."

Skedelski ducks down to climb into the transport as Fister cuts Sergeant Bentley with a hurt, angry expression with watering, hateful eyes.

"Go with him if you want," says Sergeant Bentley.

"He won't make it," says Fister.

"You don't know that."

"But... if he... he..."

I take the transport into flight. Dr. Sellers is compressing Rhigas's wounds with the planet getting smaller behind us as the hatch finishes closing.

"Mason," shouts Fister over comms. "Mason, where the haze—"

I kill the comms link between myself and the ground team. I feel bad about all that has happened, but Rhigas has no time for decision-making. The doctors and tech in the Med Bay on Athanasios have a better chance of saving him than words alone.

18-2
Incoming

Doctors Wright and Utley meet Dr. Sellers next to the medical shuttle's raising hatch as it slides in a spin across the shuttle bay to face them. I jump from the starfighter replica cockpit and race through Athanasios's corridors. I need to help them if I can.

My steps are quick. Door after door blows by. I am almost at the medical shuttle. Panic in distant voices. I cannot make out what they are saying yet. I enter and await instructions.

Doctors Sellers, Wright, and Utley are trying desperately to pick Skedelski up and onto a hover gurney.

The big man pushes them to the side and stands. "I'll walk."

"I'll prep Med Bay's systems," says Dr. Wright, taking off from the shuttle bay in a jog.

"Sellers..." calls Dr. Utley. "Help me with Rhigas."

Dr. Sellers gets on the other side of Rhigas in the transport. He is unconscious, and part of his lower intestines are exposed. They lift him and exit, resting him on the hover gurney.

Morris enters the shuttle bay and freezes in his tracks with wide eyes.

"Morris," says Dr. Utley. "Find out everything you can about the incident from the ground team and anything they might have come into contact with since they gained these wounds."

Morris nods and leaves for the comms room, responding on his way out. "I'll find out everything I can."

"Mason," he says, tossing me a clean surgical cloth. "Get Skedelski to the Med Bay. Hold this on the wound."

I catch the cloth and reach high to hold it against Skedelski's chest as he walks but cannot easily reach it. I apply pressure and try to keep up with his long strides. His blood runs down my forearm, into my sleeve, and into my armpit to make its way toward my waist. I can barely reach the wound.

"I got it," he says, grabbing the cloth from me and pushing it to his wound.

Skedelski appears to be okay, but it is hard to tell with his congenital analgesia disorder. It is possible that he has suffered severe injuries but does not feel any pain. I jog ahead and reach the end of the corridor to look back and find him right on my heels.

"This way," I say.

He knows where the Med Bay is at. I am panicking. His uniform has blood seeping from its waistline. It is not a gentle flow, but the Med Bay is just ahead. We enter with the doctors running behind us with the hover gurney carrying Rhigas.

I turn to help steer Rhigas's hover gurney, trying not to bang into corners as I round them. There is not much else I can do yet.

"Hold on, Rhigas," I say, knowing he cannot hear me. "Hold on. We have you now. The doctors are here."

Dr. Wright is getting the Med Bay's full systems up and running at the station on the opposite side of the area from the beds. It lights up, and a 3D holo-image of the room and everyone in it comes to life. We are all visible in it with the beds, stations, equipment and walls.

"Get Rhigas to bed two," says Dr. Utley, turning his attention to Skedelski. "You take bed one."

Skedelski moves to the first bed, squeezing between it and the wall. He is trying to stay out of the way but remains focused on Rhigas. The pressure he is holding on the cloth against his chest relaxes as he watches. Blood pours from the wound.

"Skedelski," I say. "Sit down."

He takes a seat on the first bed. I move to his side and apply pressure to the wound on his chest again. Running blood slows as he looks over his shoulder but does not stop.

The doctors move Rhigas against the second bed. I grab his upper body to help, but he convulses. My hands slip, covering my arms and chest with blood when he presses into me.

"Get back," says Dr. Wright, stepping in to replace me.

I step away to build nerves. He is bleeding a lot and his skin... There is... It is getting darker around the wound.

"Get tier three stabilizers ready for Skedelski," says Dr. Utley. "Tier five for Rhigas."

I step to the shelving units and look for anything labeled tier four or five. My head goes right to left. Eyes searching.

Dr. Sellers moves in and overtakes me, pushing me out of the way.

"Blue or red?" he asks.

"Blue on Skedelski," answers Dr. Utley. "Red on Rhigas."

Rhigas stops convulsing. He is motionless—dead, as far as I can tell. Anxiety sets in. I am losing my calmness but remaining calm on the outside.

"What can I do?" I ask.

The Med Bay flashes red and yellow three times quickly. Everyone stops.

"Bed two in cardiac arrest," says Athanasios.

"We're going straight into surgery with Rhigas," answers Dr. Utley. "I need you to clear the Med Bay."

"Bed two in cardiac arrest," says Athanasios.

"Stop lights and cease warnings," says Dr. Utley.

They lift Rhigas onto the bed. Skedelski lays back on bed one. I move to his side.

The wall near him opens and a life-rack moves into position next to bed one. It is half my height, full of unfamiliar instruments, and resting on four legs without wheels—a mobile med unit capable of implementing dozens of procedures and operations. They are among the most valuable tools any doctor can have in the field, but this one is specific to Athanasios.

"What about Skedelski?" asks Dr. Wright.

"Induce him into a light coma," answers Dr. Utley, moving to bed one. "Dr. Sellers, you're with me on Rhigas."

"Unrecognized biological properties detected in patients one and two," says Athanasios. "Beds one and two."

Dr. Wright opens a compartment on the far wall and grabs a biohazard suit, throwing it on with haste. Doctors Sellers and Utley suit up right behind him. I have never seen them scared before this moment.

"Prepping Mizophile," says Dr. Wright.

I swallow hard, knowing I cannot help. It is painful to watch. Rhigas is flatlining and Skedelski, whom I have developed a fondness for, is being induced into a light coma. There must be something I can...

"Mason," says Dr. Utley. "Leave."

Mizophile is not a good sign and has not been used since patient zero of Kep Four Syndrome. It is an organic nano-bot-based chemical used in the medical field with many applications, including sleep aid, coma inducement, pain treatment, as well as everything else between and up to heightening senses, adrenalizing, and rendering diseases inactive. Each dose has a mixture of thousands of different nano-bots individually carrying heavy concentrations of varying chemicals. They analyze the human body with parameters given by applying doctors ... and communicate amongst themselves to release suitable mixtures needed for correction. Once the desired balance is attained, they turn solid like a hardened pea to form a protective shell around any remaining chemicals they may have; and make their way from the body via the urethra.

I backpedal to the exit as they work on the men, terrified Rhigas will not make it and unsure about Skedelski. Staying in here will only put me at risk, and I have no choice but to leave. I exit into the hallway.

"Wait," shouts Dr. Utley. "The blood."

I stop. He stares at me for a moment. "Straight to your quarters. Take a decon shower now."

I turn for the corridor.

"Athanasios," he continues as the door shuts behind me. "Initiate emergency decontamination protocols, all corridors between Med Bay and Private Mason's quarters on level—"

The door shuts behind me. Worry overwhelms my thoughts about Rhigas and Skedelski. They are both hurt badly.

Corridors around me—in front of me, behind, and those branching off to the sides along my path—flash yellow and decontamination fog purges from their sides and ceiling. I can barely see. Cold mist on my face, I feel my way to my quarters.

The door is already open when I reach it. Purging fog in my room matches the halls. I enter.

18-3
The Red Wash

I hop straight into the already running shower with my clothes and shoes on. Decontamination fog is already pouring in with water from four places overhead. Fans run strong.

My hands shake without warning. A single sob escapes me as I remove my terra boots one by one and drop them to the edge of the shower floor. I strip down to nothing but bare skin and pile my garments in the corner on top of them.

The warmth feels good on my body but will not wash away what I am dealing with inside. Their blood… Rhigas's… Skedelski's… It is all over me.

Subtle effects from individual droplets falling from the shower's ceiling cannot clean fast enough. I envision a warm rain caressing my skin, but I have never stood under rainfall. I would not know, but I think of anything to escape heart-wounding thoughts.

Sniffles slip from my chest and out of my nose. Fighting back tears, I turn my face to the flow and wash myself with soap-free hands to remove sadness. My head drops when I relax. I open my eyes and look down. A red-swirled drain is devouring another's life force as it runs from my body.

It hurts to see. What is Fister going to think if he does not make it? I cannot handle the thought. This is too much.

Tears flow to match the overhead wash. Thoughts are as foggy as the surrounding air. My spirit is breaking. My lungs heave.

A somber cry seeps out, and I lower myself to the shower floor against the wall. Cold on my back. Palms to my face. I cannot look at it anymore. All I can do is cry, and I am not moving until the red slips away.

CHAPTER 19

Recovery

All I have thought about are those with me, unconscious in the Med Bay, and how much the doctors could help them. I have been standing over them for a few teks now. There is nothing I can do. They would not hear me if I spoke.

Rhigas and Skedelski are lying unconscious on separate gurneys. The doctors have settled and are in their personal quarters getting a much-deserved rest. Slow steps guide me toward the wounded. Worry creeps through my veins like a twilight thief stealing composure.

Skedelski's vitals are not perfect, but he looks a lot better than his roommate. Attached to a ventilator, Rhigas bleeds through the bio-wraps that bind him. A force field up around his lungs holds them in place. The holo-feed floating above him displays his organs ... several of which are severely damaged and meshed back together.

Dr. Wright enters to work at the station on the far side of the room for a moment and scoots to the inlaid medicator (a medical distribution device filled with thousands of chemicals which mix and make small, chewy, medicated balls for oral delivery).

"Sperkon," says Dr. Wright. "Five timed doses. Set drug release rate to spread evenly over five rotations."

The circular inlaid medicator's display scrolls the word across the topside of its ring:

Sperkon

I love its design. It prompts me to think about wedding bands in Kep Four's Capital Museum people once adorned to signal they were in a relationship. I think they were called wedding rings. Or bands. Either way, I find its black and silver trimmed outer ring lovely.

The inlaid medicator stops, and a small door slides open. There are five orange pill balls inside lying on a transparent plate. He grabs them and faces me with one outstretched.

"What's this?" I ask, taking it from him.

"It'll boost your immune system," he answers. "Me, you, Morris, Utley, and Sellers... we're all taking them."

I pop the pill into my mouth and chew it up. He does the same as I glance to our wounded friends.

"How are they?" I ask.

"Dr. Utley thinks Skedelski is going to pull through in time," he answers. "I second his opinion."

"And Rhigas?"

He shakes his head. "I can't answer that yet. We're hopeful at best."

"Has anyone told Fister?" I ask.

"Not yet."

"Not yet?" I ask. "What do you mean, not yet? You realize that's his cousin. I think he's entitled to—"

"Mason," interrupts Dr. Wright. "We need to see how stable we can get him before we know what to tell Fister. He'll know soon enough. We all will, but they need to stay sharp down there. This would be too much of a distraction. Especially for Fister."

I look at him, piercing the back of his eyes, mad that any of this happened, worried for Skedelski and Fister; and frustrated that we have a young … something … captured, which we know is not a mindless animal; and I am bothered no one is telling Fister his cousin's condition. I take my eyes off Rhigas and turn them to Dr. Wright.

"Armada principles say little to our humanity's existence," I say, taking a few steps back and turning to exit.

19-2
Silk-Like Hair

I work my way through Athanasios's corridors and to the science lab where they are holding their young prisoner. If someone is torturing or cutting on him when I get in there, I am going to pull out one of their eyes, freeze it, sharpen it, and use it to stab their other eye. I am not in the mood.

The door slides open with the touch of my hand. Doctors Utley and Sellers are both there. Relief hits me like a warm wave of purified water. Dr. Sellers would let nothing bad happen to the young creature.

They stand near the caged humanoid. Poor thing looks terrified. My eyes lock onto it as Dr. Sellers holds up a finger, motioning me to stop.

Dr. Utley never looks my way. "Afraid you can't be in here right now, Mason."

"I just want to see it," I say.

"No," he says. "I'm not comfortable having a former A.R.S. extremist in my lab while we run these tests."

Dr. Utley must sense my glare. He turns to face me. "I will not be responsible if—"

"Just…" interrupts Dr. Sellers. "She's fine, Doctor. Really."

Dr. Utley sighs. "Don't get too close and please, keep your sticky A.R.S. fingers off of everything."

Dr. Utley and I will not be making amends soon. He knows what I did while he was studying me as a research scientist for my H-SAM. I know what people like him do behind closed doors. One of us is a traitor to the Armada, the other a traitor to life.

He goes back to preparing a set of small vials and places them into a device. He snaps it closed and brown liquid fills a pair of thin tubes on top of it. I recognize it.

It is the same type of tubular injector I have seen scientists use in labs in the past. At least he is safe for now. I ease my way to the cage while Dr. Sellers chews his fingernails and paces.

"This is..." Dr. Sellers pauses. "This is..."

My eyes have not left the humanoid yet. He is curled up in the cage with his back to me. My breaths halt as I approach, glancing back at Dr. Utley to see if he is hawking me. He and Dr. Sellers are in their own world and paying me no mind. Dr. Utley presses a button on the tubular injector and the tubes take on a gaseous brown state.

"This is..." continues Dr. Sellers.

"Unnerving?" asks Dr. Utley.

"That'd be close..."

What are they talking about? I ponder their conversation while squatting down next to the cage and reaching my hand toward the humanoid's fur.

"What happened down there..." says Dr. Sellers. "It was—"

"Nobody's fault," Dr. Utly interrupts. "That's what it was."

The humanoid jumps and moves to the other side of the small cage when I try to touch it, wiping its watering eyes. I am captivated by it, but I think it feels the same way about me. I can see it in its eyes. He must realize my empathy enough to understand no harm will come his way.

I tilt my head and wait until it makes eye contact with me. He studies me. We were as alien to him as he is to us.

"They attacked our team first," continues Dr. Wright.

"We took one of their children," says Dr. Sellers. "I mean, we didn't know, but we did. Of course, they came after us."

I look the Doctor's way for a moment and back into the cage, reaching my shaking arm into it with my eyes locked onto him with compassion. An unintentional gulp plops slowly down my throat. My heartbeat... My breaths... They match my nervousness as I check on the doctors one last time.

"That's correct," says Dr. Wright. "The small one here attacked you. I read the field report."

"I could give a ton of dyogg droppings what the field report says," replies Dr. Sellers. "It didn't happen that way."

"You know we need this planet. Not for us. For our world."

"But it doesn't have to happen this way," says Dr. Sellers. "What happened down there was reminiscent of the old tales from the Battle of Laqmier on Kep Four."

"Let go of your troubles," says Dr. Utley. "I am sure we'll be returning it to the surface."

"And the damage we've already caused?"

Dr. Utley turns and goes back to work.

I return my attention to the humanoid and lay my arm on the floor of the cage, submissively placing my head on the table where the cage is sitting. The young humanoid reaches out and touches my fingers like a curious child, but stops and pulls back, allowing me to maintain eye contact while turning my palm up.

Dr. Sellers is right about what happened on the surface echoing the Battle of Laqmier. Though once semi fertile and full of mineable resources, Laqmier has become a place no one visits. It lies at the Suicide Fields' heart and is where the Battle of Laqmier waged. War over initial dwindling resources left it a radiated graveyard hundreds of cycles ago. With Kep Four already in a failing state before humanity's arrival, it did not take long for the Suicide fields to claim it.

I sigh while thinking about it. Humanity depresses me, and many things about it need to change for us to persevere. Extinction is the alternative.

The humanoid reaches for my hand and touches it again.

Young humanoids like the one they captured are laughing as children do while playing an unknown game with a foreign ball made from something I cannot make out. It is all blurry. They are kicking it about and running to different points while the others try to tackle or hit them with the ball as they go.

Three of the young humanoids are rushing after the ball. Two in the background cheer as another runs from object to object under an unknown part of the game's play. One of them goes for the ball, but another tackles him. They hit the ball when they fall, and it bounces into the air. A third rushes for it, but it ricochets off an invisible wall.

The young humanoid chasing it stops in wonder and uncertainty and takes a few slow steps forward with a raised arm reaching out to feel the invisible object.

"Mason," shouts Dr. Utley.

My body jolts away from the cage.

The young humanoid in the cage looks at me with imploring eyes and releases a series of syllables. *"Dexlee pes gingo woo cea."*

It was a sentence. I am shaking at my core. My eyes widen. My breaths cease.

"Mason," continues Dr. Utley. "You can leave."

I face him silently and glance at the cage.

Dr. Utley points to the exit. "Now, Mason."

I take defeated steps to the door and look back one last time as I exit, only to find its eyes still glued to me ... making it harder to leave.

Dr. Utley holds the device up to the cage. A pair of tubes at the end of it moves. Dr. Sellers eases toward me as I watch, frozen and unable to move. I open my mouth to say something, but Dr. Sellers beats me to it.

"I'll make sure no one hurts him," he whispers. "You know that."

I look to Dr. Utley while shaking inside for his captive, then back to Dr. Sellers and give a nod. I need to leave before he gets suspicious of Dr. Sellers's A.R.S. involvement.

"It spoke," I say.

Dr. Sellers glances at the humanoid and back at me. "You sure about that?"

I cut him a look.

"Of course you are," he says.

Dr. Utley watches us for a moment under high suspicion and places his focus back on the humanoid. Two small lasers from the device lock onto its nostrils and follow his frightened movements. He pulls the trigger. A pair of tubes shoot into his captive's nostrils. The young humanoid panics and backs into the bars as the tubes fill with brown gas, forcing it to sleep.

"I'll let you know when it's clear," says Dr. Sellers.

"But—"

"Out, Mason." Dr. Sellers pushes the door shut on me and turns back toward the lab. "Sorry about that, Doctor. The beliefs in her will never die."

"I see." Dr. Utley's eyes harbor suspicion as the door closes.

19-3
Thinking

I move back to the security feed room thinking about the vision I had and sit to think about not being able to get to know our furry extra crew member better.

"Activate all panes to last recorded settings," I say.

Panes come to life—thirty-two visuals and I only care about one. I watch Dr. Utley carefully. Knowing Dr. Sellers is in there with him is comforting, but not much with me separated like this. What if something happens, and I am here on the other side of the ship?

"Wait. What?" I sit forward in the chair. "What are they doing?"

Doctors Utley and Sellers are loading the humanoid onto a hover gurney and strapping it down.

A yellow medical alarm flashes from the Med Bay as I stand, forcing me to pause. A subtle beeping accompanies it. Dr. Utley looks up.

"Go ahead," says Dr. Sellers. "I got this."

Dr. Utley walks from the room. I watch the feeds as he makes his way quickly through the corridors. Something is wrong. He would not be in such a hurry otherwise.

My eyes switch panes. Dr. Utley enters the Med Bay. Rhigas is waking but remains restrained. His wounds are severe, and the recent surgery was extensive. His pain is understandable and high enough to rouse him. I thought it was going to be something much worse.

Dr. Utley reaches up and turns a dial resting under the single word:

Mizophile

Its digital readout climbs from 226 to 273 as he raises it. Rhigas falls back asleep. Dr. Utley turns his attention to the other side of the room.

Skedelski is sitting up in bed.

Dr. Utley's lips curl. His face wrinkles with the most emotion I have seen from him yet. No doctor wants to lose a patient.

Dr. Sellers's voice comes over the Med Bay comms. "Do you need my help in there? How are they?"

"I have it under control for now," answers Dr. Utley. "The automated system's reconstructing his damaged organs, but it's having trouble locking onto his DNA. Doesn't make sense. He's at four times the safe Mizophile dose for his body weight, and the coma still won't hold."

"Do you think he is going to be okay?" asks Skedelski.

"No, Skedelski," answers Dr. Utley with raised brows. "I do not think he's going to be okay. Now lay back down and rest?"

Skedelski looks at Rhigas with sensitive, unblinking eyes and lays back down. A big man with a big heart. I watch them for a bit ... but I am still too worried about Rhigas and Fister to concentrate on anything else.

I need to get my mind off it and stop watching the Med Bay feeds. Surface-side will be an excellent distraction. Then again, Fister might be in a mental and emotional haze right now.

# CHAPTER 20

Fister's Rage

The crew stands in a large clearing next to Argos, patiently waiting with worry. Bell and Sapp stand on its tracks. No one talks.

Gusts of high winds rip periodically through the area, carrying purple and pink leaves from nearby trees to float around the ground team. Trunks of distant trees are strong and do not sway to match random shakes in their canopies. A flock of black and green birds with large bills fly effortlessly against the wind.

Static-laced comms fill the air for a moment, ensnaring the attention of our ground team.

"Are you getting me down there, Sergeant Major?" asks Dr. Wright.

"It's distorted, but I hear you," answers Sergeant Bentley.

"Copy that. I'll set auto-pilot to bring us in for a tighter orbit until the storm passes."

"Sounds good. Any word on Rhigas and Skedelski?"

"They were both still under the last time I heard. Dr. Utley thinks Skedelski will be in recovery soon."

"What about my cousin?" asks Fister. "What about Rhigas?"

It is a question I am not sure I want to hear the answer to. None of us do. We all know it is bad. None of us want to face it, not when we are so far from home and with so much at stake.

A long moment of silence passes. Each of those on the surface looks at one another with great concern. Dread fills their hearts. We are all thinking the same thing but waiting hopefully for confirmation of the opposite.

"Hey," continues Fister. "I asked about my cousin?"

"Fister..." says Dr. Wright with a long pause. "I don't think he's doing well. Utley has him at elevated doses of mizophile, and he's still having trouble keeping him under. The more he moves, the more he damages newly regenerating tissue."

"What are you saying?" asks Fister.

"I'm sorry," answers Dr. Wright. "We don't think he's going to make it."

"Mason," shouts Fister. "You wait until I—"

"Tighten that lip," says Sergeant Bentley. "Mason's the reason he's still here at all."

My heart sinks as they go back and forth. Fister does not mean it. I can tell. He is lashing out at anything and everything. A cold pressure fills my chest; water fills my eyes. The mission has been a disaster so far.

Fister throws a piece of his gear into the side of a tree and fires a few blasts from his onium rifle into the woods.

"Fister," shouts Sergeant Bentley.

My heart rate elevates. Disquietude sets in. I stand as if to run away from the instant when another blast rings out.

"Fister," continues Sergeant Bentley.

"No," shouts Fister.

"Hey," says Sapp. "Ease up."

"Don't *Fister* me. That's my blood dying up there."

Despite the ground team's attempts to comfort him, he walks toward the faraway tree line and fires another volley in the direction where Rhigas got wounded. I jump with a startle in the security feed room as if I were his intended target.

Dr. Wright steps from the visual feed in the forward as Sergeant Bentley, Sapp, and Bell grab Fister to stop him. A brief scuffle ensues. They fall to the ground.

Delgado steps from Argos as Chubb hops from its turret. Fister punches Sergeant Bentley, but the others pin his arms to subdue him.

"That's my blood…" Fister falls into a cry, and they pull him to a seated position to embrace him.

"Sergeant Bentley?" asks Dr. Wright.

"It's fine," answers Sergeant Bentley. "He's fine." He locks eyes with Fister. "We have it under control, Doctor."

"Are you sure about that?" continues Dr. Wright.

Sergeant Bentley watches the woods for a moment as if he saw something we did not. "Yes." He stands and looks at Delgado. "We're a go in twenty."

20-2

Impossible Findings

I get up to take a breather. Snacks are in order since I cannot remember eating a meal since we left Kep Four. Jerleanian would be nice. It is a shame I could not bring any aboard Athanasios.

My self-created snack table makes a hard choice with prickle fruit—a sour fruit that turns tart after chewing for a tek, lizzles—a compressed Armada M.R.E. (Meal Ready to Eat) beverage that comes in a small, flavored pouch, and Armada M.R.E. rations in a respectable variety. I grab an M.R.E. without paying attention to what kind. None of them are anything special. The need for sustenance keeps knocking at my stomach's door.

The chair in front of the video feed panes finds my rear back onto it while I eat and scan the panes. Dr. Sellers removes a small hair from the humanoid. I watch curiously as he sets it on a clear disk. A transparent cylinder lowers down over it and guides the hair to lift and spin. The cylinder glows a momentary yellow before it stops, and the hair falls back to its base.

This stuff has always interested me. Science... biology, in particular. I have not taken the time to learn much about it.

Dr. Sellers looks at the DNA with doubting eyes. "Results?"

"Genetic profile unknown," answers Athanasios.

A breakdown of its genetic code comes to life in a rotating holo-projection fashion above his equipment.

Dr. Sellers ponders. "Nearest match?"

"Homosapien," says Athanasios.

I choke on my M.R.E. and sit upright. "What?"

Dr. Sellers studies the genetic code for a moment with a frozen expression. "How close is the match?"

The calculation floats up and rests next to the DNA strand:

99.9999%

"Ninety-nine point nine, nine, nine, nine, percent direct," answers Athanasios.

Dr. Sellers turns back to the humanoid strapped to the table and then ponders further over the DNA sequence. "Run it again. Speculate at factor eight before determination."

The holographic image disappears as the hair rises to the center of the cylinder and spins again. Factor eight is going to take a while. It is the deepest level of research we do in the Armada, and it runs all records in recorded history.

"Delgado," says Dr. Wright. "We're a go in fifteen."

I watch the hair spin for a moment, knowing Athanasios is going to be calculating much longer this time.

What are they doing in fifteen? I redirect my attention to the other panes to find out.

20–3
Bad Moon Rising

A distant horizon spins to move the fiercely blue binary suns from sight as the planet rotates around them. I lose myself in a plausible theory watching. The possibility needs to be investigated more, but differences in our worlds may explain the humanoids' silk-like, flowing hair if DNA is as close of a match as predicted.

This planet orbits in the Goldilocks belt for sustaining life but must vary significantly in temperature from season to season. The humanoids I have seen so far's hair are primarily brown with random patterns and colors. However, there were variables. This could be a natural evolutionary adaptation in such an eccentric system.

Their thin coats are enough to keep them warmer when the orbiting binary stars are horizontal to the planet and further away, but not dense enough to burn them up during phases where the stars are closer and vertically in line with the planet. Surely, we are going to be in for some rapid and interestingly hot/cold seasonal shifts if we stay here.

The panes reveal our ground team driving along the edge of the clearing. Chubb tosses small silver boundary orbs from a box every two hundred paces as they ride. The orbs tumble through quarter-pace-high grass and roll for a tek, before popping up to hover above the ground. Small tripods eject themselves from their bottoms and jab into the ground. The orbs on top of the tripods glow a faint green as the crew pulls away from them.

A bit of watching this and they come to an orb they have previously activated and stop. Chubb flips a switch on a small, black, palm-sized transmitter. Green lasers surge from each side of the nearest orb to those closest to it, causing the next in line to do the same. The process continues down the line until a green ring forms around a forested area standing in the center of what would otherwise be a massive clearing.

One by one, the orbs stop glowing. Lasers linking them fade until they cease to be visible. The small tripods beneath them turn black as pitch, take on a mirrorlike state with their surroundings, and render themselves invisible to match.

"You should get an image now," says Sergeant Bentley.

Dr. Wright patiently waits at his station in the forward. The feeds have his attention. "Nothing yet. Still waiting."

"Want us to check over the link?" asks Sergeant Bentley.

The forward feed flashes white.

"Negative on that," answers Dr. Wright. "It's coming through now."

An overhead shot of a thickly forested area shaped like a donut appears with a green circle surrounding it. The massive structure and smaller ones those humanoids emerged from on the rotation Rhigas and Skedelski were injured is at the center. The detail is higher than I thought it would be. Swaying leaves glisten with the rising moons' glow as if to hypnotize.

I look to mountaintops concealing a far-flung landscape no longer sheltering the planet's moon from sight. It casts the once-green mountain into an unconventionally deep shade of darkness.

I can still see a few small fires flickering below, but it will get difficult to make out the details as night falls.

"Got it," says Dr. Wright.

"What's the word from topside?" asks Sergeant Bentley.

"Give me a tek. Switching to thermal."

Fires, once a faint flickering orange, now glow white hot within the boundary orbs when he makes the switch. A pair of humanoids are making their way into their primary structure. Their bodies glow white enough to match the fire's intensity.

Ground team waits outside the perimeter ring, but Armada suits conceal body heat, and their images relay as a barely visible faint gray. Thermal detection is nice at this range, but it will not be picking up cold-blooded life. We have encountered none yet, but the possibility of its existence here is high.

A faded white dot with shaded edges comes onto the forward view, making its way toward the ring with two more behind it. They glow brighter as they near the boundary orbs' parameter line.

"Ground team," says Dr. Wright. "Hold for a tek. I have something here."

"Let me hear it," says Sergeant Bentley.

The dots turn a white-hot as they grow closer to the signal amplification ring. He zooms in on one of them. It is the humanoids. They are running right for the ground team.

"I think you've got company," says Dr. Wright.

A rustle echoes across comms.

"Whoa," says Bell. "You getting this?"

Several more gray dots appear on the forward view and become brighter as they rush closer toward the ring. They are speeding up as the night falls. Bell looks up. Both suns are gone, with the large moon rising fast in the backdrop. His head whips down as the humanoids run past him and dart into the woods for the large stone structure.

"Must be afraid of the dark," says Bell.

"I doubt that," says Sapp.

"I'm with Sapp on that one," says Delgado.

"Don't get relaxed yet," says Dr. Wright. "Looks like we got about thirty of those things running toward the structure they came from, and they're doing it in a hurry."

"Confirmation on that," says Sergeant Bentley. "We got—"

He ducks for cover as several humanoids blow past him.

I watch on, not knowing what is to come. Fears for both the ground team and the humanoids are high. I would beg the universe to help us … if it will listen.

One slams into an invisible perimeter tripod and tumbles into the woods, forcing it to phase mirrored, black, and visible again as it powers down. The other tripods and orbs do the same. The green laser connecting them becomes visible and disappears one section at a time from the point of collapse.

Delgado is looking at an onboard monitor in her vehicle. "We're losing enhancement perimeter."

Ground team looks down the tree line as the last green lasers connecting the orbs power down. A cascade of failure rounds the tree line out of sight. The enhanced image disappears from the forward view, but Dr. Wright already imported data to save what we received.

This is neither efficient nor acceptable in smoothing out and helping Rhigas. We need a different approach. Anything.

I stand and exit the security feed room.

20–4

Game Plan

I make my way through the empty corridors and sneak into the forward. If we are ever going to communicate with them, someone must make the first move. The way they are going about everything is only going to lead to more bloodshed.

Dr. Wright has his back to me. He is busy sorting and dissecting incoming video feeds. I sneak to a nearby console, pull up pictures Dr. Sellers took from the planet's surface, and remove a drive from the station's holding bay. It releases a purple light when I move it closer to the console. Then it stops, signaling it has already downloaded the images.

I place the drive into my pocket, thankful Athanasios's system is fast.

Dr. Wright stops for a moment and pulls at his collar, stretching and rubbing his neck. He is under a lot of pressure. Life as we know it is counting on us, and that weight rests on his shoulders as the leader of Expedition Anchor.

Dr. Utley walks into the cabin and heads his way.

I sneak through the exit and stop behind its frame to listen. After ten cycles involved in espionage rescuing so-called nonsentient captives from testing and research labs, I have learned it is a shorter path to truth.

"Yes, doctor?" asks Dr. Wright.

"It's Rhigas..." answers Dr. Utley. "I need to talk with Bentley on a sheltered signal."

Dr. Wright patches him through. "Sergeant Major?"

The P.O.V. from Sergeant Bentley's Eye-Cam displays on their forward view when he answers. He is walking away from the ground team for privacy on the sheltered line. An empty field is on screen with a partially rising moon in the backdrop.

"Bentley here," he says. "Loud and clear."

"Dr. Utley needs a moment of your time."

"Go ahead," says Sergeant Bentley. "Comms open, doctor."

"Listen..." says Dr. Utley. "Thought it best to say this directly here with you and Dr. Wright. Skedelski's going to make it. He's not having a single reaction, and he's responding normally to medications."

"And Rhigas?"

"He's resistant, and it's making it difficult to keep him stabilized. He won't pull through unless we get a blood sample from one of the adult humanoids that attacked you. I have to figure out exactly what's happening to him. I need at least one sample to do it."

"Forgive my ignorance, Doctor," says Sergeant Bentley. "Can't you get a sample from the one you have up there?"

"I did," answers Dr. Utley. "But the changes taking place in Rhigas's DNA don't match up with that of the younger humanoid. It appears to be shifting though."

"Elaborate," says Sergeant Bentley.

"I don't know the how's, why's, and what's yet," answers Dr. Utley. "I think the one we have up here's beginning its transition into adulthood."

"Puberty?"

"You could say that, but the answer to what's happening to Rhigas is not in the younger one."

"I'm reading you down here," says Sergeant Bentley, looking over his shoulder to make sure he is alone. "But we may have to go into the structure for something like that. No way those things are going to stay outside when they see us coming."

"This is option number one, Sergeant," says Dr. Utley. "There is no option two."

All grow momentarily quiet. My attention is unyielding in waiting for them to continue. Those on the surface must be wondering who he is communicating with and what about. After being in the heat of battle when everything happened and seeing Rhigas get so badly hurt, there must be distress.

"Is there any way you can—"

"I'll be abrasive here," interrupts Dr. Utley. "If I do not get a blood sample from an adult to draw a comparison with, Rhigas is one hundred percent going to die."

"Everyone listen up," says Sergeant Bentley, turning back to his team. "We need R.B.C., W.B.C., and DNA from one of the adult humanoids to find a cure for Rhigas."

Fister locks, loads, and powers up his rifle. "Then let's go kill some of these things."

"Nobody's killing anything unless they have to, Fister," says Sergeant Bentley. "We'll get your blood, Doctor. Hopefully without incident."

"Be careful out there," says Dr. Utley. "I need to check on Skedelski and Rhigas."

"Sergeant Major," interjects Dr. Wright. "Morris has an idea I'd like you to hear."

"Go ahead, Morris," says Sergeant Bentley.

"Yes, Sergeant Major," says Morris. "I think you should reverse the field generators on your onium rifles to see if we can get a disruptive charge out of them."

"Field tasers?" asks Sergeant Bentley.

"Correct," answers Morris. "The weapons your crew is carrying work off sixteen-fifty-based energy principles for Expedition Anchor. The conversion should be the same for all of them."

Dr. Wright pulls our ground team up on the forward view for Morris to see.

Sergeant Bentley nods to his team and they grab their weapons. "We're ready."

"Start by unlocking the aft surge mixers and disconnecting the C.F.F. wires," says Morris. "I'll guide you from there. Just remember, if you must fire them, it will cause temporary disruptions in your phase suit each time you pull the trigger. They'll be able to see you for about one tik."

"I'm down two squad members, Morris," says Sergeant Bentley. "I'm going to need you down here. Walk us through the conversions when you arrive."

"Sergeant Major," says Morris. "I'm mainly here for—"

"You're here for the mission, Morris," interrupts Sergeant Bentley. "End of story. I don't need you for firepower. These field tasers are your idea. You need to be here if something goes wrong. Grab a phase suit, have Dr. Utley fill you in, and set a drop pod to our coordinates."

"Yes, Sergeant Major."

"Chubb," calls Sapp. "See if you can get that perimeter back up and running when we're done here. We need to head into that structure. It'd be nice to have it up beforehand."

I cannot keep listening to this. My knowledge of rifle engineering and field manipulations is subpar, but I plan to educate myself in the future. The current idea in my head is something only Dr. Sellers would appreciate, and it has nothing to do with field tasers.

I need to be quick in my game plan to communicate with the humanoids. Part of me feels the battle that led to so many injuries was no one's fault, but the logical side of me knows otherwise. We came here, moved into their territory, and abducted one of their children. It is our responsibility to defuse the situation on both sides of the equation.

I turn and exit the forward to move through Athanasios's corridors. I have got a date with a hairy captive about my size. He does not know it yet, but he is about to have a conversation with an alien.

CHAPTER 21

Linguistics

I walk into the science lab. The captors have restrained the captured humanoid juvenile on the table. It is not right. They should have at least unstrapped him.

I ease over and brush his cheek. "Poor thing."

His eyes open and lock on me.

"It's okay," I say. "Let me find the release, and I'll get you out of here."

He tries to snatch away from me but cannot move. His whole body is shaking. There is no way for me to imagine what he is going through right now. Petrified would not do his situation justice.

I look for a tik and move to the other side of the table. A release comes into view near his feet. I raise its cold lever. Telescoping latches wrapping its left ankle detract, and, for the first time, the humanoid shows trust for me with unbreaking eye contact. He knows I am not here with hidden malice.

The lever to release its left arm is at my right. I lift the lever, and he pulls his arm free and rolls away from me. Slow steps take me to the other side of the table. Two more levers. I throw them both, and he is free.

The young humanoid hops from the opposite side of the table from me and ducks behind it.

"You don't have to hide," I say, easing around its edge.

He stays low and out of sight while matching my movements around the table. I climb up and sit on the spot he was strapped at and have a seat to watch. A solid five teks pass with him remaining still and neither of us making a sound.

The top of his head creeps into view. I watch and wait for him to be ready on his own. His eyebrows, then his eyes... He moves slowly up, peeking over the table's edge at me.

"Hi," I say. "Feel like talking yet?"

No response.

"I'm not going to hurt you," I continue, holding out my hand to him. "And I'm not letting anyone else hurt you either." I pause, waiting for a response. "Are you going to help me down like a gentleman, or not?"

The young humanoid looks back and forth between my hand and eyes a few time.

"It's alright," I whisper.

He takes my hand, and I slide slowly off the table toward his side without breaking eye contact. His grip is loose. The lack of hair on his palm reminds me of the flagert I rescued and allows skin-to-skin contact.

"That wasn't so hard," I say. "Was it?"

I guide him to a video pane in the back of the lab. He stands nervously at my side, looking around at the wonder of the mighty Athanasios science lab.

His eyes follow my hand as I raise the golden drive toward the pane. It lights up, and his fixation moves to the now brightly lit image. One of the flying animals that tore the camp apart comes onto the pane.

I point to it, tapping the pane a few times before turning back to face him. His head cocks as I bring my hands gently together to form the shape of a bird, flapping my fingers to simulate flight.

"Bird," I say.

The young humanoid looks at the pane for a bit. There is magic in his eyes, and he is momentarily in awe before turning back to face me. I motion from my mouth to the viewing pane with my pointer finger.

"Bird," I repeat.

He touches the viewing pane as if he can touch its wings.

"Come on," I say. "I know I heard a language in there somewhere."

I motion once more from my mouth to the viewing pane. He is still unsure what to think of me. Patience is needed here, but I do not have a lot of time for it.

"Bird," I say again.

"Blazee," he says with a raspy, otherworldly voice.

"Yes," I cheer, turning to see Pru'Cet hiding behind me. "No. It's okay."

I motion him back to me.

He eases back toward the pane. "Blazee."

I give a victorious smile. "Blazee."

He does not find it amusing, and my happiness is not reciprocated. Dr. Utley's captive is probably worried the doctors will come back. His eyes keep flicking toward the door.

"Hey," I say, pointing two fingers at my eyes. "Look here."

He looks me in the eyes.

"It's okay," I say. "It's okay."

I slowly take his hand and place it on my cheeks. His eyes sparkle in reaction to our similar bone structure, but my lack of hair captivates him, and he brushes the side of my partially shaved head.

He smiles, and I change the image to some of the crew members standing around a large, sharp-petaled white flower covering them like an umbrella. He leans in to examine them and touches their faces.

I point to the pane again and single out the flower, motioning from my mouth to the pane again. "Flower."

"Peelota," he says.

"Peelota," I say. "That's a funny word."

I switch images and stop at one taken from Argos of the four-legged chicken-looking birds we saw running around upon the ground team nearing the structure.

"Yeena," says Pru'Cet. "Yeena."

The young humanoid looks at me with great interest as I switch images again and point to each of the crew members, one at a time. "Chubb, Sapp, Bell, Fister, Morris, Delgado, Bentley, Utley, Wright." Then I point to myself. "McKayla." Tapping my chest with an open palm. "McKayla."

I move my hand toward him a few times, but he does not respond. My hand to my chest again, I repeat my name. Then I touch his chest and motion for him to respond.

"Pru'Cet," he says.

"Pru'Cet," I repeat with a giggle. "Your name's Pru'Cet? That's actually kind of cute." I move his hand tenderly to my chest, then to his. "McKayla... Pru'Cet..." Back and forth between us. "Friends. McKayla... Pru'Cet... Friends."

"Blenya," says Pru'Cet.

Blenya? I am not sure if it means friend, together, or safe. It could mean a lot of things, but I am confident it means we are not enemies. That is what matters right now.

I hold my hand up and step in for a high-five, but he ducks under my swipe. "No?"

I smile and change the image on the viewing pane again. It is a picture of Dr. Sellers digging up a small plant with a pile of dirt next to him. I point at different things, singling them out in rapid succession to speed things up.

"Sun," I say. "Tree, dirt, clouds."

Pru'Cet points to the objects in the same order. "Heeza, staog, tos, ooves."

He points to my hand, then to other parts of my body rapidly. I mouth everything he says as if I am saying the words myself to memorize them.

"Uneger," continues Pru'Cet, "letrow, nit, pota, lazzaz, aryan, flazee, ga, swil."

"Well," I say, "at least I know some of my body parts now."

Pru'Cet looks at me with excitement and points out everything in the pane, calling out all the details at a quick pace. My mouth moves with everything he says until I switch the image without either of us missing a beat.

He stops me after a few more images, pointing to himself and to a picture of the extensive structure on the planet's surface. "Lessdelop."

"This is your home?" I ask.

"Lessdelop," he repeats.

"Home it is," I say, shifting to an image of the Planetary Conference Hall—one Dr. Sellers must have taken before we left. There are thousands of people in it. I point to one. "Human." Then run my finger over all of them. "Humans."

He looks at me, and I touch my chest.

"McKayla, human," I say, pointing to all the people in the image again. "Humans."

"Huemon," says Pru'Cet.

His pronunciation is not perfect, but we are getting somewhere. I smile and give him an encouraging wink. He mimics me with a single perplexed clap as I pull up an image of his people chasing Argos and place it side-by-side with the Planetary Conference Hall.

My hand goes to my chest. "Human."

His eyes follow as I run my finger across those seated in the hall. "Humans."

I guide my finger through his own kind before motioning back to him.

"Kla'Wah," says Pru'Cet, motioning to himself. "Pru'Cet. Kla'Wah. Dah'Sel." He points back to his people in the image and runs his finger over them as I did. "Kla'Wah."

"Pru'Cet," I say. "Kla'Wah."

He runs his finger over everyone in the conference hall. "Kla'Wah."

"Good," I say.

Pru'Cet circles a small portion of them and places his palm on his chest again. "Dah'Sel."

Perhaps Kla'Wah is his race, and Dah'Sel is his section or branch of it. My grin turns into a cheek-splitting smile. This is going to work. I am going to fix this.

21-2
Wrapping Up

We have been going at it for three taks. I have everything in every photo on the planet memorized. A good chunk of time was spent playing charades, trying to figure out words like *and, but, love, anger, because, civilization, culture, family, sit,* and a slew of others not capturable by video files. It was fun. We were playfully pushing one another at the shoulder by the time a few taks went by.

"Push," I say, giving him another nudge.

Pru'Cet returns the nudge. "Zotka."

A glass basin catches my attention and I push it to slide a hand's length across the table. "Zotka."

Pru'Cet pushes the basin, only it keeps sliding. It is not stopping. I shoot my arm out to catch it, but I am too slow … and it crashes to the floor to shatter.

"Whaul," he shouts.

Dr. Utley enters the science lab, startling us both. We dip toward the back to hide, but I trip and make a smacking sound when my palms meet the hard flooring to catch myself. Pru'Cet takes off to hide, realizes there is nowhere to go, and crawls back to my side. Neither of us moves. I flick my eyes left and right to listen.

"Hello?" says Dr. Wright with a baffled expression.

Two snaps. The sound of filling vials. Dr. Wright is preparing another tubular injector. He rounds the corner of the table. Pru'Cet cowers behind me as Dr. Wright freezes in place when he sees us. He eyes Pru'Cet as I stand.

"Mason," says Dr. Wright. "Back away from—"

"It's okay," I interrupt.

"These things are dangerous," he continues. "Ease this way."

"Kuzsoec," I say.

Pru'Cet steps behind me and stays close. Dr. Utley is momentarily speechless.

"Fascinating, huh?" I ask.

Dr. Utley looks around the lab and back to us. "How?"

"He's been teaching me for a few taks," I answer. "My head literally, physically hurts from information overload. Really. It's amazing when you—"

"How did you do it?" he asks.

"We went through the surface pictures," I answer. "He pointed out everything in them and told me what they were. After that, we started filling in the blanks, mostly. I mean, it's not perfect yet, but he trusts me. I think he's bonding with me."

"That's remarkable," says Dr. Sellers. "And you remember everything?"

"Yes, sir," I answer. "I can't have a regular full-on conversation or anything yet."

"How many pictures did you go through?"

"All of them. I think it was—"

"There were over a thousand images," he interrupts. "Almost fifteen hundred."

I squint my eyes and rub my aching temples. "Feels about right."

"Outlandish."

"And you're sure that thing is safe?"

I nod. "One hundred percent."

"Dr. Utley," calls Dr. Sellers over comms, "Rhigas is up again."

"On my way," says Dr. Utley, cutting me an unconvinced look. "Get that thing back in the cage."

"His name's Pru'Cet."

"Pru'Cet?"

A thrashing sound fills the scene as Dr. Sellers shouts over comms. "Doctor, I really think you need to get in here."

Dr. Utley grabs a few things from the shelf and looks my way as he heads toward the door.

"Oe en aryan," I say.

Pru'Cet takes my hand.

Dr. Utley stops outside the door and looks our way again. "Inconceivable."

He rolls his head in concern and turns back down the corridor toward the Med Bay. I move to follow him with Pru'Cet in hand.

Dr. Utley halts me. "Mason, find out what's going on planet side and keep me informed."

"Yes, sir," I say. "Got it."

Dr. Wright comes into view from the left corridor on his way to the science lab.

"Dr. Wright," calls Dr. Utley.

"Yes?" he answers.

Dr. Wright is looking down, trying to remove his outer jacket as he approaches us, but the comm link on his right arm and the vital sign monitor on his left keep it from coming off.

"I'm going to need your help in the Med Bay," continues Dr. Utley.

Dr. Wright unclasps the two bands from his arms, sets them on the floor, and slides off his jacket. He looks up to see us. His breaths halt. His body freezes.

"What's going on here?" he asks.

"Dr. Wright," I answer. "Meet Pru'Cet."

"Specap," says Pru'Cet.

I am not sure what that one means. I hope it was a, '*Hi*,' and not a, '*You look like another evil human that wants to experiment on me.*'

Dr. Wright is staring. "How?"

"No time to explain," says Dr. Utley. "I need you in med-bay."

Dr. Wright locks unwavering eyes onto Pru'Cet. I watch his wide-mouthed expression and searching eyes.

Dr. Utley moves toward the Med Bay. "Now, doctor."

Dr. Wright eases past me and my hairy new friend, cutting us a puzzled look before he jogs down the corridor after him.

We part ways. He heads to whatever emergency is going on in the medical lab with Dr. Utley. Pru'Cet and I move toward the security feed room. I am routing all communication back to it as soon as I get there. I have a feeling the dyogg turds are about to hit the fan.

CHAPTER 22

32 Panes

I enter the security feed room and pull the only other chair in it next to mine. "Lilimensa."

Pru'Cet takes a seat but never takes his eyes off me. He is still taking in the technology and trying to accept me as a newly found friend.

"Armada voice clearance," I say. "Mason, five, Sinote, one, four, McKayla, three, six, reactivate video feeds, previous sequence."

"Video feeds back online," says Athanasios.

"Intercept all communications and reroute to my location."

"Communications systems rerouted."

Pru'Cet jumps back with a loud gasp when they come to life as if those in the feeds could come out and grab him. It is understandable. He has never seen such a thing, and those displayed on the panes are the ones that captured him.

"Shh..." I say, placing my hand on his silky forearm for reassurance. "It's okay."

He settles and accepts his overstimulation to watch the feeds with unblinking eyes.

Chubb catches my interest when I turn back to the panes. Stars litter a now dark sky over the ground team's heads as the planetary ring system shines brightly beneath a still-climbing moon. He repairs the last perimeter orb and tries to stand the tripod, but its leg is broken. It falls to the ground.

"Shit," he says.

"Someone's full of righteous words," I say.

I turn to Pru'Cet, who does not know what I am talking about. He turns back in wonderment to the video feeds, watching on as Chubb takes the orb apart, pulls back a panel, and touches a trace-tool to the inside of it.

Sergeant Bentley approaches. "I thought you had that fixed."

"As did I," answers Chubb. "But I—"

Sparks fly from it. He jumps back. "Great. We might as well round them up now."

"Can we adjust the spacing on them to compensate?" asks Sergeant Bentley.

"If you're only looking to set up an alert perimeter," answers Chubb. "But they're already stretched too thin for detailed scans."

"Morris," calls Sergeant Bentley.

Morris is working on a rifle with the rest of the crew. "Yes, Sergeant Major."

"How much longer on the field tasers?"

"I'm reprogramming on the last one now."

"Come help Chubb when you're finished."

"Yes, Sergeant Major."

Sergeant Bentley walks away from the group. "You got a copy up there, Dr. Wright?"

No response.

"Sergeant Bentley to Dr. Wright, copy?" He pauses. "Bentley to Mason."

"Mason here," I answer. "Go ahead, Sergeant Major."

"Where's Dr. Wright?" he asks.

"He's with Dr. Utley."

"Patch him in for me."

"I don't think they can answer you right now."

"Elaborate."

"There was an emergency in the med lab," I say. "He had to assist Dr. Utley."

"What kind of emergency?" asks Sergeant Bentley.

"Unknown."

"Is it Rhigas?" interjects Fister.

"I honestly don't know," I say. "I really don't."

"Do me a favor," says Sergeant Bentley. "Keep me informed," says Sergeant Bentley.

"Yes, Sergeant Major."

"Everyone else," he says, "you know the drill. You know what it's time to do. We got a man dying up there, and we aren't going to let that happen. But no casualties unless there is absolutely no other choice. We need one blood sample. Not a hundred."

Delgado fires up Argos.

"Let's do this," says Fister.

Sergeant Bentley enters the vehicle and takes a seat next to Delgado. "Drive."

She pulls Argos into gear and carries the ground team into the woods toward the structure.

22-2

Changing

Skedelski is sitting near the edge of Rhigas's bed on the 25th pane, intently watching his wounded friend as Dr. Sellers secures a final strap around him. Rhigas's breathing is rapid and in distress when the doctors walk in.

"Skedelski," says Dr. Utley. "I need you in the forward with Mason to make sure she's safe with that thing while I talk with Dr. Wright."

"Thing?" asks Skedelski.

"You'll understand when you get there."

"I'm in the security feed room, Skedelski," I say.

Skedelski says nothing. He simply turns, ducks under the door, and walks from the bay without further question. He is quiet, gentle, and powerful; but I would not want to see him angry. He might be my first man crush before this mission is over.

Dr. Utley plucks a hair from Rhigas's head and looks at it. "I am going with your theory on matching DNA, Dr. Sellers. Grab the other hair from the science lab and get it back here. I want to compare bulbs, skin tissue, and blood samples."

Dr. Sellers nods and exits the bay.

"What's happening here, Dr. Utley?" asks Dr. Wright.

"I think Rhigas is undergoing a metamorphosis," he answers.

"Metamorphosis? How so?"

"He's turning."

"Into what?" asks Dr. Wright. "One of those things?"

"They're called Dah'Sel," I interject.

"Dah'Sel?"

"Yes, sir," I explain. "Their species. That's what they call themselves. Maybe Kla'Wah in totality, but Pru'Cet is Dah'Sel."

"That's good to know," says Dr. Wright. "Thank you, Mason." He turns his attention back to Dr. Utley. "But I need to know what's happening to Rhigas."

"I'm not sure yet," answers Dr. Utley. "We need to run some more tests."

He moves to the other side of the medical bay with Dr. Wright and talks about things I am not educated in, but it does not sound good.

Dr. Utley hands him the hair he plucked from Rhigas. "Here. Run this while I set up the comparison."

They go to work and remain quiet. My eyes go to the other pane with worry. Nothing good is going to come from them going after a blood sample.

22-3
Approaching the Structure

Argos is in the backdrop of the woods with all but Sergeant Bentley, Delgado, and Chubb on foot. The large moon is no longer hidden by the distant horizon. It is casting a dense glare upon the planet's surface. Treetops high above ground team lean toward it like growing flowers to a star.

"Stop here," says Sergeant Bentley. "We're making the rest on foot. You and Chubb hold back here."

"Yes, Sergeant Major," she says, stopping Argos.

Sergeant Bentley exits to approach his team. "Let's keep moving."

Sapp takes point as they walk. "Man, I feel light."

"Dr. Wright said the moon's gravity's unusually strong because of its dense core. Mix that with what he said about its rotational speed and..."

"Think that's why these things don't come out at night?" asks Sapp. "Tidal surges?"

"No," interjects Sergeant Bentley.

"Why not?" asks Sapp. "You'd think that—"

"Tighten your jaw."

The crew comes to the edge of the tree line. The field surrounding the structure is evenly lit, revealing several young Dah'Sel playing amongst it.

Sapp stops and raises a fist to halt ground team. "Didn't expect to see that."

"What do you guys have up there?" asks Delgado.

"Youth," answers Sergeant Bentley. "About seven of them."

Argos's interior is glowing fluorescent as Delgado works diligently for a better visual. "About to have some serious eyes for you over here." Windows around her and Chubb act like advanced night vision goggles, lighting the surrounding woods brightly for those inside to see like the sun is high overhead.

"You said youth?" asks Delgado.

"That's an affirmative," answers Sergeant Bentley.

"Doesn't sound right at this time of night from what we've seen so far," says Delgado. "Let me double-check before you move in."

Chubb sits in the back of the vehicle running a program.

Delgado powers up a small, radar-type viewing pane. "Connection clear. There are a few younglings around the backside of the structure."

22–4

Watching

Skedelski enters the visual security feed room and stops. Pru'Cet jumps behind me.

"Thing…" says Skedelski with a smirk. "Okay. I see now. You have a new friend."

"His name's Pru'Cet," I say, motioning him from behind me. "Blenya."

"Blenya?" asks Pru'Cet.

"Yes. Blenya. Kuzsoec. It's okay."

He eases out from behind me. Skedelski smiles.

"You want my seat?" I ask.

"No," he answers. "I'll stand. Thank you, Mason."

He towers over me and crosses his arms to watch the thirty-two panes in front of us. Pru'Cet is on edge, but he will get over it. I do not mind the big man looming behind me. He makes me feel safe, at ease, and glad he is here.

Ground team is moving ahead with stealth to post at the edge of the clearing.

"And we are a go," says Delgado. "I got you linked up. We'll come in if you need us."

"Understood," says Sergeant Bentley. "We're going to get low." He looks across the field. "Time to mask up."

He and the others press a few buttons on their forearms and their suits phase in the same manner the tripods and orbs did earlier. They pull a small wire from their firearms and plug them into the suits, rendering their weapons invisible as well.

"Are you reading us through the mask, Delgado?" asks Sergeant Bentley.

"Clean and easy," she answers. "Just like I like it."

Skedelski and I smirk at her comment and watch the ground team move from the inner tree line and into a small section of grass. They leave only footprints and moving grass as a disruption in the meadow for signs they are crossing it.

Bell and Sapp are walking in front of Sergeant Bentley with Morris on their tail. A unique, partially transparent aura outlines their silhouettes so they can see each other while masked. Their names float on the screen above each of their heads for identification.

Sergeant Bentley turns and watches the younger Dah'Sel in the distance as they kick a primitively made round object.

"This is so wild," says Morris. "What the haze are they doing out here alone at night after everything that happened on the other rotation?"

"Wondering the same thing here," says Bell.

Sergeant Bentley looks at the structure's edge and notices several primitive weapons and spotting devices leaning against it.

"Looks like they're supposed to be standing guard," says Sergeant Bentley.

"But where are the adults?" asks Bell.

"Something's off here," says Morris.

"Come on, guys," says Sergeant Bentley. "Stay focused."

The side of the structure reaches up toward the night sky with impressive effort. It grows heavier with cracks and its color gets lighter near its base. Grass clings to its side. Footsteps appear near the wall as the cloaked team makes their way along its edge.

The young Dah'Sel laugh as children do while they play an unknown game with a foreign ball. I am clueless about the material it is made from. It looks like a head of lettuce wrapped in an animal's dried, cured stomach. Maybe it is leather.

Two of them kick it at the same time and run to different marked points on the field. The others try to make a tackle or hit them with the ball as they go. Pru'Cet bounces up and down in his seat when he sees them.

A countdown on Sergeant Bentley's Eye-Cam flashes in the upper-right corner while highlighting an entrance into the structure:

'104 paces'

'103 paces'

'102 paces'

'101 paces'

"We have an opening at a hundred," he says. "Stay sharp."

The young Dah'Sel continue laughing and playing in the backdrop. Sergeant Bentley looks in their direction. One of them kicks the makeshift ball, and it sails directly for the ground team.

"Heads up," says Fister.

They spread out as the ball flies between them before hitting and bouncing off the structure.

Three of the young Dah'Sel rush after the ball. Two in the background cheer as another runs from object to object under an unknown part of the game's play. One of them goes for the ball, but another tackles him. The ball ricochets off one of their legs when they fall and bounces into the air. A third rushes for it, but it rebounds off Sapp like it hit an invisible wall.

The young Dah'Sel chasing it stops in awe. It cannot see Sapp but looks directly at him. A haunting P.O.V. Eye-Cam feed fills the pane I have him routed to as it approaches.

"That's not good," I say.

The young Dah'Sel is taking slow steps forward with a raised arm reaching out. The two that were wrestling on the ground are now motionless as they watch in partial fear mixed with wonder. Sapp continues to move backward. The Dah'Sel looks back at his friends as they stand to their feet. Sapp backs into a protruding piece of the structure and stops.

"Delgado," says Sergeant Bentley. "How about a little distraction here?"

Delgado's fingers are rapid as she enters a code with the crew's P.O.V. images displayed in front of her. "Already on it."

Chubb slides on a small headset with visors. A pair of controls pop up in front of him, and a small A-Drone—an unmanned surveillance device specific to the Argos and its systems—lifts from the invisible transport vehicle and takes off.

The advanced drone zigzags through the air as it dodges several small trees before pulling high above them. It clears the tree line and fires a flare that lights up the night sky. The young Dah'Sel are mesmerized. Their concentration goes skyward.

The drone is heading right for them. A few youths move for the primitive weapons, but there is no time to grab any. They run down the side of the structure and go for the entrance, but the drone cuts them off, and they continue toward the back of it.

The drone pulls up hard and comes a finger-width away from impacting the structure as the last Dah'Sel youth rounds the corner.

Chubb sits in the seat, working the controls. "That was close."

"Where'd they go, Chubb?" asks Sergeant Bentley.

"Other side of the structure."

"Follow them and make sure there's not another entrance. I don't want these things to know we are coming."

"Keep them corralled back there," says Sapp.

"Good call, Sapp," says Sergeant Bentley.

He turns the drone. "One step ahead of you, Sergeant Major."

The group reaches the entrance and takes formation. They are about to go in, and I just realized I am not breathing as they near the entryway. I take a deep breath and turn to check on Skedelski.

My mighty protector pops his neck and stretches his arms. I am sure he wishes to be there with them, but maybe it is best as is. How well he would be at something this delicate is unknown. Skedelski is a magna-rail spike, not a finishing nail.

Ground team is almost there. Less than a tek out. Fingers crossed.

CHAPTER 23

Blood Sample

Sergeant Bentley halts his team outside the open stone entrance. Each looks over their shoulders for threats. The coast looks clear beyond the Dah'Sel youth playing outside, but I trust nothing in this situation to be as it appears.

"How are the suits doing," asks Dr. Wright.

"Links are holding up so far," answers Sapp.

"Standard formation," says Sergeant Bentley. "No bursts. Dr. Wright said the electrical surges will cause temporary disruptions in our phase suits. We need to remain obscured as much as possible, preferably indefinitely."

"En blenya-zis ka tadak," says Pru'Cet, pointing to a pane with excitement.

Chubb has a shocked, open-eyed expression on his face. "Wow, those suckers are quick!"

The young Dah'Sel are climbing the side of the mammoth structure with impressive speed. The unmanned drone buzzes over and beyond them.

"Sergeant Major," says Chubb. "Get a load of this. The ones I chased off are climbing the side of this thing."

Delgado finishes entering her codes. "Signal enhanced to compensate for atmospheric abnormalities. High-altitude flight's a go."

Chubb pulls up on the controls. "Here we go."

The unmanned drone overtakes the young Dah'Sel. They duck, watch it go by, and continue climbing.

My eyes, along with Pru'Cet's and Skedelski's, flick about the visual feed panes.

23-2
Cloaked Entry

Sergeant Bentley halts his ground team at the structure's entrance. There are multiple hallways carved throughout it like the pyramids once were on Ancient Earth. Each section breaks into separate rooms and other various sections of their home. Reflective mirrors adorn the ends of the hallways. The interior walls are semi-reflective. The walls look obsidian, a naturally occurring volcanic glass that becomes highly reflective when sanded and polished smooth. Etched hieroglyphs cover the walls.

"Some of the writing..." I say, zooming in on a section of the wall. "Not possible."

Portions of writing match what we deciphered and translated for the Armada back on Kep Four cycles ago. The humanoids have pale green horns with naturally forming nodules mounted throughout the halls. There are many room entrances and corridors on both the left and right sides along their path.

A larger opening to the right reveals several wounded Dah'Sel recovering from their last human encounter. Dah'Sel males and females alike are tending to the wounded—some bring water, others food, a few are in the corner grinding up herbs or smoothing I cannot see. An older female sews together a wound on the shaved portion of a male's leg.

"This is incredible," says Sergeant Bentley. "You getting all this up there?"

"I am," answers Dr. Wright, "but I'll be damned if I can explain it. Just stay the course. Everything you're seeing's being recorded for examination later."

Sergeant Bentley continues through the structure. "Affirmative."

Another group of Dah'Sel comes into view in a large open area with high ceilings. They are eating plates of unknown fruits and vegetables near tiki torches burning a soft yellow behind brass cage-style encasings.

Two are entertaining the eaters by performing a scene of some type with one another. A play. The Dah'Sel spectators watch them for a tek and laugh.

Fister's suit flickers to life for a brief tik and goes invisible again. One of the performing Dah'Sel notices it. He stops performing his role in the play, looks in the ground team's direction, and creeps toward them. The other Dah'Sel watch on with silent curiosity.

"What the..." whispers Fister, turning to Sergeant Bentley. "What just happened?"

They take slow steps backward from the structure.

"I don't know," answers Bell. "Looked like you just phased out for a tik."

"Keep falling back," says Sergeant Bentley. "Regroup outside."

The Dah'Sel who noticed Fister grow closer. Others move in behind him. The Dah'Sel leading them reaches out in front of him for a moment and looks down. Ground team's footsteps leave marks in the sand-covered floor as they exit.

I turn to Pru'Cet. He locks his eyes onto me with worry. His lips quiver. Skedelski moves closer to the visual feed panes to watch.

"Why'd that happen?" I ask.

"Feed surges can happen with unintended modifications to certain energy principles," answers Skedelski. "It's a calculated risk."

I turn back to the visual feed panes with apprehension.

The young Dah'Sel reach the top of the structure. Dozens of highly polished, mirror-like plates matching the structure's obsidian interior walls rest at its top. Pipes atop the structure are beneath them. My first thought is a ventilation system designed to funnel wind into the structure from all possible blowing directions. A flap rests on each, and a rod running across their bases connects to a rope of some kind through makeshift pulleys.

One of the young Dah'Sel reaches for the rope and pulls it taunt, causing it to tighten up at the flaps covering each tube. The unmanned drone buzzes by them. "Uh," says Chubb, "Sergeant?"

23–3
Sandstorm

The Dah'Sel approaching Fister leans down to look at the prints in the sand and brushes his hand across them, grabbing some of it as he looks up and stands.

Chubb watches the youth on the rooftop.

"Ummm… Sergeant Major?" he asks.

The Dah'Sel in front of Fister takes a step forward and casts sand high into the hallway. It covers him, Sergeant Bentley, and Bell before most of it falls from their sleek suits and leaves them standing like sandy silhouettes.

"Bizmon," says the sand-wielding Dah'Sel with a lunge forward that tackles Fister.

His high-tech suit permanently fails when he crashes into the ground. The Dah'Sel in the backdrop spring to life and rush to the fore. Shouts in their alien language fill the structure near and far.

An electrical blast from Sapp's rifle renders him visible for a moment but stuns the Dah'Sel on Fister and drops it on top of him. The others stop as it rises back to its feet. Another charge electrifies the Dah'Sel again, and he falls to the sand-covered floor next to Fister.

"Sergeant?" asks Chubb, still watching the rooftop youth.

"Not now, Chubb," answers Sergeant Bentley.

Two Dah'Sel tackle Sapp to the floor and bash into his suit. It fails when damaged. Sapp pulls a silver cylinder with three spikes from the side of his suit and plunges it into one of the Dah'Sel. It screams out in pain.

"I got the sample," shouts Sapp.

Occupants of the structure rush the ground team to attack, filling the corridor in a matter of tiks. They grab at the air and throw random strikes toward their invisible invaders. A few more enter behind them. Two in the back grab clubs from the left wall's base.

"Dalasa," shouts the first Dah'Sel with a club, tossing the weapon to his comrades.

A Dah'Sel at the front of the pack catches it and swings wildly with fast steps forward. Ground team backs away without firing until Sapp is in danger of being hit with the club.

"Let 'em have it," shouts Sergeant Bentley.

Ground team unloads on them with their modified field tasers, revealing themselves with each blast. Sapp stands and hits the control plate on his forearm a few times. His suit phases invisible again as the Dah'Sel swarm the rest of those inside.

"Ma," shouts Pru'Cet. "Ma, ma, ma."

He buries his face into me to advert his eyes. I comfort him for a tik and look back to the panes with Pru'Cet in my arms. Electrical discharges continue dropping the Dah'Sel.

The drone buzzes by as all but two of the young Dah'Sel team up to pull the thick, braided rope on top of the structure.

"It's not for ventilation," I whisper.

They snatch the rope again, but it does not move. The group pulls hard. Their feet slide on the rooftop's surface until the other two join the effort, pivoting up the flaps covering the obsidian tubes and angling the moonlight's shine into the tubes beneath it.

Moon's beam bleeds from the bottom of the tubes and into the structure. Light bounces off its reflective obsidian walls until it reaches the Dah'Sel. A terrible sight unfolds.

Dah'Sel within the structure transform when the moonlight reaches them: palms, feet, fingers, and toes elongate, claws protrude, heads and bodies grow to twenty percent of their original mass, mouths and jaws stretch to form snouts with four pointed fangs—two at the bottom, two at the top— alongside the rest of their human-like teeth.

It happens fast, almost in an instant, and I jump back from my seat with Pru'Cet in my arms. We land next to Skedelski with the chair, eyes still on the 32 panes, and get to our feet. Pru'Cet buried his eyes back into me against my racing heart.

"Holy Armada," says Skedelski, stepping back from the panes.

"Get ghost," shouts Sergeant Bentley. "Get ghost."

Get ghost—an Armada term. When it is called, you are to leave your current location and any situation you are involved in while fending for yourself until a regrouping can occur.

The crew back-peddles toward the entrance as they fire. The Dah'Sel no longer resemble anything known. Ground team's rate of fire increases four-fold to keep up with the new and more resistant threat. More transformed Dah'Sel pour in, some attacking each other mindlessly.

Rapid fire from ground team's weapons expands the gap between them and the crew. They make it out of the structure but maintain their line of fire into it. Two of the creatures attack one another as they exit after my teammates and roll off to the side, fighting in a primitive state of rage. They are trying to kill each other. Savagery at its finest.

A red light activates at the front of Fister's weapon with a beep.

"Overheating," calls Fister. "Switching to secondary firearm."

"Negative," says Sergeant Bentley. "Don't go live."

"I have to if I am—"

"Do not go live."

Fister resumes fire. Three more beeps signal his suit's failing state.

"Overheating," says Bell.

"Same here, Boss," says Sapp.

Morris's weapon sparks and stops firing. The shorted-out firearm renders him visible. "I'm done." He disconnects his weapon and drops it to the ground, sending his suit back into an invisible state.

Bell's weapon releases a plume of thick white smoke. The short circuit leaves him in a permanent state of visibility. He unplugs and drops it. His suit goes invisible again before the rifle hits the ground.

Each time their taser-rifles fire, the ground team becomes visible. They resemble strobe lights, periodically flashing into existence within the glossy obsidian halls. It is imperative for them to stop firing and exit immediately, but they cannot get out if they stop firing.

Sapp and Sergeant Bentley remain in the area with Fister to keep whatever those things are at bay, but there are too many of them. The team is losing ground. Fister's suit is in a constant state of visibility. Worst-case scenario.

Sapp's rifle sparks and fries out. He disconnects but can still be seen. He dips out the exit and squats with his back against the structure's outside wall, leaving only Sergeant Bentley to hold them off.

"Morris," calls Sapp. "I need you."

Morris rushes to his side and unlatches a brown flap at the lower rib area of his suit, plugging a port-wire from his wrist into a receiver on Sapp's suit. They both go visible as a 3D hologram of the failing suit's electrical system rises above it.

Sapp looks at their suits and at a pair of transformed Dah'Sel fighting each other in the clearing. "Brother, you'd better hurry."

Morris maintains his focus. The 3D image zooms to a flashing red section of circuits. He inputs a series of quick commands into his wrist. The red section of circuits stops flashing, and he unplugs from Sapp. They go invisible again.

"Done," says Morris, stepping to fire more taser bursts into the structure over Sergeant Bentley's right shoulder.

I look back and forth between the panes transmitting visual feeds of ground team and the young Dah'Sel high atop the structure, hoping they will close the tube's flaps before it is too late. We could lose Sergeant Bentley and Fister if something does not change soon. The Dah'Sel are gaining ground on them.

A transformed Dah'Sel makes it past their shots and tackles Fister with a hard hit. They fly from the entrance and tumble across the field. Fister is rag-dolled for a moment before another creature attacks the one on top of him.

Fister is hurt but pulls himself to a kneeling position and removes the sidearm from his hip. It is a small, hand-held, live round weapon that fires classic steel projectiles. All Armada personnel carry them for backup during dangerous engagements. They never fail.

"No, Fister," says Sergeant Bentley, looking over his shoulder into the field. "Not yet. Not unless you have to." He aims down the structure's hall and fires more electrical surges at the transformed Dah'Sel. His weapon beeps with a red light but continues firing single-shot energy bursts at multiple targets.

Dah'Sel drop left and right until his rifle spits a small flame from its rear and over his helmet. He backs from the structure, disconnects himself from the weapon, and drops it to the ground to go unseen.

They surround Fister in the field. He points his sidearm erratically at them. They close in on him while dozens more exit the structure—attacking each other—intending to kill. Three creatures are engaged in a mindless brawl until one kills the other, causing the remaining two to fight and tumble further from the entrance and into the trees.

"I'm going back for Fister," says Sapp.

"I'm with you," says Bell.

"You're ghost for now," says Sergeant Bentley, walking toward them at the tree line. "Get back to Argos and stay there."

"There's no way we can leave—"

"I said get ghost!" shouts Sergeant Bentley.

I have never seen nor heard Sergeant Bentley so angry, serious, or stressed. He stares his team down until they turn into the trees for Argos. They are ten paces ahead of him as they walk.

Sergeant Bentley stops a few paces later. "Haze."

He turns back as the others continue. I study his eye cam. Fister is in the distance with several transformed Dah-Sel fighting around him.

Fister's eye cam reveals a moment of Sergeant Bentley heading his way with a sidearm in hand... then his pane fills with snarling teeth.

"They're up to something else," says Chubb.

Nobody responds. I check the drone's visual feed pane.

"What are they doing now?" asks Skedelski from over my shoulder.

Young Dah'Sel atop the structure turn the mirrors skyward again. Moonlight disappears from the reflecting obsidian walls. Transformed Dah'Sel in the structure return to their normal Dah'Sel states.

Their faces hold bewildered expressions. Eyes glancing at one another, looking around to figure out where they are. They do not appear to remember anything that happened during their transformation state.

Dah'Sel near the exit stop and jump away from the moon's shine near its edge. They stand in the shadows and watch their comrades kill each other in the clearing. The transformed Dah'Sel outside continue their rampage, destroying animal pens to get to the living food inside. Their four-legged yeena—as Pru'Cet called them—are the first to get eaten. A pig-like animal with ill-proportionally tiny heads and a single eye are attacked next after their pens of wood and dried mud are destroyed.

Sergeant Bentley is thirty paces out from Fister. He raises his sidearm and prepares to fire.

"They're changing back," says Chubb.

"Confirm," says Sergeant Bentley.

Chubb studies the drone's feed. "Confirmed. They're changing."

Sergeant Bentley studies the scene, halts, and does not fire, but keeps his sidearm raised at the ready.

Fister looks at the three creatures approaching him. Their focus shifts back and forth between him and their desire to fight over his human flesh. They stop to stand over him, but two tear into each other in another blood-spilling fight.

Fister looks into the eyes of the remaining creature and raises his secondary sidearm to his temple. A shot rings out as it tackles him.

23–4
Capture

A pair of Dah'Sel in the structure look to the outside. The creatures, possibly family members, are killing each other. A creature fighting over Fister in the moonlight sees the third trying to eat him through his protective combat gear. It breaks away from the fight and attacks to protect the meal. The third creature approaches him with slow steps, trying not to draw attention from the two now fighting. Its body bleeds from a mess of claw marks. Blood drips from its mouth. It spits a hairy piece of flesh Fister's way as it approaches.

Two Dah'Sel struggle to wheel a large container of soil into view from the back. They pour water into the container. Their hands move fast to mix it into a muddy, slimy, sticky state.

A few Dah'Sel with cloth wrapped around their ears pull ivory horns from the walls. Others are wrapping their heads and ears. I am not sure how many. My only eye to the inside of the structure is what I can see from Fister's Eye-Cam.

The humanoids in the structure rub the mixture onto two of the Dah'Sel until they are coated with it, and the others blow the horns. The sound they release is beautiful, but the creatures around Fister, and all inside the structure without their heads wrapped, cover their ears and fall to the ground in pain.

Fister sees them falling and attempts to stand. He tries to escape but has sustained an injury to his leg and only gets to a knee before collapsing. His Eye-Cam whips visuals on the viewing panes from tree line to structure and back, looking for the rest of his ground team.

The two Dah'Sel covered in the mixture come from the entrance and brave the moonlight without effect, lifting Fister from the ground as those that were killing each other roll around them, clutching their heads in agony.

The unmanned drone flies over the mud-covered Dah'Sel's heads as they drag him into the structure.

"They got Fister," says Chubb.

The horns stop. Those in the clearing's moonlight stand when the sonnet dies and attack each other, along with their livestock, before bolting into the woods.

"What the haze are these things?" asks Sapp. "They're destroying themselves."

"Delgado," says Sergeant Bentley. "We're going to regroup and rendezvous with Athanasios."

Fister looks over his shoulder while they drag him into the structure. No one is coming for him. His squad mates cannot turn their heads from shared eye cams like I can. If the Dah'Sel kill him, they are going to watch him die.

I wipe a few tears from my eyes over Fister, the civilization we have disrupted, and those who have fallen on our actions in this world. None of them… None of us deserves this.

Pru'Cet cries next to me. I look his way as I stand.

"It's okay," I lie. "We're going to figure this out."

"Wazme," he says. "Wazme licea ver takiep seblak pisip?"

"I'm sorry," I answer, knowing only a portion of what he says.

Pru'Cet shakes. He is hurt. Scared. Same as me. I am going to hold him for a moment and listen to the ground team.

They are arguing about what to do for Fister. Everyone is talking at once. It is hard to make out what they are saying.

"All right," Sergeant Bentley's voice raises. "Everybody quiet."

The bickering continues.

"Listen up," he shouts.

They grow silent.

"Now, we can't just go back in there the way we are right now," continues Sergeant Bentley. "There's too many of them. They're too fast and too strong."

"Let's go live," says Sapp.

"I don't think we can do it without risking Fister's life at this point. If they see us coming, they may tear him apart."

"We have to do something," says Bell.

"I feel you," says Chubb. "But we can't just sit here and hope they don't kill him."

"Or eat him," says Morris.

"They're right," says Delgado.

"Doesn't matter. We got a man dying on Athanasios and his cousin having who-knows-what done to him in that structure. We need to stay—"

Dr. Utley's voice sings out in desperation, "Rhigas is—"

A loud impact, shattering glass, and a partial scream cuts him off.

"Dr. Utley?" I ask.

"Everything okay up there, Doctor?" asks Sergeant Bentley.

We wait. He does not respond. I swallow a sinking feeling to find it slithering slowly down my throat.

"I'll go check on him," I say.

"I'll meet you there," says Dr. Wright.

"Okay. I've got Skedelski with me."

"Dr. Sellers," says Sergeant Bentley. "What's your current location?"

"I'm headed for the Med Bay," he answers. "What was all that about?"

"Unknown," answers Sergeant Bentley. "Skedelski, you have point with Mason. Escort her to the others and don't mess about. If something's going on up there... If someone's breached Athanasios, show them what the Armada's about."

Skedelski nods. "Yes, Sergeant Major."

"I'll be topside with a—"

The feed cuts.

"Sergeant?" I wait in silence and turn to Skedelski. Fear pours from my chest, beating its way out. "Let's go check on the doctors."

"I got you, Mason," says Skedelski, ducking under the door.

I take Pru'Cet by the hand and follow him from the surveillance room toward who knows what. If Skedelski were not with me, I remain unsure if I can muster the courage to enter the corridors. I mean, I would, but something does not feel right about this.

We move down vacant passages, but it is going to take a tek to reach the Med Bay. We are trekking all the way to the other side of Athanasios. I am concerned for Dr. Sellers and the others, and these quiet, empty corridors are not helping.

All is still. I cannot stop wondering why we are out of communication with Doctors Utley and Wright. I only know where Dr. Sellers was at last and where he is heading. What is going on? Where are the others? My mind races without a destination as we near the Med Bay.

"Hold up," I say. "I don't know about—"

I rush into a corridor as a man screams out in pain behind us. Flesh is being torn back there. I must keep running.

Bell is sprinting toward us from the opposite end of the corridor and instinctively raises his firearm when he sees us, then lowers it. Pru'Cet surges past me. A loud crash sounds out. A breaking door.

Something is coming after us. It impacts the walls in the corridor as it enters. I hear it, but I am not looking back. Bell hears it and turns, stopping to get out of my way. His eyes inflate with an inhaling a breath of air upon seeing whatever it is behind me. A roar releases.

Skedelski shakes me gently by the shoulders, and I release a partial scream.

"What's wrong?" he asks.

I breathe very fast, as if I have been running away from the suicide fields. My heartbeat matches it. I spin a 180 in panic to look down the corridor behind. Nothing. I turn back to face Skedelski.

Pru'Cet's eyes go back and forth between mine in worry.

"I don't want to be here," I say. "Let's get out of this corridor."

Skedelski and Pru'Cet gaze upon me as if I am crazy, and he huddles behind me.

"Now," I say. "Please."

I follow the big man until flickering lights from within the Med Bay appear around the next corner. Its negative pressure door reserved for surgical procedures shuts part-way and opens repeatedly over the main door. Something is blocking it. Blood lines its edges.

Skedelski comes to a halt and gives me a bass-filled whisper. "What do you think it is?"

"I don't know," I answer.

He looks back toward Med Bay. The surrounding area grows darker as we proceed. Something happened to the power here. Comm station two's door across the way is bent at the top and cracked open. Someone has busted out the frame latch.

Skedelski lumbers to the chopping slide door's frame and stops. His hand goes back, motioning me to remain in place.

He stares into the Med Bay for a moment. "Don't come in here."

I watch him hold the door open and duck under it into flickering lights. I am getting nervous. Whatever is happening, it is dreadful. I cannot take it anymore. Pru'Cet and I are alone in the flickering corridor, looking back and forth down its daring depths.

Darkness. Light. Darkness.

I am discomposing while standing in visual shifts of light and dark with Pru'Cet's death clutch on my arm. He is adding to my nervousness, but I cannot blame him. Athanasios is alien to him, and something terrible is happening onboard that we are not yet aware of.

I move forward with Pru'Cet until I am at the door's frame. Blood comes into view as I enter. Lots of it.

Med Bay's door chops open and closes at nothing. The bed Rhigas once laid in is torn apart. Random splashes of blood line the wall next to it. An unknown force wrecked much of the room's equipment. The surgical door continues chopping.

"Can you please do something about the door?" I ask.

Skedelski grabs and bends it until it jams.

A random piece of equipment is active, with no one to wield it and bouncing about on the floor. It is a complete disaster here. A battle took place. The shelves have been cleared without delicacy, shattered glass fragments are scattered everywhere, and someone... something... forcefully broke the thick windows separating the surgical observation room from the Med Bay.

Skedelski turns back to face me. "Something happened here."

"You think?" I ask. "Mason to Dr. Utley? Dr. Wright?" I pause. "Mason to Dr. Sellers?"

No response. Something must have happened to him. I look to Skedelski, then to Pru'Cet, and back to the big man praying for a delayed response that never comes.

A bashing sound echoes from an unknown location. Our heads whip to the door as if it is upon us. Quietude follows a distant, quivering growl. We turn to each other for answers we do not have.

"What do we do?" asks Skedelski.

"Avoid whatever that was," I answer. "But we need to find the others. I'll check the comms station."

Skedelski ducks under the door and I follow him out, pulling Pru'Cet's hands from my arm and intertwining my fingers with his to lead him out.

"Blight o glotren," he says.

I stop. He holds out his right hand with his palm down. It is shaking.

"Yeah," I say. "I'm scared too."

24-2
Further Investigation

We follow Skedelski a few paces down the corridor. He reaches comms station two's open door and turns back to me for a moment before passing in. I worry about him entering first, but if anybody can handle themselves, it is certainly Skedelski. He once entered the professional Galactic Combat circuit on Kep Four and could not continue competing. Nobody could hurt him, and his strength is the greatest in our world. Skedelski is an anomaly.

I peek my head into comms station two. It doesn't look as damaged as our Med Bay, but it appears rough. Someone knocked the audio intensifier that Morris set up to the floor, the one that all communications were routing through. It is frightening, but at least makes sense of our current inability to communicate with the others.

"Strange," says Skedelski. "They are not in here. Either they—"

A loud bang somewhere in the distance reverberates through corridors with songs of terror. Our heads whip to the door, faces become motionless, breaths twist to shallow states and hearts pause to listen. We are no longer alone on Athanasios.

"Sellers was in the science lab," I say. "Where's your weapon?"

"On the surface," answers Skedelski.

"There's more on Athanasios though, right?"

"Yes. But I need Delgado's, the Sergeant Major's, or overseer's clearance to access the munition hold."

"Armada voice clearance, Mason, five, Sinote, one, four, McKayla, three, six, unlock munitions hold."

"Inferior authority classification," says Athanasios. "Access denied."

"Armada voice clearance, Mason, five, Sinote, one, four, McKayla, three, six, override security clearance protocols to the munitions hold."

"Inferior authority classification. Access denied."

"Great. Mason to Delgado." She does not respond. "Okay. Let's just get to Dr. Sellers and figure it out from—"

A roar of untold magnitude echoes through the ship. My eyes go to Skedelski for assurance, but his reflect the same worry I have in mine.

"Sounds big," says Skedelski.

"Unfortunately," I say.

"You ready?"

I give a lying nod. I am not ready ... unless you count an overwhelming urge to soil my clothes.

"Come on, Pru'Cet," I say, following Skedelski unhappily back into the corridor.

24-3
It

The science lab corridor is silent when we enter. An overhead light sparks. The roar grows closer. A loud bang follows with the clanking of toppling metal.

I stick my head back out the door. My heart stops. A massive thing is before us. It looks like the ones that entered the moonlight only without as much hair. It is patchy with bald spots and big. Really big. Much larger than the others. Larger than Skedelski.

"Uh oh..." I barely say.

It sees me, squares off, and releases another deep roar again. I fall into the lab.

"There's..." I say, getting to my feet. "There's a..."

Several thuds. It is coming for us. I lock the door behind me.

Another door at the back of the lab beyond the tables opens. It is Dr. Utley. Relief fills my veins.

"In here," he says.

Skedelski moves to the entrance door with protective instincts.

"No," I shout. "That thing's..."

My eyes go full open with fear, trying to talk. I cannot. Horror has stolen my words.

"Hurry," says Dr. Wright.

"Go," I say.

We move to Dr. Utley. A thunderous bash vibrates throughout the lab. I turn back. The door is failing us.

Skedelski runs toward it, and the door gives way a step before he slams into it, but he knocks it back shut.

"Go with Utley," says Skedelski.

I hesitate. Creepy entertainment has never been my strong suit. I cannot handle the terror, and this is much worse.

I rush to Dr. Utley and enter the back room, turning back to Skedelski as he fights to hold whatever that thing is at bay. Another impact knocks the big man to the ground. He rolls up into a sprint for us as that thing squeezes in, never taking its eyes off Skedelski.

It rushes across the lab as Skedelski surges through the back door, turns, and drops his butt to the hard flooring. His back slams against fixed shelving units.

"Shut it!" he shouts.

I close the door. Dr. Utley locks it. Skedelski turns to brace his back against it, propping his feet against the shelving. The creature bashes into it, but it does not give with the lock in place and Skedelski bracing it from the ground.

I back away with Pru'Cet, hoping it does not falter. Skedelski gives me a wink. I take a breath of relief.

The bashing stops for a tik, and a twisted roar unlike anything heard before sounds out. The beating recommences. Each time it hits my ears, my blood pressure spikes. It is hard to focus on anything. I do not know what to do.

I glance down to see Dr. Wright on the floor with a serious leg wound puddling blood under a tourniquet. He is Pale and unsteady. He must be lightheaded from loss of blood. Sweat beads on his forehead.

"Are you okay?" I ask.

"No," answers Dr. Utley. "He's not."

Dr. Sellers runs through input codes on a holo-info typesetter as fast as he can. The bashing stops for a tik. Skedelski looks up from the floor. The doctors listen with us.

"Please tell me you're onto something," says Dr. Utley.

"I am," says Dr. Sellers. "There is definitely something in Skedelski's blood that kept what happened to our buddy Rhigas out there from happening to him."

"Rhigas?" I ask.

"Yes," answers Dr. Sellers. "That thing out there is him. At least it used to be. Some molecules, DNA strands, and various other things..." Dr. Sellers points to the pane. "See these cells?" He types quickly. "I just have to isolate the properties that are—"

Another twisted roar clashes into our eardrums. Dr. Sellers stops and looks up for a moment before going back to work. Things are breaking and being tossed about the science lab again.

Skedelski still has his back against the thick door. He stretches out one of his legs for a brief instant and the bashing recommences. Surprise fills his eyes as the force nearly knocks his enormous frame from the door. He repositions himself to hold it fast.

I run my palms over my face in distress, cup my right fist in my left hand, and bite at my thumbnails. "I don't think it's going to hold much longer."

"Let's hope it does," says Dr. Wright.

"I have to get a weapon, or we are going to die in here," I say.

"How?" asks Dr. Wright. "I can't link the overseer with munitions."

"Pretty sure that thing damaged part of Athanasios's O.S.," I say. "But I think I can hack it if I can get to it."

"You think?"

"I can. I just don't know how long it'll take. I'm small. I can get there through the ship's baker-channels."

Dr. Wright looks up to the baker-channel access panel. "Without a baker's suit?"

He is right. It will be hotter than Haze in there, but I must try.

"The engine room's not far from here," I say. "I'll head straight for it and make the rest of the way on foot."

"No," says Dr. Wright. "Not with that thing out there."

I look out the reinforced door's clear lead window. The monster stares at the door Skedelski is holding shut.

"It's in here for now," I say.

"Bad idea, Mason," says Dr. Sellers.

"Agreed," says Dr. Utley.

"Well," I pause. "I'm the only one here small enough to move quickly through the baker-channels. You're out of your minds if you think I'm going to sit in here until that thing eats one of us, and I'm sure as haze not going in there to escape and watch you die if it gets in. I can do this."

"Maybe," says Dr. Wright. "But we won't have a way of letting you know if it leaves the science lab."

"The overseer," I say. "Give it to me."

"It won't reach ground team through the upper atmosphere."

"It can crack and hack the cams on Athanasios," I say. "I can open the munitions hold with it. Activate it and give it to me."

"Armada law states that—"

"Just give me the damn thing already. We're two-point-five million light cycles from the Armada and a fricking ... something's trying to kill us. Give it to me."

He looks to Dr. Utley to receive a nod, then cuts his attention to Dr. Sellers.

"I hate to say it," says Dr. Sellers. "But I think she's right."

Dr. Wright unclasps the overseer and puts it on my left arm. It tightens down to match my smaller bone structure. My forearm grows warm.

"Don't let us down," says Dr. Wright. "Armada voice clearance Wright, three, Zinto, eight, two, William, three, transfer operational clearance to P.F.C. McKayla Mason."

The overseer activates with a dim hue.

"You need to accept it," he says. "Your voice clearance. Final input—accept overseer operational clearance transfer."

I wrap my right palm around it. "Armada voice clearance Mason, five, Sinote, one, four, McKayla, three, six, accept overseer operational clearance transfer."

Its lights go black.

"Ah." I shake my arm.

"Stings when it bio taps, doesn't it?" asks Dr. Wright.

I climb up without another word said and remove the baker-channel access panel, handing it to Dr. Wright. An echoing impact forces a jump from me when the creature bashes into the door again.

"Go," says Skedelski.

I nod and head in.

"Mason," calls Dr. Sellers.

I turn back.

"Watch out for exposed electrical lines," he continues. "We haven't run inspections since Athanasios went down in the Ein-Rosen bridge."

I eye them for a moment before moving into the hot crawl ahead. Skedelski's eyes are that of fear for my safety, and he will not take them off me. This is either a brilliant idea or suicide. Hopefully, the former.

I am making my way through the baker-channel with warming knees and palms, distracting me from the hot-wiring smell. It is hotter than I expected. Then again, I have never been inside a baker-channel before. It is cylindrical with a small foot-width grading on the bottom side of it to scurry upon. Nobody of reasonable size could navigate this thing without putting their feet on the hot hard-wiring encasing or bumping against its top side.

It gets darker as I move further from the science lab. I stop to think. "Activate overseer to visual feed, motion detection parameters."

My gained overseer activates to project a hand-sized three-dimensional image of the Med Bay over my forearm. Static washes over it. It is not what I was hoping for but gives me enough light to see what I am doing in here.

An upcoming turn on my right is going to be my first of two when I get to it. Subtle noises I cannot make out send me to freeze in place. Something is in here with me. I turn to look back the best I can, holding the overseer just out of eyesight to have a clear visual and light the area behind me.

Four Dah'Sel stand guard under turquoise candlelight mounted into a stone wall. They flicker in the room with a

beautiful ambiance that does not match the scene. Fister is on his knees in a primitive holding cell. He has been badly beaten and is not doing well.

Pru'Cet's mother enters and kneels in front of him, slapping Fister across the face when he looks up. "Likiedasno!" She breaks into a heavy, emotional cry. "Pru'Cet, mabap ot en fit."

She is amid a hard fight against the four Dah'Sel guards struggling to remove her from Fister's cell.

"Blight hasta en fit!" She shouts.

One of the Dah'Sel looks back at Fister while dragging her away, as she screams the same thing over and over.

"Blight hasta en fit! Blight hasta en fit! Blight hasta en Pru'Cet ledasno-zim!"

Pru'Cet shoves my arm.

A screech slips from my lips when I jump. "You scared me."

I take a tek to compose myself. Truth be told, I am glad he snapped me out of it. My hands and knees are burning. I must have been out of it for a tek.

Pru'Cet smiles the widest adolescent grin he can muster when I motion him to follow me. I make it only a few paces and stop to lie on my back for a moment. My hands and knees need a break from the heat. He copies my action and lies on his back behind me at my feet. His eyes question my actions before looking around the baker-channel.

"Give me a tik," I say, waving my hands to cool them off. "You should have stayed in there with the others."

"Utlu ot fesnop?" asks Pru'Cet.

He must be curious about something, but I am unsure what. I find his language simple, yet difficult to comprehend with connective pieces of it missing from my vocabulary. Of the words he spoke, I only understood "*fesnop*," which means "*this.*"

I raise my head to look over my chest, stomach, and terra boots to see what he is talking about. Pru'Cet is reaching up toward the baker-channel's ceiling. My eyes go up. He is about to grab a burned, finger-width cable.

"No," I say, changing to his language to ensure he understands. "Ma, ma, ma."

He looks at me, and I shake my head. Pru'Cet's arm lowers back to his side. There is no way to tell if it would have hurt him or not. I see no exposed wires from where I am at. Better safe than sorry.

"Don't touch anything in here," I say.

He looks over his shoulders at me from his back.

"Ma vasika-zic," I continue, motioning to everything around us. "Ma vasika-zic."

Pru'Cet does not understand. He knows what I said, but nothing in here appears dangerous to him besides the heat. Haze, I do not know all the dangers in here.

I roll back over and continue crawling. "Come on."

Sweat beads my forehead as we near the upcoming junction. I stop when we reach it. The wider area of the baker-channels ahead is something I am going to take advantage of. I turn to sit on my rear for a moment. My hands and knees need another break from the heat. They are burning, and getting blisters would only slow me down. It will not help for long. My rear is burning. I need to get out of here.

25-2
Rescue?

The overseer's visual feed shifts to an exterior shot from Athanasios. An incoming shuttle reaches visual feed range above the turbulent atmosphere on the planet below. Its hull burns against the atmosphere as it ascends, only to cool off once breaking free from it and entering cooler regions of space.

"Overseer," I say, "switch visual to internal shuttle feed."

The vessel's pilot and passengers come into view. It is Sergeant Bentley. Bell and Morris are with him. The signal blinks out and stops.

"Sergeant Major," I say.

No answer.

"Bell?" I continue. "Morris?"

Pru'Cet watches me hide the worry from my face, knowing I am doing it for him. He is intelligent, that is for certain. He understands the circumstances and knows what it is doing to me.

The overseer should be able to cycle through various parts of Athanasios. A better grasp of what we are dealing with here will be helpful, and I would like to know if there are more of those things on board with us.

"Cycle Athanasios visual feeds," I say. "Various."

Some areas are in a trashed state, presumably because of that thing that used to be Rhigas. Others have remnants of conflict that most likely happened while Dr. Utley struggled to help the critically injured Dr. Wright reach the science lab to join Dr. Sellers. Several areas of the ship are eerily unscathed. Many have no signal or reveal nothing more than static. Silence fills them all.

"Toggle feeds to the shuttle bay," I say, crawling through the baker-channel, shifting the placement of my palms to prevent them from further burning.

There are no signs of life as the massive bay doors close behind Sergeant Bentley's shuttle. It comes to rest. Brackets on the floor clamp them into position to power down safely. Sergeant Bentley, Morris, and Bell exit the craft with curious expressions, unaware of what has happened on Athanasios.

"Where's the welcoming party?" asks Morris. "You piss Mason and the doctors off, Bell?"

"Bentley to Dr. Wright," says Sergeant Bentley. "Dr. Wright? Sellers?" He paces for a moment and stops. "Sergeant Bentley to anyone."

"Sergeant Major," I say. "It's Mason. Can you hear me?"

He turns to Bell and Morris. "Let's get changed out and catch up with the others."

They strip away their phase suits and continue without knowing I am trying to communicate with them.

Morris walks to a comm station and activates its manual input option. A glass pane rolls out with an options menu. He selects:

FORWARD

"Dr. Wright?" he asks.

The image on the screen remains black. He moves back to the options menu and selects:

SHIPWIDE CALL

"Morris to Athanasios," he says. "Anyone copy?"

"Looks like comms are down," says Bell.

They move into the cabin area. It is still and void of life. The men look around for clues under high caution.

"Open comms while we change," says Sergeant Bentley.

Morris steps to the cabin control feed and selects:

HOLD OPEN CHANNEL

The cabin is still. Quiet. Sergeant Bentley notices the cargo bay's communication system flashing green words across its pane:

ANSWER CARGO BAY CALL?

He answers the call. Static.

It flashes periodically with a simultaneous beep as the men move through the cabin.

"Dr. Wright?" calls Sergeant Bentley.

They enter the ship's forward.

"Mason?" he continues.

"Where the haze is everybody?" asks Morris.

Bell climbs up to my cockpit door and opens it. "It's empty. I can't say I'm feeling too comfortable about this." He turns with tight, squinted, thinking eyes to Sergeant Bentley and Morris.

Sergeant Bentley sees Dr. Wright's comm link and vital bands lying on the console. "Neither am I." He picks them up, and his comm link lights up to match Dr. Wright's.

"Comm link test..." says Bell.

Sergeant Bentley turns to face him and shakes his head. "It's not coming through."

"I'll try to get everything back up once we figure out what's going on here," says Morris.

"Go ahead," says Sergeant Bentley. "Get on it."

They move into Athanasios's forward. Morris pulls up the monitors on the forward screen. He shifts the feeds through room after room, but they are absent of life. He turns to Sergeant Bentley, eyes wide with unease, and shifts through a few more locations.

"Wait," says Sergeant Bentley. "Go back."

The image returns to the previous one, a small fitness room with half its equipment toppled.

"Is that blood?" asks Morris.

"Where?" Bell eases over to look.

"Push in," says Sergeant Bentley.

Morris guides the feed to zoom in. What may or may not be a smear of blood is visible at its edge in darkness, but the feed is not stable. Static laces it.

"Hard to tell what we're looking at here with the feed acting up," says Morris.

"Keep looking," says Sergeant Bentley.

Morris shifts over a few more feeds as I crawl rapidly through the baker-channel with Pru'Cet—hands and knees burning.

Morris reaches a black image.

"What room's that?" asks Sergeant Bentley.

"Med Bay," answers Morris. "No signal." He sifts through a few working feeds before coming to another blank one. The main comms station he modified comes into view. It seems like everything is broken or slashed to haze and back. "That explains the comm issue." He continues searching. "Science lab's down as well. So is the quarantine room."

"Okay," says Sergeant Bentley. "Enough of this. You check the science lab and quarantine area. Bell, get to Med Bay. I'm going to head for the munitions hold and grab some gear."

"Good," I say to myself. "I'll meet you there."

I do not know if the others I left behind are still alive, if that thing is still in there with them, or if they are in the science lab at all at this point. At least Skedelski is there with them, but Sergeant Bentley and the others have no clue what they are walking into.

"Ah," I say, scowling through burning pain. "Hurry, Pru'Cet."

It is getting hotter in here by the tik. As we approach the engine room, I feel increasingly like we are being cooked alive. I roll to my back for an instant, but not long. The skin on my face feels like fire. Pru'Cet cannot keep his palms and knees on the baker-channel flooring any longer. He moves them up and down in quick succession—the scent of burning hair.

Burning hands and knees hasten me into a crawling sprint through the baker-channel until I reach the engine room. Its grate is on my left. I need to open it to get out of here. My face scrunches like a firecat crossing a hot steel roof as I pry its corner to open it.

The grate holds fast, preventing me from removing it. I lean my back against the large hard-wire lines to push it open with my feet. Red streaks burn a left-to-right run into my back.

"Ahhhhh..." I shriek out in pain with a push.

Pru'Cet pushes it with his shoulder to help. We scream through the agony. Pressing... Straining until it pops off and clanks loudly onto the engine room's metallic flooring. Pru'Cet falls in with it. I surge headfirst into the engine room behind him and land hard.

25–3
Engine Room

I hop up to fan the back of my shirt. Pru'Cet is still on the ground. His hands, feet, and knees have singed hairs to the point he is partially bald in the areas. He rubs them as I shed my pants down to my shins for a moment to fan my knees. They are bright red but not as damaged as my hands, which are near the point of blistering.

My nose crinkles at the scent of burning flesh and alien hair.

"Pru'Cet," I ask, "are you okay?"

He picks himself off the floor and taps his chest as if he saved the rotation.

"Alright then," I say. "Let's get to the munitions hold."

The engine room is a breath of fresh air. Not the smell. It stinks like burned fabric and hair in here as I wipe sweat from my face, but the air is cool on my skin.

We move beyond damp, pink, cloth-like, odd-shaped engines resembling tubes. The external design of these engines casts the perception that they are kinked and melting in several places. Their centers alternate to pulse waves of golden glows. Their technology and architecture are one behemoth of human accomplishment.

Pru'Cet glowers over it. "Friveka."

"I know," I say. "Only one of its kind." I watch him for a tik. "Come."

He does not move.

"Kuzsoec, Pru'Cet," I say. "Kuzsoec."

He moves to my side, eyeing the wavering engines as he walks. Then, he freezes. Pru'Cet knows something I do not.

"What is it?" I ask.

The roar. It sounds out again. The creature is close.

I check my overseer. The thing is in a corridor a few over from our location. It is probably hungry. Or just angry. I doubt it would turn down a McKayla and Pru'Cet sandwich. I am hoping to stay off the menu as we ease through the next door toward the munitions hold.

The corridor is ghastly in aura. I can physically feel trepidation settling on my skin. Hyperventilation is imminent if I do not regain control. I concentrate on steadying my nerves. Pru'Cet takes my hand again.

Each step is a nightmare waiting to happen. The thought of breathing loudly scares me. My lungs shake with each passing step.

I peek around the corners of the first intersection we come to. The area is empty. Our destination is a few more paces ahead and to the left. I pull Pru'Cet through the dark corridor with quick steps. It is the longest in the ship and provides a great vantage point for being seen by whatever that thing is hunting us down.

The doors are just ahead on our right. We are almost there. Just a few more...

A snarl of heavy reverberation rips through the corridor. I spin a quick 180 to see it at the far end of the passage. It wastes no time rushing toward us with heavy, thudding feet.

"Kuzsoec," I shout.

Getting into the munitions hold is going to have to wait. That thing is coming, and I am one hundred percent sure it is not coming for dinner, unless I am that dinner. Pru'Cet is babbling about something, but I do not have time to pay him any mind. We rush into a storage bay.

A gray, empty, organic food crate on our left... I go for it and waste no time straining to flip it, but I cannot move it enough to get it to topple. Pru'Cet grabs it and helps dump it over. We move to the other side of it to pull it on top of us.

The edge of the crate lands on the bumper lining the walls at their base. It leaves a half-hand gap between the floor and crate on one end of it, but I cannot adjust it. That thing will hear or see us and know what part of the cluttered room we are in if I do.

The creature's steps have slowed, but it is still coming. I can hear its footsteps—its breathing. Its drool splatters the floor upon its death march.

"Power down overseer," I whisper.

It powers down to emit no light source as it nears. There is nothing for us to do but hide. We are trapped ... and I can smell its musk approaching us.

Pru'Cet peeks from underneath the empty crate we over-turned upon ourselves against the wall. He puts his fingers together like a karate chop to his mouth and motions for me to stay quiet, as if I did not know.

That snarling beast... Its adrenalizing breaths... The thing comes partially into view, and I place my hands over my mouth. I shutter my breathing and lean back. A thin line of light shines over my right eye through one of the crate's cracks. A terrified tear rolls down my cheek and into my mouth. Salt is the taste of fear.

Something breaks. No idea what. It sounded like something destroyed in one of the other rooms fell over. The sound of arching electrical currents...

The creature moves through the area we are hiding in and makes its way to the back of it, moving some sixty paces away. It is angry without reason. Another roar... It smashes a few unseen items. Sergeant Bentley, Bell, and Morris should be equipped with weapons.

Morris enters the storage hold we are hiding in, turning toward the beast. It is looking for something. Anything it can kill and possibly eat.

"Sergeant Major," says Morris. "We have a problem."

The nasty thing turns to face Morris and snarls, flipping a few crates into the air. Pru'Cet and I lift the crate concealing us and dart across the room. It charges.

"Morris!" I shout.

He opens fire. I look its way long enough to wish I had not and scream. The riddle-effect the rifle has does not slow its advance. It pushes through toward Morris with heightened rage.

"Bell," says Sergeant Bentley.

"Meet you there," says Bell.

We tear into the corridor and bounce off its inner wall. I slip and catch my balance. My turnover in stride is faster than it has ever been.

More gunshots... Morris screams out behind us. Flesh tearing is a horrid sound, especially when it involves a person you know—someone you have just abandoned and left to die.

Bell runs toward us from the other direction and instinctively raises his firearm when he sees us, then lowers it. Pru'Cet—who is apparently much faster than me—overtakes my position and runs ahead. This is further unsettling. I am going to be the first of us to get eaten.

A loud crash makes it worse. I force myself to look back. It busted down the door and will soon be in the hall behind me.

Pru'Cet nears Bell on a collision course, but Bell dips to his side so my young Dah'Sel friend can blow past him.

"What the..." says Bell.

The creature impacts both sides of the corridor walls when it enters. I hear it, but I am not looking back again. Bell's eyes grow huge with an inhaling breath of air when he sees it chasing me. Another roar releases as I close the gap between us.

"Run!" I scream, running to and pass him in a desperate sprint.

"Holy Armada," he says.

"Don't shoot!" I continue. "Just run!"

Thuds. Footsteps. Fast ones.

I turn to look back once I am past Bell and near the entrance to the records room at the end of the corridor. The beast is coming for us and carrying Morris's limp, flailing body with it. It is a colossus thing, bigger than I remember it being. It is still hairy in some areas, yet it is bald in others—a terrifying, deformed sight that is still growing and changing.

It stops and drops Morris's body when it sees Bell, letting it splat on the floor at its feet. Bell volleys a few shots at it with no effect. The creature releases a growl and beats back and forth between the corridor's walls. Bell fires again, and it surges our way—death coming for us.

I wait at the end of the corridor for him, ready to close the security door and lock myself in the mission records room at its end.

"Come on," I shout.

Pru'Cet is jumping up and down behind me. "Bleku, Bleku, Bleku."

It is too fast. The gap between it and Bell is closing as if he were not running away at all. He will not make it. That thing is about to grab him, and I am going to have to shut the door on him before he gets here.

"Bell..." I whisper, knowing he will not make it.

The creature is on him. It grabs the back of Bell's uniform and stops him in his tracks next to an adjacent corridor.

"Close the door, Mason," says Bell.

I reach for the close button and pause when a deep-toned scream of aggression shoots from the intersecting side corridor. Skedelski comes into view with his head lowered and slams into the beast under a full sprint with terrible force. The creature's feet lift to become airborne with its body, and they hit the wall.

"Don't close it," says Bell, running into the records room with me.

Skedelski and the monster fall into the other corridor and out of sight. Snarling. Grunting. The sound of scuffling.

They fall from the connecting passage and to the floor in front of us again. It beats Skedelski to his feet, knocking him down with a clawing strike that runs a river of blood from his face and shoulder. It steps to get on top of him, but Skedelski gets a foot under him and launches from the floor, grabbing it in the air and slamming down on top of it. Beast vs beast.

It rolls to its stomach in front of Skedelski, who wraps his arms around its back, but it rises and charges forward with the big man hanging off its shoulders until it tumbles down several paces from us. A ferocious scramble for supremacy takes place as Skedelski's speed, power, and technique matches the creature's chaotic movements for a stalemate, until it powers itself to its feet.

Skedelski spins to its back for a rear body lock as it stands, arching into a series of belly-to-back suplexes that steer it head-first into the hard flooring behind him. It tries to break loose, but Skedelski's grip is that of legend.

The beast forces back up again. Skedelski drives it stomach first into the corridor walls, squeezing with all his might, screaming in strain. Bones crack, and the creature wails out in pain before reaching down to rip at one of Skedelski's ankles, causing them to lose balance and fall again.

Skedelski goes to reposition, but blood rushing from his ankle now matches his face and shoulder. His Achilles tendon is severed. He falls when he puts weight on it, and the creature gets on top of him, biting, clawing, and ripping up Skedelski.

Bell fires a volley. It wounds the massive creature, but not enough to prevent it from standing and facing us. Skedelski pulls himself up the wall. Anger and hate twist his face—something I did not know he had in him.

"Wrong guy," says Skedelski. "Wrong rotation."

It turns to face him as Skedelski plants all his weight on his good foot. His teeth grit to the point of crushing in on themselves. Power surges up through his thick leg, into twisting hips, through a tensed torso rocking forward with near fictitious ferocity, across a rolling shoulder, and down a massive arm to accumulate in his fist as stored energy dying to be released. The punch sounds like a 15-pace slab of flat steel hitting the surface of still water when it lands. The beast crumples to the ground like a wet cloth as the big man falls past it as the shot echoes throughout Athanasios.

Skedelski stands with the creature and grabs its leg to pick it up, but it twists and slashes him again. The big man pins it to the wall, fighting on a single leg. It cuts at him. He attempts to take control of its arms, but it is too fast for him.

Bell fires a few more rounds until the weapon runs dry and stops, but the rounds shift Skedelski's weight to his injured ankle and he falls. He has sustained serious injuries, and we cannot offer help.

"Hey!" I shout. "Over here!"

It looks my way for a brief instance. So does Skedelski. We lock eyes, and the look on his face... He does not want to let us down and rises long enough to hit it with a thunderous uppercut that sends it up, off its feet, and into the wall at an odd angle. The monster takes several heavy blows from Skedelski until a right hook on its snout buckles it like a fighter that has taken one too many shots. The big man limps in to finish the job, but it lunges off the corridor wall, driving our protector into the opposite side of their battle-zone.

It roars as it rises and grabs Skedelski by the head and face, driving the back of his head into the wall, stunning, and pinning him to it. The beast's mouth opens large enough to fit Skedelski's entire head into it. He strains to hold it back, but it is black with rage.

Bell steps into the area behind me, looking around for something. For anything. "We need some help here, Sergeant Major."

"Almost there," says Sergeant Bentley.

Bell moves back into view of the corridor, pulls his T-blade (a tactical combat slicing and piercing tool with an electric charge), and takes a few steps in as Skedelski strains—arms shaking to hold it back.

Skedelski turns to face us. "Run..." He buckles on his severed Achilles tendon.

The creature pulls him from the wall when his body drops, lifts him, and slams him back into it. He fights to hold the beast back, but it opens its nasty mouth a click wide and forces it toward Skedelski's head.

"Bell," pleads Skedelski. "Run."

Bell moves in and stabs it in the ribs. It cries out as it backhands Bell, sending him across the floor to my feet without abandoning his attack on Skedelski.

Bell, dazed from the blow, looks back toward our protector, who tries to hold the monster at bay with shaking arms. His veins swell to the point of bursting with pressure. It is no use. The beast's mouth engulfs Skedelski's head.

He looks our way again. "Ruuuuun!"

Bell takes off with me as a loud crunch fills our ears and nearly collapses me. He shuts the door behind us.

"Ahhhhh!" I stop to go back. "No!"

"No," says Bell, grabbing and pulling me into him. "No, Mason."

The creature roars as Bell drags me away screaming and crying.

"Bell," calls Sergeant Bentley. "Where are you?"

"There's..." says Bell, over my shouts and struggling to control me. "There's something in the—"

Bell drags me further into the records room and shuts the door behind him and Pru'Cet. I am still struggling. Not thinking right. Tears flow down my cheeks with salty emotion.

More bashing against the door that Bell shut behind us. Each hit from the monster after us causes a small portion of it to concave. It is coming for us.

"Cargo bay," shouts Bell. "Main entrance compromised."

"I'm close," says Sergeant Bentley. "Going to engage."

The bashing continues.

"Negative," says Bell. "I couldn't hurt it."

"Armed from munitions."

"I wouldn't—"

Shots ring out from behind the door as the creature bashes it again. It is about to come through and be all over us. I take several steps back and look for Pru'Cet. He is nowhere to be found.

Shots ring out as the door gives way, sending it stumbling through and to the ground beside us. We scream and take cover when the door falls with the beast on top of it.

Sergeant Bentley stands on the other side of the door in a B.G.C.S. (Blast Grade Combat Suit—the toughest in the industry of war designed for battlefields where air strikes and mines are in heavy use.). The creature is between us, five paces from my face, and looks down at me.

I back up with quick steps and fall into the corner of the shelving unit where digi-records are kept. It roars with a few steps toward me and stops to stare. Its eyes... There is something about them—as if Rhigas is still in there somewhere. If so, he is no longer in control, and this thing wants us all dead.

"Hey," shouts Bell.

It turns to face Bell as Sergeant Bentley slides a weapon to his feet and opens fire again. The creature is bleeding badly but turns and attacks Sergeant Bentley.

"Full shields," says Sergeant Bentley.

A metallic face shield wraps his head at the last tik, forcing the creature to bite the bending metal while on top of him.

Bell unloads into the creature's back, to no avail. He walks up to it and fires the last few rounds into the side of its thick head. The beast nearly falls and whines out in pain as Bell's gun clicks empty.

It attacks Sergeant Bentley again.

Bell steps back and looks at his weapon.

"Watch out," shouts Dr. Sellers, setting down a tub of white powder.

He pushes past Bell, stabbing a pair of huge syringes—one red, one green—into the creature's back at a 45 degree angle so the long needles meet under the surface of its skin. He depresses the plungers, mixing their contents together in the beast and boiling the area beneath them. It screams out and rolls on the records room floor ground in agony.

"Get away from it," says Dr. Sellers. "Get back."

The boiling spot spreads, liquefying the creature as it rolls about in pain and spreads the chemical, melting anything it touches.

The creature rolls on top of Sergeant Bentley as he tries to get up, pinning him again. His suit is smoking. The chemical mixture has splashed onto it. Bell snatches him up when the beast rolls off him, and they run further into the cargo bay next to me while it dissolves, releasing a horrifying sound I could not explain with a thousand cycles to do it.

Sergeant Bentley tries desperately to get out of his suit. It is melting. Dr. Sellers grabs the tub he entered with and dumps its white powder on the melting areas. The melting ceases.

Corrosive acid and strange blood-mixed fumes fill the air. We cover our noses, trying to shield ourselves from the vomit-inducing smell.

"We might want to move over here," says Dr. Sellers. "That stuff's pretty toxic."

We move to the other side of the room.

"Where the haze were you ten teks ago?" asks Sergeant Bentley.

"Cracking the serum code," answers Dr. Sellers.

Bell activates a ventilation system to suck out the toxic air. I take my first breath and wipe tears from my face. A sniffle escapes me.

26-2
Darts

Sergeant Bentley turns to the melted pile of whatever the haze that thing was on the ground and eases back to us. "Where's Dr. Utley?"

Dr. Sellers shakes his head. "He didn't make it."

Sergeant Bentley's face drops. His head lowers.

I do not know how Dr. Utley met his end. I do not want to know.

"Morris was looking for us when he..." I say, holding back tears that break my ability to speak.

"Morris is...?"

I nod. "And... And Skedel... Sk..."

"Skedelski saved my life," says Bell. "He saved all our lives."

Sergeant Bentley's face goes blank as he takes it all in.

"Dr. Utley," says Dr. Sellers, "Morris, and Skedelski. They are all gone."

Pru'Cet drops from the shelving unit housing Athanasios's schematics, digi-books, and files of all types, knocking a few off. Sergeant Bentley grabs his sidearm. I position myself between them so he cannot fire.

"Mason?" Sergeant Bentley's expression signals confusion through shifting eyes.

"Kuzsoec," I say.

Pru'Cet eases my way as I motion him closer.

"His name's Pru'Cet," I say.

"Baklee yataat woo ca," says Pru'Cet with fearful eyes.

"He thinks you're going to hurt him," I say. "Or something close to that. I think."

Sergeant Bentley looks to Dr. Sellers for an answer. "How?"

"Too much to explain, Sergeant Major."

"And Rhigas? Did he pull through?"

"That thing we just killed..."

"It killed Rhigas?" asks Bell.

"No," answers Dr. Sellers. "That was Rhigas."

"What?" asks Sergeant Bentley, head cocking in disbelief. "What about Dr. Wright?"

"Sitting on a stool in the gene lab making batches of darts with a counteragent in them. His leg's hurt pretty bad, but he'll recover."

"All right," Sergeant Bentley pauses. "I know we can't disregard the fallen, but we have a man to rescue and people on Kep Four to save. We'll pay their respects soon. I promise this to all of you." He turns to Dr. Sellers. "How are we going to do it, doctor?"

"With these," says Dr. Wright.

He limps in, pushing several boxes of thumb-sized, dart-tipped projectiles on a cart. Half are black. Half are white.

"You're not supposed to be on that leg yet," says Dr. Sellers.

Dr. Wright looks down at his leg. It is wrapped in an azure, rubbery, gel-like compound.

"It'll be fine," he says, turning to face everyone. "When you load these, they need to be alternated. One white. One black. The compound will fuse under the skin to take effect. Keep your shots tight. Two round bursts."

"You heard him," says Sergeant Bentley. "Drop the live mags and hook in tranq receptors for the darts. Maximum capacity." He glances at Dr. Wright while loading them. "How long will these darts need to take effect, because those things are going to rip us apart when we go after Fister."

"They're charged with a shock, that upon impact—"

"Tried the shock thing once—"

"If you'll hear me out, Sergeant Major," cuts Dr. Sellers. "I've set them in sequence with the electrical impulse frequency that runs through their nervous systems. Once the charge is released, the compound should begin mixing and neutralize the transformation process they undergo, just as it did in Skedelski. Should happen fast. Technically, they will still be infected for a short time, but their nervous system will be blocked and prevent the change while the cure works on eradicating their symptoms."

"How did you find this?" asks Sergeant Bentley.

"It's complicated," answers Dr. Sellers. "Short answer, it had something to do with the bite on Skedelski's finger he received from that flying insect and how it reacted with the compound he took for the congenital analgesia disorder he suffered from."

"Are you sure it'll work?"

"It's why Skedelski didn't share Rhigas's experience," he answers. "It should also render them non-contiguous once administered."

"I have a better question," interjects Dr. Wright. "Are you sure you can rescue Fister?"

"No," answers Sergeant Bentley. "But we need to try."

Dr. Wright nods.

"I'm coming with Pru'Cet," I say.

"Negative," says Sergeant Bentley. "You're staying here."

I look at the dissolved thing on the floor. "I can promise you that will not happen."

"Mason—"

"And Pru'Cet wants to go home."

"Sorry," says Sergeant Bentley.

"O blight ledasno-zic ti'it Lesdelop ti'it renasa?" says Pru'Cet.

I am not sure about that one. He said something about home. I am sure he wants to return surface-side.

"Tirqesa, Pru'Cet," I say.

Pru'Cet grows louder with me. I understand why he is upset and try to reason with him through broken dialect. We are bickering. I am emotional. It is turning into an argument, and I am no longer trying to speak in his language. He is yelling at me in his, and I am returning fire in ours.

"She communicates with them better than we can," says Dr. Wright, "and he likes her. It may be the key to doing this peacefully."

We get louder in our blindly firing debate.

"Okay," says Sergeant Bentley. "Okay..."

We grow quiet.

Sergeant Bentley sighs. "You can come, but don't leave Argos unless I say so. Got it?"

"Yes, Sergeant Major." I nod.

"Utlu ka ohrap pes-zic?" asks Pru'Cet.

I motion from the ship to the planet below. "Lessdelop." I shake my head, looking for the right words. "Uhm..." I pull Pru'Cet to a video feed with his planet on it, gesturing from him to the planet as I speak. "Lessdelop."

Pru'Cet smiles.

"I'll set the ship to auto-orbit until we get back," says Dr. Wright.

"You're hurt," says Sergeant Bentley. "You stay on Athanasios."

"I'm sorry, Sergeant Major," says Dr. Wright. "This time, I'll have to pull rank on you. I'm the commanding officer on Expedition Anchor. This problem is mine to solve as much as it is yours."

"Understood." Sergeant Bentley bumps boots with Bell. "Let's load up and get Fister."

I t is not long before we are at our landing site near the original base camp. We remained silent during our descent. It was tense at best with all we have lost and suffering to come.

Rhigas is no longer with us. If he had known that his last moments were spent trying to kill his squad mates and friends, it would have crushed him. Perhaps he knew. Some small part of him could have remained trapped within the beast he became, helpless to do anything but watch from within as he killed those who wanted to save him.

I desire it not to be the case, but I cannot think positively with him gone, Morris fallen, and Dr. Utley—our best medical doctor—lost to the tragic situations that have unfolded since we arrived in Andromeda. To top things off, the Dah'Sel still think Pru'Cet is a captive hostage, and they have Fister in their clutches. I do not want to be the one to tell him about his cousin ... if we can get him out of there alive.

I am watching his Eye-Cam while Delgado transports us to the structure in Argos. We all are. We want to help our Expedition Anchor comrade but believe it is impossible without further loss of lives. Pru'Cet's Dah'Sel sect has suffered more than us in this unintentional fallout, and none of us are sure whether we can reason with them at this point.

The land, sky, and everything else about this planet are beautiful, though I pay it no mind on the ride to Fister. An occasional bump lets me know I am still in a transport, but I cannot get my concerns off what lies ahead. For now, all I can do is watch Fister's Eye-Cam and have faith the Dah'Sel do not kill him before we arrive.

They stripped Fister to his undergarments and tied him to a pole. Severe gashes from the creature attacking him left him weak—blood has been lost. He appears dehydrated when glancing at the reflective walls and struggles to hold himself up.

There are four Dah'Sel standing guard over our comrade. A turquoise candlelight mounted on a stone wall flickers in the room with a charming ambiance that does not match the scene.

Pru'Cet's mother enters and kneels in front of him, slapping Fister across the face when he looks up. "Likiedasno!" She breaks into a heavy, emotional cry. "Pru'Cet... Mabap ot en fit."

A nearby Dah'Sel grabs and pulls her back.

She removes a large, paper-like object from her pocket and unfolds it—a brilliantly detailed drawing of her, Pru'Cet, and his father—as she cries. "Ama e'o en whattka. En Armona. En beLa!"

Fister lowers his head in shame and sadness. More Dah'Sel step in to drag the upset mother from the room.

"Bea ca, Nala'Cet," says an elder Dah'Sel, stepping into view adorned with exotic furs and bones. "Nala'Cet. Kuzsoec."

Kuzsoec... I know that one. It means *to come.* Nala'Cet must be the name of Pru'Cet's mother. Perhaps the *'Cet* in their name represents their family's bloodline?

She fights hard against those removing her from the hold. "Blight hasta en whattka ledasno-zim, Wat'Uza!"

I recognize only the word whattka in that sentence, which means *family*. She shouts it again. Wild arm movements signal her distressed, terrified emotions for Pru'Cet. Wat'Uza may be their elder and leader's name. I am unsure what they label him as, but it is transparent that he is in charge.

One of the Dah'Sel looks back at Fister while they drag her away, and she screams the same thing repeatedly.

"Ohrap hasta crez whattka ledasno! Ohrap hasta crez whattka ledasno! Ohrap hasta crez whattka ledasno!"

Her last shout is more of a cry than anything else and hard to understand as we come to a stop. I wipe a tear from my eye. Nobody else needs to see it. I am unsure whether the others understand yet, but they will soon.

"Delgado," says Sergeant Bentley. "You, Chubb, and Mason stay here. Bell and Dr. Wright, you're coming with me."

"Splendid," says Dr. Wright with sarcasm.

Sergeant Bentley studies him for a tik. "You have the authority to say no."

"No," says Dr. Wright. "I want to come, but I'm as unsure of how all this is going to go as everyone else is."

"If you let me go with you..." I clear a lump from my throat to speak. "I can—"

"This isn't a discussion, Mason," interjects Sergeant Bentley. "Stay in Argos."

27–2

Hopeful Approach

We pull to a stop one hundred paces from the enormous structure. A group of young Dah'Sel stand guard in the moonlight near its entrance. Their heads lean into one another for whispers as they ease closer to the building's ingress.

"Look alive, ground team," says Sergeant Bentley.

Delgado opens the Argos doors.

The young Dah'Sel guarding their structure shout when they see us. Two of them run into the structure. The others point their spears our way with brave intent.

Ground team exits and makes their way across the field toward the stone structure, leaving me, Delgado, Chubb, and Pru'Cet in Argos to watch.

"Everyone on burst?" asks Sergeant Bentley.

The squad double-checks their onium rifles.

Bell watches the others finish checking their firearms. "We're good to go."

The team lines up outside of Argos and moves toward the new world's inhabitants with cautious steps to appear non-threatening. Sergeant Bentley and Bell are at point and less than fifteen paces into their march before the young Dah'Sel reach a point they can no longer remain still.

The young ones shake their spears. One acts as if he is ready to launch it Sergeant Bentley's direction like a javelin.

"Icci aday," shouts the young Dah'Sel on the right. "Icci aday."

"I told you we should have worn phase suits," says Bell.

They get closer to the structure, and the remaining young Dah'Sel run inside, then come back out to the entrance and stop. Several adult Dah'Sel step forward but stop just shy of stepping into the moonlight.

Sergeant Bentley raises his hands. Dr. Wright and Bell do the same. They are armored and ready for anything but trying to appear as docile as possible. I swallow hard, watching as Delgado closes the Argos doors.

Pru'Cet glues himself to the window. I cannot imagine what he is going through or how hard this is on him. It would mortify me.

All we can do is watch with hopeful optimism as my squad mates near those standing at the structure's base.

"We aren't here to fight," says Sergeant Bentley. "We don't want anyone else to get hurt."

"Ama ka," says the elder Dah'Sel. "Trestaluk-zeg su crez drost."

The rest of the Dah'Sel raise a fist and shout in unison, "Trestaluk-zeg."

"Okay." Sergeant Bentley looks at his crew. "The haze with it. We need Mason out here."

The thought of exiting Argos makes me nervous. I look to the Dah'Sel, to Pru'Cet, and to Delgado. Her lips part, but words do not come out. Chubb is on the Argos turret, not within eyesight, but I am sure he shares our concerns.

"Sergeant Major..." Delgado looks back at me with apprehension-laced eyes flicking back and forth between mine. "Mason's only wearing a flight suit."

"I'm aware of that, Delgado," he says with a stressed voice.

Delgado looks at the structure, Sergeant Bentley, and then back at me with a baffled expression, as if she wants me to stay and go simultaneously.

"I'll be okay," I say, dissecting the unconvinced look Delgado is giving me. "Really. I'll take Pru'Cet with me."

"Negative," says Sergeant Bentley. "Your friend stays in Argos for now."

I look out the window to Sergeant Bentley and back to Delgado. "Maybe I'll be okay?" I force a smile.

Chubb lowers enough to peek into the Argos cab. "You got this, Mason. You can do this."

I nod through a racing heart. "Love the optimism."

Delgado watches as I reach for the lever to open the door. Pru'Cet moves to go with me. She stops him.

"Bea ama," he says.

He watches on with worried eyes as I exit without him to make my way across the field in a thin flight suit. The Dah'Sel watch until I reach the others.

"Tell them we offer trade and truce," says Sergeant Bentley.

"I don't know how to say truce," I say. "Or trade."

"Then just be nice if they—"

"Bizeemon," says the lead Dah'Sel. "Lokodee reema teedoe fusite."

"Um... Ama ka..." I pause. "I'm not sure know how to say all this."

"Try," urges Sergeant Bentley.

I take a shaking breath and look back to Argos for a moment before facing the Dah'Sel. "Fister is my..." I point to myself. "Fister en blenya. Nesplu? Ot whaul?"

The Dah'Sel look to one another with wrinkling eyes and puzzled gestures upon hearing me speak their language.

"Fesnop," says their leader. "Op gingo tom ledram sa wagthra. Mabap ot crez whattka!"

He motions to one of the Dah'Sel, who heads back into the structure.

"What did he say?" asks Sergeant Bentley.

"Something about peace," I answer.

"Good." Sergeant Bentley stares at the Dah'Sel. "And you?"

"I told him Fister was our friend and asked if he was broken."

"Broken?" he asks.

"That's the best I can do right now, okay?" My gaze goes to those near the structure in wonder of what they are thinking or planning. "I learned from pictures. And I think I told him we had Pru'Cet."

"You think?"

I raise my brows. "You want to talk to them?"

"No," says Sergeant Bentley, turning back to the structure. "You're doing fine."

The Dah'Sel member that their leader sent into the structure returns with a piece of Fister's phase suit and tosses it far into the moonlight. "Ohrap uptru gingo ledasno ver moolawell bizeemon."

"What's that mean?" asks Sergeant Bentley.

"No idea," I answer. "But he said something about mean, or evil. Fairly sure he's talking about us."

Pru'Cet's mother steps between the others and stops just shy of the moonlight. I turn back to Argos, knowing bad things are soon to follow. Emotions never lead to intelligent reasoning.

Pru'Cet's eyes grow wide when he sees her. His face presses against the glass. He screams through it, and his mother looks up.

"Pru'Cet," shouts his mother.

She makes a dash toward the moonlight for her son, but a pair of Dah'Sel grab her before she hits the night's shine.

"Rita," shouts Pru'Cet

"What's rita mean?" asks Sergeant Bentley.

"Could be her name." I answer. "I'm not sure. Might mean sister or mother."

She reaches Pru'Cet's direction from the ground. The two Dah'Sel on her struggle as she battles to her knees and lunges forward. All three drop to their bellies again... and her forearm goes into the moonlight.

It takes but a tik but her body changes beneath those holding her down. The rest of the group backs away as she tears from the entrance. Young Dah'Sel in her vicinity scream and rush up the side of the structure.

She is heading straight for us, bigger, stronger, and nastier than she was before hitting the moonlight. Her mind is no longer in control. She could hurt both us and Pru'Cet.

"Lock and load!" shouts Sergeant Bentley.

Ground team powers up their firearms. Dr. Wright eases behind them as Pru'Cet's protector-turned-threat closes in.

Sergeant Bentley motions from Dr. Wright to his weapon. "I hope these things work, Doctor."

"Me too, Sergeant Major," says Dr. Wright.

He backs away from the rest of the squad and eases toward the Argos as Sergeant Bentley and Bell fire a few darts. Pru'Cet's mother is jolted with electrical currents. They wrap her body from head to toe like trapped static charges, and she drops. A moment of silence follows.

"She's okay." Dr. Wright looks toward the Dah'Sel in the structure. "She's okay."

Her body remains motionless to the point she appears dead in the grass. Pru'Cet screams, opens the door, and bolts from the vehicle.

"Pru'Cet!" I shout. "Wait! No!"

"Can't let you do that." Chubb leaps from the turret and tackles Pru'Cet to the ground to keep the situation from escalating.

Chubb wrestles with Pru'Cet, but the young Dah'Sel slips from beneath him and makes a break for his mother. Chubb trips him by the ankle and climbs back on top of him. We cannot let the Dah'Sel kill Fister.

Young Dah'Sel in the structure release screams and shouts in equal measures of anger and fear when they shoot the mother Dah'Sel and tackle Pru'Cet. They run toward her fallen body in the field. Sergeant Bentley and the others raise their weapons out of reflex and nothing more.

The Dah'Sel leader's eyes grow wide when the men aim at the younger ones. "Seblak!" He runs from the structure and changes instantly when he hits the moonlight.

Young Dah'Sel ahead of him in the field scream when he transforms. They split in multiple directions and run as far away from him as they can. The crew opens fire with the darts, dropping him. Dah'Sel in the entrance—not knowing the darts are not lethal and could cure their transformation—scream and rush the field. Their human-like war cry turns into a terrifying roar as dozens upon dozens of them break into the moonlight and change.

The squad has no choice but to open fire as the transformed Dah'Sel charge. Their electrical medical darts drop them like a flock of womosa bats crossing the Suicide Fields. I turn and rush across the field for the Argos. Delgado fires it up and meets me halfway as electrical blasts ring out to light the surrounding area.

I reach for the Argos door, but an electrical charge hits it.

"Ahh..." I scream and fall back to the ground, turning to look.

Sergeant Bentley is on the ground with one on top of him. His rifle discharges again into the trees as he struggles.

"Bell..." he calls.

Bell turns and fires a burst into the creature's side. It falls off Sergeant Bentley.

"Let's get Fister," shouts Sergeant Bentley, rising to his feet.

Dr. Wright jogs through chaos to check the mother Dah'Sel's vitals as the crew moves forward with rapid fire. A horizontal rain of darts showers the Dah'Sel. The heavy flow of creatures coming from the structure slows to a drizzle until there is fifty down for the count in the surrounding field.

Dr. Wright watches Pru'Cet's mother. She changes slowly from her larger, monstrous state and back into her normal Dah'Sel state of tranquility.

"Almost out of darts here, Doc," says Bell.

"That's all we got," says Dr. Wright. "So, I suggest you pick your shots."

A few creatures leap high into the air, while others keep charging on foot. Ground team's fire splits between them and is no longer focused. Bell gets tackled. His thick suit is saving his life but failing quickly as he is rag-dolled about the field.

Delgado opens Argos and fires a few rounds from its interior. Darts dig into the side of the creature attacking Bell. He disappears beneath bright currents of electrical shock before it falls off.

He stands and gives a quick salute to Delgado. "Thanks."

She fixes her gaze on his stomach. Bell's stomach is exposed and bleeding. She aims down her onium rifle's sights.

"Wait," says Bell.

She fires a two-round burst into his stomach, forcing his body to tense and fall. "Sorry, Bell."

I watch over the madness, half in/half out of Argos with no way to help. The field is strewn with transformed Dah'Sel drifting back into their state of normalcy.

Pru'Cet breaks free from Chubb and rushes to his mother's side. Chaos ensues around them, and I rush from Argos to be next to him. His mother looks at me with fearfully fluttering eyes as he holds her.

Chubb moves in behind me to help the others with their raining of darts. A pair of transformed Dah'Sel jump over me to attack him, scratching my shoulder with a claw as they pass overhead. Chubb drops them both and advances forward.

I stand to check my surroundings. Ground team is still laying down suppressive darts on our attackers, dropping them one by one.

"Mason," calls Delgado.

I spin to face her. Delgado's rifle is aimed right at me. She fires.

Two darts pierce my upper right shoulder near the claw marks. Electrical charges fill and surround me. My body tenses … and I fall.

27–3
Hostage

My eyes open. Every muscle in my body feels like they are at the ending stages of cramps. A grunt escapes me as I sit up to see Pru'Cet still holding his mother.

"Po ot jelq," says Pru'Cet. "McKayla po crez blenya."

His mother stares at us and gets to a knee amid battle, amazed by the appearance of her limbs to the point she cannot notice the war waging around her. She looks up at the blue moon and planetary ring system lighting the night sky. "Tret'tret?"

Pru'Cet turns his palms up, not understanding enough to know the answer to her question.

Dr. Sellers looks our way for an instant and turns his attention to the stunned Dah'Sel lying on the grass-covered field. My eyes follow his. The others lying in the field are returning to their normal state of existence. A few of them are waking.

"It's working," says Dr. Wright. "It's working."

The crew drops the last few creatures.

A group of hardened Dah'Sel approach the structure's entrance with Fister in hand, remaining safe from moonlight's kiss. The one dragging Fister has a deep, hair-less scar across his shoulder.

"Blight desme fradus soooo," he shouts.

All in the field look his way. He places a large blade on Fister's throat.

"Wait!" shouts Sergeant Bentley.

Delgado steps from Argos and nears Chubb with unease. The hardened Dah'Sel wrenches back Fister's head and tenses to draw the blade across his neck.

"Ma," says Pru'Cet's mother. "Hueton."

He looks his mother's way.

"Ma," she continues. "Crelo ama matao deca?"

She steps aside and holds out her hand, revealing other Dah'Sel walking in the moonlight. Her eyes go toward the night sky and back to the others. The Dah'Sel holding Fister and the surrounding others are spellbound.

He releases Fister. The blade clanks to the ground as he walks forward to step under the night sky. Everyone, human and Dah'Sel alike, shouts and motions for him to stop. He halts before hitting the moonlight but is perplexed.

His inability to exit with the Dah'Sel rising to their feet in the clearing is something he does not understand. He looks back into the structure. A tek later ... he looks back outside and takes another step away from the moonlight.

I walk halfway toward him and stop. "You can't step out until we... Not until you've been..." I grunt in frustration. "Ver suetrow crelo mola woo ama leprev fesnop brotma."

More Dah'Sel have gathered at the entrance. They are staring at me—all of them. All within the structure and standing around me are looking at one another with con-fusion upon hearing me speak their language. Despite my limited knowledge and fumbling of their words, the Dah'Sel must understand my effort here.

I try for a moment, shake my head, and realize I cannot do this alone.

"Pru'Cet," I say. "Kuzsoec."

Pru'Cet runs to my side and explains everything he can to those still in the structure in his native tongue, gesturing as he talks. He is doing a much better job than I was. Those on the outside watch intently as he tells the story of what happened, how we ended up in this situation, and why those inside cannot enter the moonlight yet.

Bell is just getting back to his feet. The technology in his combat suit must have held the darts charge to wrap him longer than it did me, and the others hit with them. Delgado walks over to help him up.

"You're not angry," she asks. "Are you?"

He shakes his head. "No, but do you have any idea how bad that hurt?"

Delgado releases a smart-aleck smirk. "Couldn't have you changing on me."

I smile and watch them for a tik and look at the others in the field, unsure if peace is amongst our people yet. We are closer than we were, but I will take it. A warm sensation sets into my heart as we watch Pru'Cet point to the sky, physically reenacting some of what he has seen on the ship. It takes a solid ten teks for my little, hairy friend to get through his excited retelling.

When he ends his charade of explanations, the Dah'Sel in the structure take a step back and help Fister to his feet. The male that once held a blade to Fister's throat holds his hands high above his head and stares at him. Fister is untrusting. He looks at the others for an answer.

Pru'Cet and the other Dah'Sel motion for him to raise his hands like the tall one in front of him. Fister holds his hands high over his head in pain. The Dah'Sel standing before him places their palms together and lowers his forehead to Fister's, but he is far from comfortable and backs away. The Dah'Sel, with the others, coax him. A moment passes and those outside raise their arms as he watches on.

Pru'Cet's mother raises hers to Sergeant Bentley, and he matches her movements, smiling when they touch foreheads. The other Dah'Sel do the same with the rest of the ground team.

Pru'Cet looks at me and raises his arms. I cut him a funny look, open my arms wide, and dive in for a hug, tackling him without warning. We roll around in a playful embrace as he wraps his arms around me and laughs. The others laugh and cheer.

Those in the field finish their traditional embrace and look to one another in examination. None of them can believe it. A gasp escapes their lips as they stand in stunned silence. Others cannot stop talking. A few around me laugh uncontrollably after spending a lifetime living with the fear of transformation.

They're cured. I can barely accept it myself. And I cannot stop grinning about it. Soon, those gathered in force at the structure's entrance will walk under the stars with their friends and families for the first time.

Small transport shuttles land in the distance and take off to the sky again. They are being loaded with basic tools, limited personal items, Armada rations, and general equipment in the black and unloaded here on the surface. The Dah'Sel are carrying some M.R.E. crates into their structure and assisting us in stacking others in the clearing.

Dr. Wright organizes the logistics of everything. I think he enjoys this sort of thing. He comes across as someone who loves being in control of things around him.

My mother Maddie and brother Comilo would have been proud of me. I had a hand in saving humanity, and they will never know. There is nothing I would not give to have them here with me now.

I teach younger Dah'Sel how to play games like freeze tag when I have free time. We are having a blast. Many thoughts occupy my mind, but I feel an immense happiness in this world.

There are many events, games, holidays, and traditions I am looking forward to experiencing here. Placox, Fak sa pasho, Sishwa, and Unsha come to mind. Rench-snech, for example, is an herb growing here—potent and trippy to inhale. The Dah'Sel smoke it during the Fak sa pasho, and it is something I am curious about. Not to try it with them during the upcoming Fak sa pasho would be an insult to them. Armada members will try it soon.

Of the places I wish to explore, Besawe, Misdela, and Zasaza are a few I want to see. Pru'Cet says Besawe is a large cove surrounded by mountains that lies at the edges of an immense gulf. This is where the unsha hunt takes place and an animal known as the wakoa dwells. Misdela is another and will be a feat to climb. It is the highest mountain on the planet and in its most dangerous region. Its deadly wildlife makes it rarely traveled, but there are seasons when it is safe. Out of all the places on my list to explore, Zasaza is number one. Pru'Cet's mother, Nala'Cet, says it is a beautiful place where the trees come together to form a shingled canopy over the forest floor, so effective it remains dry during the monsoon season, and its interior is boundless with life. The trees in the area are called zasaza staog-zis, and its canopy's dome shape is tight, making it hard to enter from any point. These are but a few of the things I wish to experience.

The Kla'Wah language was the first thing I mastered here, and I found learning proper names for flora and fauna exciting. Though we have been told it is best to avoid some of it.

Those angry flyers that attacked our camp are one such thing. The Dah'Sel call them *benvata*. The second animal I learned the name of was the four-legged chicken-like birds with large beaks. They are called *yeena*; and the pig-like animal with ill-proportionally tiny heads and a single eye kept behind pens made of wood and dried mud, they are *memsa*.

My visions have not stopped and remain a mystery to scientists who have made it here so far. They are also happening more often, but it is not as horrible as it sounds. I do not talk about it with the others. There is no reason to. It is obvious when I have them—freezing in place like a corpse is a good giveaway.

I try not to think about Dolofónos and what his Uprisers are doing back on Kep Four. Recent Armada arrivals say the war is getting bad back home. They claim it to be near a tipping point. The more Armada that come here, the less there are on Kep Four to stop the Uprisers from overthrowing the government and taking over its buildings and resources.

Most of the time my visions have to do with our involvement with the Dah'Sel. Other times they are an inside look at what is happening back on Kep Four, which is not good. The Uprisers attack the innocent without fear of repercussions and head-on now. We hear there have been 20,000 or more lost on both sides, and the brown is making ground skirmishes difficult.

The Uprisers have been lying low for the last fifty-four rotations but maintain their actions of intercepting Armada transport vessels. Their primary targets are munition hauls and armament supply vessels. They are planning something big, and I am getting glimpses of it. Though, I am unsure what.

Like my visions, I do not talk about what the Uprisers are doing back on Kep Four. People get heated about the subject and often question the accuracy of what I am saying. To make things worse, there are fewer and fewer patrol vessels to protect the streets of places like Najasa with each intergalactic vessel that makes it here.

These visions come in waves. Sometimes I get a few a rotation. Other times, I go many without. They are unpredictable and typically involve something important or a major event soon to take place.

I get them if someone is soon to become deathly ill, about to get pregnant—which happens a lot with the

Dah'Sel—or about to die; but I do not get visions of incidents surrounding emotional struggles. Normally, it is the aftermath I see: group joy, sadness, excitement, dread.

What I see happening back on Kep Four is always bad. There is nothing good left there, and we are leaving it behind. Two interstellar Armada vessels are on the surface here now—Wurrukatte and Columbas. The plan is to convert them into housing units. Athanasios, the smallest of them, and Uno are orbiting us here in Andromeda.

More are to come in the next forty rotations, with several more following, each carrying 10,000 hand-selected people and heaps of supplies. It may take a cycle to get everyone off Kep Four with each vessel. They can make it here but not return. What happened to Athanasios in the wormhole is happening to them all. It causes no detectable signs of damage but renders them unable to reopen the Ein-Rosen bridge. Even with full system sweeps and engine rebuilds, our ships refuse to make the jump for us again.

It has been 170 rotations, measured by our time on Kep Four. The Dah'Sel have let no one from the Armada enter the structure they once held Fister in. They call it Lessdelop ti'it renasa, which translates as *Home to all*, and they are protective of it.

Pru'Cet's mother, Nala'Cet, told me they were talking about letting my squad enter to look around it at some point. It could not happen soon enough for me. I am dying to decipher whatever is written on the walls in there.

I spend a lot of time standing in the field and taking in the planet's beauty, like I am now. The night sky is still a favorite of mine because of its moon, stars, and stunning ring system. Studying this world—one they call *Wah'Lor*—is my favorite pastime. The Dah'Sel have told me many things about it, and I am thankful for that. There is so much to learn here.

Dr. Sellers watches me. I can always tell when someone is staring—pins and needles in my back. I look his way. He gives me a wink to get a smile in return.

Sergeant Bentley and Bell are growing crops in a clearing and tending the land. They are working side-by-side with several of the Dah'Sel and exchanging water bottles to drink from. It is quite the sight, considering how it all began.

We joined the Dah'Sel to bury Dr. Utley, Morris, and my beloved Skedelski a click away under one of the sad-looking trees called dofabes. Belief holds that one's spirit is liberated when death occurs as a direct cause of a transformation or protecting another's life. They lay evil spirits far from the good to eliminate afterlife confrontation and contamination from those who died fully transformed.

Delgado rides up on an A.A.T.V. (Armada All-Terrain Vehicle) with an open center seat and four small tracks to guide it like a miniature Argos without the cover. She stops next to Sergeant Bentley and watches him work for a tek. A crooked grin eases across her face.

"You going to ignore me, or what?" she asks.

"Now," says Sergeant Bentley, walking over to her A.A.T.V. "Why would I ignore a pretty little thing like you?"

"Permission to speak freely, Sergeant Major," she says.

He smirks. "Go ahead."

Delgado motions to the field behind and to her right. She cuts him a sultry look and fights to hold back a smile.

"That's the last of what we have in orbit on Uno," she says. "There should be enough dried food to last everyone half a cycle. Also, I brought down a full medical facility with its supplies and enough weapons to equip a few squads."

"Thanks," says Sergeant Bentley. "Let's keep the weapons locked up for now. Any word from home?"

"The last Ein-Rosen probe left a few taks ago," she answers. "They should be here in a cycle if all goes well."

"How many ships do they have left to build?"

"Five more to move everyone on the planet, minus the criminals. Everyone in the Armada left on Kep Four are everyone teaming up to get it done before Kep Four's demise."

Sergeant Bentley looks over his shoulder to make sure he is not within earshot of anyone. "Sounds like we have plenty of time to get acquainted then, don't we?"

She smiles. "I guess we do."

He pulls her in and kisses her gently on the lips.

"You sure you're ready to let go?" she asks.

"I'm not letting go," he answers, kissing her hand. "I'm just wanting to take you up on those dancing lessons."

"I didn't say anything about lessons."

"Stepped on a few toes in my life," says Sergeant Bentley. "I think Laura would tell you she insists on the lessons."

A beaming grin overtakes her before she drives away. Sergeant Bentley turns to the Dah'Sel with a scar on his face that once held Fister hostage, Din'Mos as he is called, and notices him trying to make a kissing expression with a puzzled look on his face.

Sergeant Bentley laughs and goes back to work. "It's hard to explain."

Din'Mos studies him and Delgado for a tik as she rides away and joins him to tend the land. They have much to learn from us. We have much to learn from them.

Many people that have arrived so far came with life-partners or one of their kids. I, myself, have found nothing in the way of love, but there is someone that has managed to catch my eye. Her name is Tila'Cet, and she is Pru'Cet's sister.

I have not asked much in the way of their thoughts on different relationships or what is acceptable, but thoughts of her are a regular thing. Sometimes, I wonder why she has not paired up with anyone. It is not her looks that are holding her back. She is closest to being an albino in the Dah'Sel sect with a silky silver coat of flowing perfection almost wholly hiding a light brown undercoat.

The Dah'Sel sect tend to pair up at an early age, not much older than Pru'Cet. Yet, she is about twenty-five cycles into her life, alone, and has not chosen a mate. I try to ignore her when she is in sight. It is hard. Almost impossible. Tila'Cet is friveka at its finest. Heart and soul, I find her perfect.

I walk toward Les del op ti'it renasa in thought of all that is going on around me. Dah'Sel children are playing with those from Kep Four, we are learning how to cook the Kla'Wah way—which is alien to me—and transplants to this world are impressing its native dwellers with their work ethic. Though, I am unsure how much of it is the desire to perform manual labor on the land. I feel they are just happy there is life here.

The last sun begins to set. Shade drifts across the extensive field as the moon rises. Sergeant Bentley stops working when he notices him looking nervously into the oncoming night sky, patting his silky back for reassurance. Din'Mos nods, smiles, and goes back to work.

Though we lost a few along the way, I never dreamed of an outcome and transition between our cultures going this smoothly. We will no longer know the fear of dwindling resources, lack of food, and a poisoning atmosphere; with humanity's latest advancements, Wah'Lor will be safe in our hands.

We conquered intergalactic travel but unintentionally started a small-scale war with an already established culture—one that turned out to be more like ourselves than we could have possibly known. In the end, it was a young Dah'Sel named Pru'Cet that brought us together and explained that our doctors found a cure for the disease. Named after the first Kla'Wah to have it before the split of their sects, they call it *Klaz'Dra*, and it held their culture captive to themselves and prevented advancement for many an aionas.

They are now free to move about Wah'Lor without sheltering themselves from the night. Adults can stand under a sparkling night sky with their youth, and their population will soon flourish without the unintentional rage and self-destruction brought on by the disease, but this alone was not enough to win their trust and friendship. It took time, leaps of faith, and courage on both sides to build unity.

It came easier to me than Fister. His resentment toward both the Dah'Sel and the Armada for Rhigas's death. It was something none of us could have seen coming, and he knows that. He accepts it, but it has been hard for him to move on.

The hardest part of everything that is keeping Fister from moving forward is the fact that his sister, Bo, has not arrived. She was supposed to be on Barrows when it reached orbit here. That was not the case. Nobody knows where she is now.

Overall, I would say it feels good to be here, but there is another sect that will not be accepting. Who could blame them? Humanity is a proven, world-devouring parasite.

The Dah'Sel believe our arrival displeases another Kla'Wah group, and I fear they may be correct. A sect known as the Vee'Sal views the *black-sky transformation* as a historical lineage. We will not be able to change their minds. Our goal is to stay with the Dah'Sel, who keep to themselves as a separate sect and interact with Vee'Sal culture as little as possible.

Dr. Sellers taps my shoulder and points across the field at the horizon atop a small mountain. I look around to see others in the field talking to each other. They stop and fixate on something, causing me to turn and see what the commotion is about. A large group of white-undercoated Vee'Sal are at its peak and mounted on some type of animals I am unfamiliar with.

They watch us for a bit without approaching our direction. It is unsettling. A tek later ... and they turn to leave. Whatever they were thinking, it did not project a positive aura. I hope they come to accept.

"Come on," says Dr. Sellers. "I need you to translate for me again."

He guides me toward the Lesdelop ti-it renasa structure's outer left exterior where some of his supplies are being placed. My mind is stuck on the Uprisers and Vee'Sal as I walk. For the first time in rotations, I feel unease about possibilities to come, but the possibility of living a good life on Wah'Lor is still high.

I cannot predict the future but wish for the best. I love this world and, good or bad that comes from it, this is our home now. All I can do is hope.

LANGUAGE TRANSLATIONS
WolfStar Universe

Kla'Wah to English Translator— (Alphabetic order):

Abaz = Trouble/Problem

Aday = Back

Ama = You

Armona = Love

Aryan = Hand

Axta = Better

Azata = End/Stop

Banra = Lift

Bea = With

Beena = Sleep

Besta = Crazy

Bex = Separate

Baklee = Evil

Bela = Life

Benja = Apart

Bizmon = Demon

Blagrah = White

Blakabak = Announce

Blenya = Friend

Blenyas = Friendship

Blazee = Bird

Bleku = Hurry

Blight = I

Cakou = Run

Caves = Else

Cea = Me

Chant = Best

Chasta = Since

Cre = Can/Could

Crelo = Can't/Cannot

Crez = Our

Da = At

Dada = Thank

Dalasa = Catch

Dasa = Trust

Dase = About

Delt = Need

Dexlee = Please

Deyar = Ready

Dez = Nothing

Dind = Find

Disen = First

Dit = Did

Dita = Dad/Father

Diti = Hold

Dolpoz = Demand

Dotin = Next

Drost = World

Dubol = Ground

Dwaloc = Strong

E = The

Elo = Sky

En = My

Ena = From

Enlasa = Miss

Eo = Took/Take

Erif = Free

Ersee = Bye

Erude = Heart

Exes = Look

Fak = Rotation

Fax = Lose

Fesnop = This

Fejaz = Worse

Feld = Animal/Wildlife

Fit = Child

Flazee = Head/Mind

Flis = Control

Flowcee = Drown

Fradus = Kill

Falsa = Bring

Frat = Open

Fraza = Sad

Frex = Accept

Friveka = Beautiful/Pretty

Fusite = War

Ga = Eyes

Gane = Part/Portion

Ganta = Proud

Gate = Off

Gav = Ask

Gazno = Last

Gecsapasa = Impossible

Gessah = Message

Gingo = Not

Glenoda = Help

Glezlock = Bitch

Glotren = Scared

Gof = Meet

Gomee = Up

Gona = Able

Gopo = Write

Grag = Believe

Gratalua = Permission

Greh = School

Grenas = Think

Grinsapes = Tradition

Gwampa = Change/Switch

Gwan = Their

Gwana = There

Kook = Black

Haka = Oath/Promise

Hakio = Blood

Hakiya = Bleeding

Hama = Natural

Haman = Nature

Hamp = Well

Hasta = Want

Haza = Wall

Heeza = Sun/Star

Heg = Lay

Helkla = Area/Region/Zone

Heltno = Dream

Hempa = Sorry

Henkadi = Follow

Himan = Past

Hitto = Reach

Honkea = Different

Hue = Sister

Hueton = Here

Icci = Stay

Ikkida = Try

Illa = Odd

Inbem = Enter

Inots = Like

Intom = Least

Ipasag = Also

Irina = Become

Isacaz = Truth

Iscafo = Violence

Itofdrec = Might

Jambit = Leader

Janest = Gone

Jappa = When

Jesen = Go

Jazaxe = Then

Jelq = Okay

Jem = Win

Jezafe = Soul

Jipwa = Transformation

Jo = Be

Jokata = Rise

Jotap = Alive

Ka = Are

Kalps = Agree
Kav = Over
Kawen = Wake/Awaken
Kela = Word
Keleo = Magic
Kena = These
Ki = As
Kimit = Toward
Kipoa = Other
Kiskil = Bless
Kit = Should
Klava = Same
Klaz'Dra = Disease
Klis = Sick
Klota = Forward
Kurka = Lucky
Kuzsoec = Come
Lab = If
Lassabax = River
Lazzaz = Foot
Ledad = Was
Ledasno = Return
Lekde = Snow
Langaea = Pangaea
Lats = Start
Ledram = Time
Lep = Red
Leprev = Under

Lessdelop = Home
Letrow = Leg
Licea = Must
Likiedasno = Bastard
Lilimensa = Sit
Lipfa = Yes
Loilcim = Breathe
Lokodee = Prepare
Loudac = Happy
Ma = No
Mabap = Where
Maner = Remain
Matao = See
Mecee = Every
Meceete = Everybody/Everyone
Mesp = High
Meva = Doctor
Miga = Yesterday
Mola = Moon
Muto = Save
Nacas = Or
Nasig = Decide/Choose/Pick
Natroqfel = Tonight
Nax = Only
Ne = And
Neeb = Been
Nemons = Crops

Nery = Worry/Concern

Nesplu = Understand

Nest = Soon

Niss = Wait

Nit = Chest/Torso

O = Am

Ohrap = We

Ola = Before

Oladi = Elder

Olov = Step

Olsa = Make

Opacha = Large

Onas = Long

Onast = Longer

Ooves = Clouds

Orsplap = Know

Ot = Is

Ox = Extremely/Very

Ozalt = Check

Pacala = Keep

Pac = Another

Pasho = Reflection

Peelota = Flower

Peca = Thing

Pegnada = Dance

Pes = Do

Pilim = Get

Pisip = Us

Pizta = Use

Plafoh = Visit

Plako = Forbid/Forbidden

Plama = Let

Plenta = Grave

Plett = Because

Plup = Fall

Po = It

Polasa = Speak/Talk

Polasap = Said

Pota = Arm

Prajet = Pass

Qala = Between

Qua = Almost

Quipa = Amazing

Quamza = Careful

Quena = Water

Ralaha = Correct

Rarge = Union

Ratim = Generation

Reema = For

Refet = Still

Relee = Brother

Renasa = All

Pest = An

Retsu = Were

Rilc = Hair

Rita = Mom/Mother

Rolt = Harvest/Gather

Roser = Done

Rot = Now

Sa = Of

Saca = Has

Saftic = Those

Saisay = They

Sawez = New

Seblak = Attack

Sexti = Alone

Seza = Join

Sinol = Baby/Infant

Siwbe = Them

Skarm = Fight

Smetlac = Happen

Soo = He/Him

Sopet = Drink

Specap = Hello

Staog = Tree

Stafor = Represent

Su = On

Suetrow = Body

Swil = Mouth

T = Share

Tacab = Just

Tadak = Fast/Quick/Rapid

Takiep = Sect

Tanza = Care

Tar = Fear

Tatam = Danger

Teed = Dead

Teedoe = Deadly

Teefa = Death

Teeza = Die

Teilis = Silence/Quiet

Tese = Set

Tigeth = Together

Ti'it = To

Tirqesa = Relax

Tom = A

Topcal = That

Tos = Dirt

Tralama = Good

Tralea = Monsoon

Trampt = Younger

Trang = Plus

Trensapa = Nobody

Trestaluk = Welcome

Tret'tret = How

Tribeka = Translate

Troqfall = Tomorrow

Troqfel = Night

Tump = But

Turahan = Accident

Ubido = Small/Tiny

Ulapra = Finish/Complete

Ulat = More
Ulaula = Approach
Uneger = Finger
Unel = Tool
Unsha = Hunt
Uptru = Will
Utlu = What
Vasa = Wrong
Vasika = Touch
Vel = Game
Ver = Your
Volna = Remember
Wab = Give
Wabuki = Have
Wagthra = Peace
Wams = After
Waq = Scale/Size
Watt = Aside
Wazme = Why
Wazo = Drunk
Wella = Light
Wena = Send
Whattka = Family
Whaul = Break/Shatter
Wist = Never
Woo = Hurt/Harm
Ya = In
Yama = Her/She

Yamag = Mad/Angry
Yapo = Excite
Yata = Self
Yataat = Man
Yaw = Feel
Vemp = Who
Yelta = Name
Vut = Hungry
Yetia = Out
Yilp = Safe
Yirit = Banish/Exile
Yom = Way
Yop = Had
Zama = Walk
Zamba = Leave
Zasta = Heal
Zenta = Hi
Zindoc = Enough
Zotka = Push

-Zap = less (as in useless)

-Zal = 's (Possessive)

-Zeg = un (as in unnecessary)

-Zel = ment (as in movement)

-Zic = (Present tense -ing)

-Zim = (Past-tense)

-Zis = (Plural)

-Zõk = Re (as in replay)

-Zut = ly (as in accidentally)

NUMBERS (CONSTANT INITIAL SEQUENCES)

Toop = 0	**Qu** = 5
Qa = 1	**Za** = 6
Qe = 2	**Zi** = 7
Qi = 3	**Zo** = 8
Qo = 4	**Zu** = 9

"Tens have singles rotating to the front of word as in 10-20 below"

Qa-toop = 10	**Qe-Qa** = 21
Qa-Qa = 11	**Qe-Qe** = 22
Qa-Qe = 12	**Qe-Qi** = 23
Qa-Qi = 13	**Qe-Qo** = 24
Qa-Qo = 14	**Qe-Qu** = 25
Qa-Qu = 15	**Qe-Za** = 26
Qa-Za = 16	**Qe-Zi** = 27
Qa-Zi = 17	**Qe-Zo** = 28
Qa-Zo = 18	**Qe-Zu** = 29
Qa-Zu = 19	**And so forth…**
Qe-toop = 20	

Numbers (100+ initial sequences)

Toopa = 100 -(Hundreds)
Toope = 1,000-(Thousands)
Toopi = 10,000-(Ten-thousands)
Toopo = 100,000-(Hundred-thousands)
Toopu = 1,000,000-(Millions)

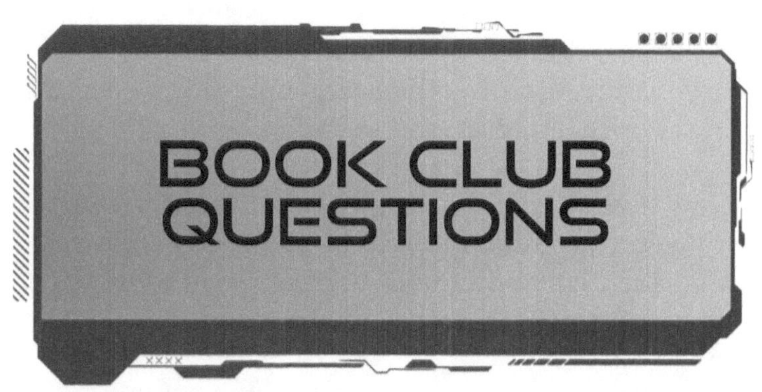

1. On an already doomed planet with no hope for humanity in site, was it morally right for Mason to free animals being tested on that could potential cure Kep Four Syndrome someday?

2. What do you think made Dolofónos come to change his opinion of the Armada to such a degree he would betray them and form the Uprisers?

3. Do you think Sergeant Magor Bentley has had enough time for closure since the loss of his wife Laura to move on and be with Delgado, and how do you feel about them being together, considering Delgado was Laura's best friend?

4. Do you think our planet, referred to as Ancient Earth, is headed in the same direction as depicted in the WolfStar story?

5. What international superpowers do you think were the founding fathers of the Armada on Ancient Earth during global war, and what would you think finally happened to bring them together?

6. What historical references from Ancient Earth stood out to you the most in WolfStar, and how did you feel about the scene painted around them?

7. Now that humanity is present on the Kla'Wah planet, how do you think they will be accepted by the Vee'Sal after their encounter with the Dah'Sel, and how will it affect tribal relationships moving forward?

8. What do you think is going to become of the Armada, civilians, and Uprisers still remaining on Kep Four?

9. After what unintendedly happened upon the Armada's first encounter with the Dah'Sel, with blood shed on both sides and no way to communicate, should the Armada have gone in peacefully to try and obtain the needed blood sample to save Rhigas?

10. Which character's loss of life, of all that died in WolfStar, did you not see coming, and which one affected the story for you the most?

11. We are all products of our environment. Born in the districts of poverty, or into Armada blood, how would your life have differed under different circumstances, and would you have joined the Uprisers if desperate enough to save your family?

Jason Diamond and C R Buchanan:

Combined, Jason Diamond and C R Buchanan have a long history of writing with a friendship that spans over a decade. From a television series in development, to multiple feature film options, completed films, and several features incoming from adaptions, it all started when they got together to expand Jason's original concept of the "WolfStar" world... bringing it to the point that the story was so big it could no longer be told in just a few books.

C. R. BUCHANAN

C. R. Buchanan's website: www.crbuchanan.com

JASON DIAMOND

Jason Diamond's website: www.vondiamondink.com

Discover more at
4HorsemenPublications.com

10% off using HORSEMEN10